Edge of Sanity

Cindy Horrell Ramsey

LOGGERHEAD
PRESS

Published by Loggerhead Press

ISBN-10: 1978406061
ISBN-13: 978-1978406063

DEDICATION

This book is dedicated to all women and children who suffer from sexual, mental, or physical abuse. May you find courage, strength, safety, peace, and love.

Also by **Cindy Horrell Ramsey**

Boys of the Battleship NORTH CAROLINA

John F. Blair, Publisher

600 Letters Home

Loggerhead Press

Maddie in the Middle

Loggerhead Press

Trying Not to Drown

Loggerhead Press

Beyond the Edge

(Book 2 of The Edge Series)

Loggerhead Press

Continue reading at the end for a sneak peek of the continuation of Emily's story in the second book of *The Edge Series*, **Beyond the Edge**.

CONTENTS

ACKNOWLEDGMENTS

A huge thanks to my readers Jennifer Edwards, Patsy Rivenbark, and Charlotte Baggett. Your gifts of time, enthusiasm, and encouragement are invaluable. I thank my family for always loving and supporting me. To my five beautiful granddaughters—who are far too young to read this book—may your world be filled with laughter, love, and happiness. May you grow in strength and courage to face adversity, for it will come. Never be afraid to chase your dreams. Thank you for making me the luckiest Mimi in the world.

Chapter 1

Emily felt rough hands on her forearms squeezing. Shaking her. Hard. Then the jerk on her long blonde hair.

"Wake up, dammit. Quit all that whining and tossing. I'm the one who's got to go to work. The least you could do is keep your mouth shut. I swear I'll never get back to sleep."

But he would. He always did. And when he walked in the kitchen after sunrise to fluffy homemade biscuits, sausage patties, creamy grits, and eggs fried just so—with the whites solid and the yellow a perfect consistency of runny—he would walk up behind her, put his arms around her waist, kiss her on the neck, ask her if she slept well, and tell her he loved her.

He wouldn't remember anything. Or would pretend he didn't. Emily never really knew with certainty.

When Dan's breathing regulated to that rhythmic indication of deep sleep, Emily slipped silently out of their bed, wrapped herself in the big terry robe, picked up her slippers, and quietly closed the bedroom door behind her, thankful she had remembered to oil the hinges. She always laid everything exactly where she could find it in the dark. For nights like these. Nights that were coming with uncomfortable regularity.

She moved with thief-like stealth through her home, opened the door to her boys' bedroom and listened for their breathing, watched for movement, any motion or sound to assure her they were alive, that they would wake up in a few hours and come rushing down the stairs shoving at each other with their eyes still full of sleep and their hair tousled and tangled. Arguing about breakfast, or games, or whose turn it was to feed the dog. Normal sounds.

3

She softly closed their door, tip-toed down the stairs and into the kitchen where she finally slipped on her shoes. She poured herself a glass of milk. Added Hershey's chocolate syrup. She liked it warm, but digging out a pot might make too much noise, so she drank it cold. She chastised herself for not remembering to take out the small pot and set it on the immaculate countertop last night after Dan started up the stairs. It would have only taken a second.

The dream was coming more often now. More vivid. More terrifying. Additional details with every recurrence. Emily thought she might be conjuring it up. Willing it to come. Demanding her subconscious to tell her what she knew her conscious mind would not. But what Emily could never remember, what would not come to her no matter how hard she had tried for more than ten years, was why. How. What happened just before.

§ § §

When Emily's youngest son started kindergarten in the fall of '66, she thought, just maybe, she could go to college. It was the 60s after all, and women were doing that more and more these days, right? Wilmington College wasn't that far away from Burgaw. She could be home in time to pick the boys up from school and study at night after they went to bed. But Dan said no. She asked about working part-time. He said absolutely not.

Finally, running out of ideas, Emily asked if she could volunteer at their small local hospital where his father had once been the chief of staff, and his mother had organized the candy stripers and pink ladies. Since Emily had carefully chosen to begin that conversation when Dan's parents were visiting from their home in Raleigh, he had little choice but to say, "What a wonderful idea." Later that night, Emily silently endured the penalty for her audacity.

One tiny victory earned. Emily cherished her time volunteering at the hospital, meeting the nurses, spending time with the patients. Sometimes, she'd stop by the library to find a favorite book a patient might have mentioned. She especially enjoyed the elderly patients, reading to them or just listening to their stories of how things used to be. She loved loading her cart with flowers and pushing it down the hall, sweet scents briefly masking the stench of sickness.

The volunteering made her feel smart and special, worthy. Patients seemed happy to see her, even when they were in pain from surgery or reeling from a devastating diagnosis. They often asked her to stay and talk. But she never lingered for chit-chat in the maternity wing, and only ventured down that hall when the nursery curtains were drawn.

Emily had been volunteering about six months when the new doctor moved to town. The staff and patients all seemed to love him. His last name was foreign and hard to pronounce, so everyone just called him Dr. Z. When Emily was pushing the flower cart, she overheard whispers in the hallways, gossip that always included how gorgeous he was, how the green smock emphasized his eyes on a particular day or why his usually well-kept black curls seemed unruly some mornings. Emily stayed out of those conversations. She didn't know much about him, really, except that he lived at the beach and was young—with a new practice and no wife. No steady girlfriend either, as far as any of the nurses, aides, or volunteers could discern. They seemed to want to tell Emily all about him. But she was married, had a family; his personal life was irrelevant to her.

Dr. Z's office shared a parking lot with the hospital, and Emily knew most of the girls who worked for him, enjoyed talking to them, listening to them gush about their boss. Occasionally, he would take the exclusively female staff out to lunch at Reade's Restaurant. Emily was certain they made quite a scene walking through the small but bustling restaurant—the handsome doctor followed by his harem of attractive women.

One day, Emily was leaving the hospital just as Dr. Z and his staff were headed to lunch. He invited her to join them, and she quickly declined. But egged on by the only people she could loosely call friends, she relented. The restaurant had been owned by the same family for years, and many teenagers had landed their first jobs there flipping burgers, including Emily and Rob. The food was fantastic but inexpensive, drawing customers from every walk of life. And just as Emily had imagined, the doctor and his entourage drew stares as they sauntered to their table. Emily allowed herself to enjoy the rare camaraderie. Just as they were finishing up their lunch, a waitress handed Emily a folded note.

"The guy at that table asked me to give this to you," the waitress said.

"To me? Are you sure?"

"Quite sure. He said to give it to the one in the pink shirt."

Emily looked around the table. She was the only one wearing pink. The others wore pure white or scrub shirt green.

"What guy?" she asked.

"That one right over...oh my," the waitress replied. "I guess I didn't do it fast enough. They're gone. There were three of them, though. Young looking, construction type. Haven't seen them around here before, and I know all the regulars. Sorry."

"Don't worry about it," Emily said, tucking the note in her pocket.

"Aren't you going to read it?" Dr. Z asked.

"Maybe later." Emily was embarrassed, felt uncomfortable being singled out.

His question prompted a flurry of innuendoes from the girls that did not cease until she relented and opened the note.

I couldn't help but notice you as you walked by me. I know you will probably think I am crazy, but I really want to talk to you...

The note included a name, phone number, and address from a town at least three or four hours away. Emily knew she would never dream of calling, but she didn't throw the note away. She pocketed it and took it with her. She put it in her dresser drawer and read it every now and then. She wasn't sure why. After a couple of weeks, guilt weighing heavy, she showed it to her husband and waited for the consequences.

"Did you call him?" Dan demanded, rising from his chair and confronting her face to face.

"Of course not," she said. Instinctively, she took a step back.

"You're lying."

"No, I'm not," Emily replied, her voice growing small. "If I planned to call him, I would never have shown you the note." Not the best answer, she realized, only after those last few words came out. The backhand was swift, the ring hard.

Dan backed away, sank down into his chair and stared at her. Emily saw the look on his face—a mixture of anger, jealousy, hurt and pathetic grief. In all the years they had been together, she had never been able to figure out why he was so insecure, so jealous. She had never strayed, never even considered it even though their marriage wasn't perfect. Whose was? Marriage vows were meant to be kept, husbands honored and obeyed.

Emily saw Dan as smart, industrious, and handsome in a wholesome way. His physique had been sculpted by working out and playing football during high school and college. Golf became his sport of choice as an adult. Olive skin highlighted blue eyes with lashes black and thick, and a smile—oh, the smile. When she first saw him in their high school hallway, his smile captured her heart. They had been through so much—a whirlwind courtship, pregnancy, marriage, miscarriage—but at that moment he needed his ego massaged, and she had learned just how to do it.

Emily walked over to Dan's recliner and knelt down in front of him, separating his legs so that she fit in between. She laid her head in his lap and slipped her arms around his waist. A few moments passed, but as she snuggled closer, he began to make slow delicate circles on her back with his fingertips.

"Don't you know that I love you," she said more than asked. "There's never been anyone but you."

"I know," he said. "I do."

He ran his fingertips up her neck and began to scratch the back of her head at the base of her hairline. She thought nerve endings there must be attached to every libido-laden cell in her body. Slipping her arms from around his waist, she raised them while he pulled her shirt over her head. He released her dark hair from the golden clasp and let it fall down her back.

He brushed his thumb gently across her swollen cheek. "I'm sorry," he said, and she believed him.

She unbuckled his belt, unzipped his khakis, and pulled his shirt up just enough so that when she laid her head back down, she touched skin. He scratched her head and combed his fingers through her hair, lifting it and letting it fall across her naked back. She ran fingernails gently up and down his sides and pressed her breasts close against his jeans.

They had been married eleven years. Emily was eighteen, Dan twenty-one when they said their vows. She had never been intimate with anyone else. Dan assured her he had not either although he was a nineteen-year-old senior from Raleigh when she first met him. She a mere freshman. His family had just moved to her small southern town of Burgaw where long-leaf pines towered, gargantuan oaks lined the streets, and nothing bad ever happened.

Emily was surprised and ecstatic when Dan asked her to be his date for his senior prom. She had a curfew, and he had joined another group of boys and girls after he dropped her off. She heard rumors of what happened that night at the river cabin. She didn't expect to ever see him again.

But when she was a senior Dan called, and Emily became totally lost in the undivided attention that he bestowed upon her that Christmas he returned home during his third year at State, and the weekends that followed. The year that changed everything. They were inseparable. His jealous outbursts just seemed to her like confirmation of the depth of his devotion. At first.

All the years that followed, he would get angry, but he had never struck her face before. Never left a mark that anyone could see.

§ § §

Within a month, Emily's face had healed, but she hadn't returned to the hospital, hadn't found the courage to ask Dan if she could. After she took the boys to school each morning, she struggled to find something to fill her day so her mind wouldn't have time to wander. Even with two rambunctious boys, there was just so much cleaning, cooking, and laundry she could do. Watching and listening to the growing feminist movement, she wondered what life would be like if she could earn her own money.

And she thought about her first baby. Emily knew how to sew, how to knit and crochet. She often daydreamed of what it would be like to have her little girl to dress, thought about the cute jumpers she could make with appliqués and embroidery, the frills and ruffles she could add to Easter dresses, the pinafores with ribbon and lace. As she folded the boys' jeans, t-shirts and flannel shirts, she pictured pink and lavender in the pile of clean laundry full of blues and oranges and greens. Tears welled up and spilled over.

"Just stop it," Emily said out loud with no one to hear but herself. "Be grateful, be grateful, be grateful." Emily loved her boys more than life itself. She would do, did do, anything to keep them safe and happy, give them a normal life with two parents. That, at all costs.

But sometimes she couldn't help but wonder what if—what if she hadn't gotten pregnant and married Dan. What if she had gone to college? What if she'd met a man who really was the person she and everyone else thought he was, or what if she hadn't lost her daughter, hadn't become so sick. What if she were stronger, more like that feminist Betty Friedan. Maybe her ideas weren't so crazy after all. Or maybe they were. Maybe she should just stop thinking all these stupid things. If she wasn't married to Dan, if she hadn't had her boys when she did, she might have children, but they wouldn't be those children, they wouldn't be Danny and Bobby. How could she possibly wish for anything that would make them not exist?

A knock on the door startled Emily. She walked to the window, pulled the edge of the sheers back just enough to see Dr. Z standing on her front porch. He knocked again, louder and more persistently. Emily unlocked the deadbolt and chain and turned the knob. She looked at him through the locked glass storm door. He was wearing jeans and a light blue long sleeve pullover. The winter weather was warm, and the bright sunshine made his black hair glisten. He held her navy blue parka in his right hand.

"May I come in?" he asked.

Emily hesitated, looked around the living room behind her, heard the soap operas playing on television. She didn't really watch them, they were just background noise to keep the house from being so quiet, to fill her mind with sound and help keep the thoughts at bay. Today they hadn't worked.

"Emily?"

She had to get him off the front porch. Out of sight of the neighbors. She turned back to Dr. Z, unlocked and opened the storm door.

"Of course," she said. "Please come in." Her mother always taught her to be polite to guests, but she prayed no one saw her let him in the house when she was alone, told Dan.

"Won't you have a seat?" she said, pointing to the rocker beside the fireplace.

"No, thank you, I haven't much time. I just wanted to return your coat I found in the break room. We've missed you at the hospital. Is everything ok?"

"I'm fine," Emily said, unconsciously raising her hand to her face, then dropping it quickly when she realized what she had just done. She saw Dr. Z's eyes narrow. "I've just been very busy. With the boys and all, I just don't have much free time to volunteer right now."

Emily reached for her coat, and he handed it to her. "Thank you," she said, "but you really didn't have to go to all that trouble."

"Well, there was another reason I wanted to talk to you," Dr. Z said. "But maybe there's even more I should ask you." He reached out and brushed her cheek with the tips of his fingers. "You have a scar. That wasn't there last time I saw you."

Emily took a step back. "I'm clumsy," she said. "Walked right into the corner of the kitchen cabinet door when I was doing some spring cleaning. I know better than to leave it open like that, but I was just so busy, and I was throwing out some old cans of beans and stuff and when I turned back around, I just knocked my face right into the corner. It's fine, it's ok, really, it is. I am."

Dr. Z nodded, but Emily didn't think he believed her. Why did she have to ramble on like that? It made her sound nervous. Made it sound like a lie. She knew better. But why did he have to ask? Why can't he just leave me alone, leave my house? Dan's house.

"Susan is leaving the office," Dr. Z said. "She's moving back to Arkansas. I was hoping you'd consider taking her job. You're obviously good with the patients. They all seem to love you. What do you say?"

"I have no training. I wouldn't know how."

"That's no problem. I can teach you most of it, the other girls can help you learn, and there's always some training available where I could send you for certifications. You'd be so good at it Emily."

She didn't answer, just stared at what looked like a dirty spot on the wall above his head. Told herself to remember to clean whatever it was off the wall before Dan got home. Maybe it was just a bug that would crawl away.

"Emily?"

"Oh, I'm sorry. What?"

"The job. I think you would be great with the patients."

When she was younger, Emily had the bright idea that she could be a doctor, planned to go to college and study medicine, maybe start as a nurse. That secret dream had died. Now this. It wasn't the same, but it was a start—working with patients, helping people. What if?

"I'm sorry, I can't," she heard herself say even as she thought how much she wanted to.

"If it's about the boys, I can arrange your hours so you can take them to school and pick them up. And we're going to a four-day week when summer starts. Some of the moms at the other offices and my girls and some of the ones at the hospital are talking about setting up a place where their kids can go during the day in the summer. They might even take turns caring for each others' kids, so you could be part of that."

"I'm sorry, I can't," she said again.

"Well, Susan's not leaving for a couple of months, so I'm not going to advertise the position yet. Just think about it. I'll talk to you again and see if you've changed your mind. Or you can call me. I better be going now."

"Yes, that would be good," Emily said.

Dr. Z reached again for Emily's face, but she stepped back to avoid his touch. "Emily, you know you can talk to me, right?"

She walked to the front door and opened it. "Thank you for bringing my coat," she said.

§ § §

When summer vacation arrived, Emily's life became a series of little league games, picnics, trips to the library, and long lazy days at the beach. Emily was always relieved when summer came and the boys were out of school. Shorts and sleeveless shirts hid little, and bathing suits hid even less.

Her family loved the beach. She and the boys went to the south end of Topsail Island often during the week, and Dan joined them on the weekends. Then they usually camped next to Elmore's Inlet on the uninhabited Lea or Hutaff island or in the center of Hutaff, their favorite, accessible only by small boat on high tide. Emily imagined it her own private island. While the boys and their daddy fished, Emily would lie in the sun or walk along the beach searching for shells or staring at the seagulls.

She and the boys spent as much time on the main island as they could when the weather permitted, taking day trips with just blankets and towels, a small cooler and kites. For some reason that she didn't understand but never questioned, Dan didn't seem to mind her taking the boys to the beach on her own as long as they went to the south end of Topsail and not to the more commercialized and populated Wrightsville or Carolina beaches. And as long as she wore what he called "old lady bathing suits" instead of the maillot or two-piece she wore when they were together.

On weekends when Dan could join them, they loaded supplies into their small johnboat and pulled it to the coast, then navigated the saltwater creeks to the uninhabited barrier island off the southeast coast of North Carolina near their Pender County home. Occasionally, she and Dan would make the trip alone. One day in mid-summer that year, she was walking down the island searching for seashells, solitude, and—if she were really lucky—baby turtles hatching. Dan was fishing in the inlet. She was a mile or two down the beach when it happened.

Hutaff Island lay sandwiched between inhabited commercialized vacation spots, and small aircraft often flew overhead. Some strung advertisements like kite tails behind them—"Eat at Joe's" or "Sunglasses—Buy one get one free at Wings" or "Mixed Emotion playing at the Sand Dunes tonight"—some didn't. Occasionally Emily had second thoughts about the planes when she and Dan were enjoying the sun a bit too much. She often wondered if the pilots were equipped with binoculars, or even worse—telephoto lens cameras. Sometimes, most of the time actually, when she and Dan were alone, she didn't really worry that much about any of the airplanes. He usually kept her bathing suit or a towel handy enough to use as cover if the pilots flew too low. Often, when they had been on the beach for a few hours and he had rubbed her body with oil longer than either of them could endure, they never even heard the planes.

Dan was different at the beach. Most of the time.

That day she noticed the plane. It wasn't the first one that had flown by, but it was flying lower than most. It was the first one to circle twice. She glanced up and kept walking. The tide was low, the best time for shell hunting. And at low tide, the long flat island had a significant amount of beach. Enough, even, to land a plane. The pilot circled a third time, then brought the plane skillfully down beside her. She stopped and looked at him.

"Do you have the time?" he asked.

She followed his eyes down her red maillot with the white hibiscus splashed across her chest, down her tanned legs to sandy feet, then back up.

"Not hardly," she said. Then, as an afterthought, she added, "If you really need to know, I can ask my husband. He's just over there fishing and always wears his watch." She pointed in a vague direction that did not divulge the fact that he was almost two miles away.

"No, that's okay," he said. "I was just wondering. Have a nice day."

"You, too," she replied.

He revved up the engine, taxied down the beach and flew away. Heart pounding, Emily turned to head back toward the inlet. She saw Dan running down the beach toward her. When they met, he grabbed her by the shoulders and shook her. He squeezed hard, but not enough to bruise.

"Who was he?"

"I don't know."

"What did he want?"

"He wanted to know what time it was," Emily whispered.

"You're lying! You're always lying. You walk too far. You don't listen. You ruin everything." Dan turned around and stalked off toward the inlet. But he didn't go far before he stopped, turned around and walked back to where Emily still stood staring. "He could have taken you from me." He took Emily by the hand and dragged her back toward the boat.

Chapter 2

In early August, Emily was folding clothes and waiting until time to pick the boys up from day camp at Kirkwood, a local church camp with a pool and a pond and lots of activities to keep two rambunctious boys busy for a few hours each day. The phone rang. She hoped it was not Dr. Z again. He had called once a week since that day he came to her house.

"Just checking to see if you've changed your mind about coming to work," he would say—almost the same words every time. "The person I hired is just not working out. The job is yours anytime you want it."

He was matter-of-fact each time he called, strangely so, as if it were the first time he had mentioned it and that he had not heard her say again and again. "I'm not interested. I like being home with my boys."

The phone kept ringing, and when she answered, Rob's voice on the other end stopped her heart.

"How are you? Where are you?" she asked, after the preliminary shock of recognition had registered.

"I'm in town for a week or so. My brother's getting married."

"It's hard to believe he's that old," she said. "I remember when he was born."

"It's been a long time," he replied.

"Yes, it has. I have two little boys now. My baby starts school this year."

"I know…that you had them, I mean. My parents keep me up to date on the news around home."

"I see your mom once in a while. She invited me to the

wedding."

"Are you coming?"

"I don't know if I can. My parents are definitely going, at least Mama is for sure. I might can come with her."

"I hope you do. I'll be decked out in a tux. Irresistible, maybe."

"You never needed a tuxedo for that."

Emily had never thought of Rob as handsome in the stereotypical sense of the word—unruly black hair, eyes dark and deep-set, smile a bit awry. He wasn't any taller than she was and a little pudgy, muscles not well defined. Still, the attraction had been strong. They were the same age, grew up in the same neighborhood, participated in the same activities, went to school and church together.

She didn't think of him as a brother, though, and she knew he didn't see her as his sister. He was her best friend. Although they never actually dated, they still seemed to find excuses to spend time together, to talk about ambitions, dreams, art and literature. She had not seen him since she married Dan, did not realize just how much she had missed him until she heard his voice.

They had shared a bond unlike any she had known before or since, an intellectual intimacy, but more. They seemed to sense each other's needs before the words were spoken. Even after she married Dan and Rob went off to college, Emily occasionally felt a pain or sadness that she knew was not related to her life, and wondered what was going on with him, who had broken his heart or what burdens he was bearing.

They talked for over an hour. She told him about her family, about how married life was good, but sometimes she wondered about marrying so young. She didn't tell him the truth.

He told her he had been too crazy in college, too busy since, and now he was really ready to settle down. He wanted children. He admitted to a near breakdown when a serious relationship ended for him a few months earlier. Emily then understood that period of depression she suffered, for the dates coincided perfectly.

"Well, I guess I better let you get back to the other men in your life," he said.

"Okay, take care."

"You, too."

She sat for a few minutes with the receiver in her hand, staring at it as though she might see him there. Her mind wandered back to a time when life was simple, a time when she could speak without worrying about the consequences, when she could sleep without nightmares. With daydreams filling her mind and summer sunlight filtering through the windows, she gave in to her exhaustion from sleepless nights and dozed.

The ringing phone startled her awake. She looked at the clock and panicked before she answered.

"Mrs. Gillespie," a stern female voice said. "Did you forget your children?"

"No, ma'am, I'm sorry. I'll be right there."

When she arrived at the camp—a full hour late—her boys were sitting on the steps of the dining hall, the seven-year-old's arm around his little brother's shoulder. All the other kids were gone.

"Where were you?" Danny demanded. "Bobby was scared. You're never late."

"I'm sorry," Emily said, wiping the dirty streaks from her six-year-old's face. "I lost track of time. Mommy promises never, never to do that again. How about some ice cream?"

Emily took the boys to the soda shop at Dees Drugstore, then hurried home to finish what she had neglected during her unexpected nap. By the time Dan arrived home from work, the house was clean, the boys were settled, and supper was on the table.

During the meal, Bobby spoke up. "Mommy forgot us today."

"What?" his daddy said. "Mommy would never forget you."

"I was just a few minutes late. I got busy and time slipped up on me."

"Mommy won't forget you tomorrow, Bobby," Dan said with a stern look at Emily.

After the boys went to bed, Dan said, "You're preoccupied. What's going on?"

"I'm sorry. I was so tired. I just dozed off and was a little bit late. That's all."

"You've got no right to be tired. You're just lazy—taking naps in the middle of the day. Neglecting our boys. Something's going on I should know about. Tell me."

"Nothing, really. It's a beautiful night. Do you want to walk outside with me?"

"Why would I want to do that? Unlike some people, I have to work. I'm going to bed."

"OK. I'll be there soon."

She watched Dan head toward their bedroom, then turned and walked out the back door. The sky was clear with a million stars punctuating its depths. She sat down on the grass, drew her legs up to her chest, wrapped her arms around her shins, and leaned back against a pine tree, just thinking. Should she tell Dan about the phone call? She really didn't do anything wrong by talking to Rob. Did she? How could she possibly have fallen asleep and forgotten her boys?

Over an hour later, Emily stood to go back into the house. She was chilled and her leg muscles ached. The den was dark, the television off.

She didn't feel like going to bed. Dan would be angry that she took so long, and she wasn't ready to face him. A little more time and he'd be sound asleep, he'd never know when she slipped in beside him. At least she hoped he wouldn't. Or maybe she'd just stay up all night and when his alarm clock went off, bacon would be frying like normal. He'd never know she didn't come to bed. Emily switched on a small lamp, selected several photograph albums from the shelves, stacked them on the end table, and sat down on the couch, her feet curled up under her. She tugged down her favorite brown and blue afghan hanging behind her and draped it across her legs. She opened the first one—May 1955.

Emily had just graduated from high school—the photo of her in black cap and gown, gold tassel for honors, Beta Club ribbon around her neck. Dan stood to her right with his arm wrapped possessively around her waist. Her mama and daddy stood to her left. She remembered how much she wanted to go on that graduation trip to Myrtle Beach with her classmates, the friends she'd grown up with. But Dan had said, "You go, and you'll be raising that baby by yourself."

She found out for sure she was pregnant two weeks before graduation. When that picture was taken, her parents didn't know— that she was pregnant, getting married, not going to college. But looking at her own smiling face, eleven years younger, Emily saw a sparkle, could feel that same warmth radiate inside. She unconsciously rubbed her abdomen with her left hand—it was firm, solid, flat. An empty womb. She wept for the little girl she lost.

Wedding pictures followed, summer flowers in yellows and reds—Dan's parents' backyard garden. Emily remembered the day she tried to tell Dan she wanted to get married in her family church, that she wanted her own mother to help plan the wedding, choose the flowers, the food, the music. She told him she wanted a traditional wedding. He said she should of thought about that before she got pregnant.

"If my mother wants it in her garden, it will be in her garden," he had said.

Emily remembered telling her mama that she and Dan decided on the garden, remembered seeing the hurt in her eyes. But Mama just said not to worry, it was fine, that God would be wherever they were. Mama always saw the good in people, including Dan. And Emily had loved him so.

Emily smiled at the pictures of summer vacation at the beach, could see a baby bulge. She had felt the baby move for the first time that July day and felt an overwhelming love like none she'd ever known—not with her mama, not her daddy, not even Dan. She wanted that baby more than she'd ever wanted anything in her life. She never said it, but Dan knew, and even that made him jealous— jealous of his own baby. Emily shook her head and turned the page. Dan had been a good daddy to their boys. He had.

The first holiday pictures were difficult to see. Emily wasn't sure why she'd even put them in the books unless in an effort to convince herself that everything was fine, that she was normal. But looking at them now, she saw her vacant stares, empty eyes that fake smiles could not disguise. She hardly recognized the gaunt person as herself, but there she was with Dan's arm around her waist. Emily remembered the times he threatened to leave if she didn't straighten up. It was just a miscarriage, women have them all the time. We'll have more babies later, he promised, when the time's right.

Pictures from the next year were better—the treatments and medicine were working and Emily was learning how to live with Dan. He was the man, after all, just let him be head of the household and everything would be fine. She built her world around making him happy, then she could be happy, too. She learned what sparked the jealousy and avoided it as much as possible, which included skipping the neighborhood cookouts when Rob might be there with his family. Dan hated him simply because he had once been so important to Emily. She knew she wouldn't go to the wedding.

Dan didn't like any of her old friends, did not want her associating with them. But he made up for it by taking her out to dinner, to the movies, on trips.

"We can have fun together," he'd said, "just the two of us."

Emily spent the rest of the night looking through the albums, replacing one stack, taking down more, reminding herself of how good her life had been with Dan. Telling herself how much she loved him. She enjoyed the memories conjured up from pictures of being pregnant, bulging huge with a full-term baby. Danny. Then only an album later, another. Bobby. Pictures of smiling faces, beach trips, holidays. Pushing back the memories of jealous tirades, anger, threats, pain. All families have problems, she told herself. Dan was a good daddy, and he loved her, worked hard to support them, make a good life for them.

Emily stared at one picture that brought back frightening memories. She remembered that Friday in 1963 when she was ironing the shorts and jacket Bobby wore in that portrait. They were going to Wilmington on Saturday morning to have photos made for their Christmas cards. Dan had chastised her for waiting so late—told her the photos probably wouldn't be ready in time for them to frame one for his parents for Christmas, much less in time to have Christmas cards made and mailed. He was right about the cards.

Like she always did when she ironed, Emily was watching *As the World Turns,* the characters talking about who was coming to Thanksgiving dinner the next week. No one would be coming to Emily's home and she wouldn't be going to her mama's. Dan had insisted they would go to Raleigh, where his parents had recently returned, and spend the entire weekend. He would not hear of splitting their time between families even though her mama had said they could celebrate Thanksgiving on Saturday or even Sunday. It was always that way.

Danny and Bobby, then three and four, were playing with their Matchbox cars on the floor in front of the fireplace. When the Niagara starch commercial came on, Emily thought, *We'll see if it really works.* She had been using the spray starch for a while, but the starch that was supposed to be poured into the washing machine promised less ironing. Emily looked at the laundry basket full of wrinkled clothes and wondered if she had wasted her money.

Funny how all those little things were still so vivid in her mind, Emily thought, recalled with clarity just by the sight of a picture and a little boy's outfit.

Emily remembered that the show had just come back on when it was interrupted with a CBS News Bulletin. She heard Walter Cronkite say the president had been shot and the wounds could be fatal. Then another ad came on. Emily remembered being so scared, so worried, so angry that advertisements were running, that the show came back on, that they really knew nothing. Then another bulletin— three shots fired, the president hit in the head and the neck, Connolly hit, a secret service man yelling, "He's dead," and Mrs. Kennedy crying out, "Oh, no!"

Cronkite said they couldn't be sure who the secret service man was referring to and that the president had been rushed to Parkland Hospital. Then the television went back to *As the World Turns.* Then another commercial—Friskies puppy food. Emily remembered because her children stopped playing long enough to watch the cocker spaniels eating. Such a surreal moment.

Then another bulletin – President John F. Kennedy was dead.

Emily could feel the shield of sanity she had fought so hard to salvage being poked and prodded by the events unfolding in front of her. She couldn't keep her eyes off the television for the next few days. She watched as Jack Ruby just walked right up to Lee Harvey Oswald and shot him point blank in the stomach in the basement of Dallas police headquarters. Was nobody safe anywhere?

That weekend, her neighbor's son was killed in Vietnam. He was the fifth one in three years from their small town.

But what stood out most in Emily's mind was Jackie Kennedy in a blood soaked pink suit, then veiled in black leading young Caroline to her father's casket. The kiss. Tiny little John-John in his coat saluting his father's casket as it passed on the horse-drawn carriage. Two children forced to grow up without a father.

Emily closed the photograph book and swore she wouldn't let that happen to her children. She could take whatever happened. Her sons needed a whole family. She put the albums away and headed to the kitchen to start breakfast.

Chapter 3

The boys always visited their grandparents in Raleigh during their last week of summer break. Emily and Dan spent the time at the beach, camping alone. But this year, Dan's boss insisted he go on an emergency business trip for the entire week.

"I don't want you here by yourself," Dan said. "Maybe I should call my parents and tell them the boys can't come."

"No," Emily said, "I'll be fine. You know your mother would be so disappointed." Emily smiled to reassure him.

"Why do you look so happy about being alone—a whole week by yourself? I just don't know. You won't have enough to occupy your time and too many things can happen."

"I'll be fine," Emily repeated. "It'll give me plenty of time to get everything ready for the start of school. I can ride out and visit my mama and daddy. I don't see them enough since they moved to the country, and they're not getting any younger."

"Well, I don't have much of a choice," Dan said. "Just be here when I call you. Be here."

§ § §

Emily cleaned all day on Monday, but decided to spend Tuesday at the beach. She'd never done anything like that before—gone to the beach alone—but what could it hurt? It wasn't like she was meeting a man there. She wasn't sure where this one burst of courage—or maybe insanity—was coming from, but she took her beach bag, her chair, and a book to the south end of Topsail Island. She'd just stay a few hours.

Emily left the beach in plenty of time to get home before Dan's meetings would be over and he'd have time to call. The guilt had been trying to nudge its way into her solitude all day long, and a cold fear began to rise when she saw the long line of traffic on Hwy 17 in Hampstead. A wreck. Fire trucks and police cars were everywhere. An ambulance flew down the shoulder of the road to her right. She said a prayer for the people involved, and one for herself as well. She wouldn't be home when Dan called.

The phone was ringing when Emily entered her home. She couldn't reach it fast enough, and the ringing stopped. She was sure it was Dan. She walked into the laundry room and threw her beach bag on the floor. The phone began to ring again, and she rushed to answer it.

"Hi Mommy, we're having fun." She heard Bobby's voice followed by an ensuing argument between her children.

"Let me talk to her," Danny said. "I have to tell her."

Emily could hear Bobby cry out as Danny took the phone and began to talk with his older brother superiority.

"Hi Mom, Grandma G said she'd bring us home on Sunday instead of Saturday. Is that alright? Please, can we stay a extra night? We're going to the circus! Please!" Emily heard Bobby in the background echoing his brother's pleadings. She couldn't help but smile.

"Hey boys," she said loudly enough for anyone close to the phone to hear her. "Mommy will talk to both of you. Danny, could you let your little brother go first? Then, we'll talk about your request."

The boys took turns telling her about what they had been doing at their grandparents' home and all the presents they had received. They talked for at least twenty minutes. She needed them home, wanted to hug them, take care of them. She wanted to tell them she was coming to pick them up right then, that day, but they had only been gone two days. So she told them she loved them and that they could stay until Sunday.

"Mommy misses you," she said before she hung up.

The phone rang immediately.

"Where in the hell have you been?" Dan yelled before Emily

even spoke. "I called every time I had a break—all day long."

"I'm sorry I missed your calls," Emily said calmly, hoping the tone of her voice would help diffuse his anger. "I was running errands off and on all day." She wasn't sure why she lied.

"How's your meeting going?"

His voice was a bit calmer, but still held an edge of rage. "Fine, I just hate being away from home. You know that. And with the boys gone, too, I just don't like you being alone. You know I worry. You should be home when I call."

"I'll be fine, Dan. Really. This will give me a chance to give the house a good cleaning. You know how it piles up during the summer when I'm spending all my time with the boys. I talked to them just before you called. They're having so much fun. Your parents are taking them to the circus on Saturday night, so they're not coming home until Sunday. You'll be back Friday night. That will give us time alone. We haven't had much of that lately. Won't that be nice?"

Her rambling apparently calmed him, for when he spoke, all the anger seemed to have faded.

"Can I take my favorite girl on a date?"

"That would be nice," Emily responded. "Maybe we can take the boat out, spend the day on the island. I might be able to find a new two-piece on the sales racks at Sears. Would you like that?"

"I've got a better idea. I found a place here where I can get some movies. We'll set up the projector and spend the day in bed. Maybe I'll even bring you a surprise."

Emily cringed. Dan had started bringing home movies she didn't want to watch and toys she didn't want to play with. But resisting increased the level of pain. She was glad he could not see through the phone.

"Okay," she whispered.

"I'm sorry I yelled, Emily. I was just worried. With me gone and the boys, you know? I didn't want to leave you."

"I'm fine, Dan. We live in a nice neighborhood. You've worked hard to make sure of that. I'll be safe. I have been every time."

"It's not that, Emily. You're just so beautiful. I can't keep an eye on you when I'm so far away. I don't know where you are or what you are doing or who you are with. You don't answer the phone."

There it was again—the jealousy, the distrust. She had dealt with it for so many years, all those innocent years. He had hurled accusations of infidelity when all she cared about was taking care of her boys and making a home for her family. She had never strayed, never even thought about it, but for years the innuendoes hung in the air like a poison mist, stifling her, controlling every decision she tried to make.

"Emily, you still there? You didn't answer me."

"Oh, I'm sorry, what did you say?"

"My break's over, I have to get back to the meeting."

"Fine, ok, I'll talk to you later. Love you."

"Love you, too."

Emily checked the locks on the doors, walked to her bedroom and took off her cover up. When she stripped off her bathing suit, she saw her reflection in the mirror. She was always so careful with sunscreen—for her and the boys. But today she forgot. She saw the sunburn that Dan would surely notice, and began to cry, deep heaving sobs that strangled her breath and drained her body. She lay down on her bed, hugged her pillow to her chest, curled around it like a baby, and let the tears flow until all her energy was spent.

Startled awake by the ringing telephone, Emily rolled over and quickly answered it. She was sure it was Dan again, and she didn't want him to wonder where she was or what she was doing. She didn't have the strength to deal with the questions. But when she said hello, no one answered. She said it again and again, but still no answer. She started to hang up, but heard the faint noise, the breathing, so slight she wasn't sure she really heard it at all. She gently laid the receiver in the cradle and sat on the edge of the bed staring at the phone. Moments later, it rang again.

"Hello beautiful," Dan responded to her timid hello. "My meetings are over for the day and I needed to hear your voice."

"What time is it?" she asked.

"Six o'clock. What are you doing?"

Emily looked down at her naked body and felt embarrassed. "Oh, just cleaning. I guess I got so busy I didn't realize how late it was." She couldn't believe she had fallen asleep.

After her conversation with Dan, Emily showered and put on her favorite flannel pajamas—the ones Dan never let her wear. She didn't care if it was summer. She'd just turn down the thermostat.

The dog began to bark, and Emily remembered she had not fed him. She slipped out the back door, hoping the neighbors could not see her in the dusky shadows of approaching nightfall. The chocolate lab nearly knocked her down with excitement.

"Hey Winston, old buddy. You hungry?" He obviously wanted attention as much as food, but Emily just went through the motions—dumping the food, refilling the water dish. "The boys will be back in few days," she said, and hurried back inside the garage. "I miss them, too," she whispered, more to herself than the dog.

In the corner, she saw the sign in bright red letters above the trash can—the sign meant for Danny any other week, his first big important chore since turning seven. "Don't forget! The garbage truck comes early Wednesday morning."

Emily knew she couldn't let the trash wait until the boys came home. She pressed the button and the garage door rattled open. She lifted the can up into the boys' wagon and rolled it down the paved driveway to the street. Her eyes scanned the neighborhood, the wiggling shadows of trees, dark cavernous spaces between houses contrasted by bright light-filled windows. That phone call had really done a number on her nerves. Probably nothing, she reassured herself.

They had lived in this house since right after Dan graduated from State, a couple years after they married. It was an older two-story home in the upper middle class neighborhood of Burgaw, just a couple of streets over from where she had grown up next to her best friend Rob, and where Dan had moved as a senior in high school. A safe little southern town where few locked their doors and the older kids played kick-the-can in the streets at night. Emily had never been scared there, never worried about her boys chasing fireflies out in the yard after dark, playing hide and seek in the woods behind the house, or ain't no bears out tonight. It was a perfect place to raise a family. But she turned and hurried back to the house, not understanding the nervous tingles running up her arms.

Emily slept fitfully. Waking before dawn, she tried to concentrate on the cleaning she told Dan she was doing, but guilt weighed heavy on her heart. Why did one little trip to the beach make her feel so guilty? Why did she lie to Dan? She had every right to go to the beach, didn't she?

Emily had never had any close girlfriends the way so many women did—no one she could confide in, ask for advice. Dan wouldn't allow it. What advice could they give her anyway?

She couldn't talk to her mother; she would never understand. Her parents had the perfect marriage as far as she could tell. Her daddy never even raised his voice to her mama. Emily was positive he would never raise a hand. And she didn't want them to worry.

And she certainly couldn't confide in her sister-in-law—older by two years but as immature and demanding as anyone Emily had ever known. No, she would definitely not seek advice or even solace from Norma. She'd had three husbands since becoming widowed by Emily's brother. Emily would continue to deal with it on her own. But there seemed to be a seismic shift brewing, and she wasn't sure she would be strong enough to withstand the tremors.

She would just pretend she never had the nerve to spend a day at the beach by herself—keep it a secret from Dan. She hadn't seen anyone she knew. With renewed vigor she scrubbed and cleaned. Late in the afternoon, she was working on the living room windows, concentrating on a stubborn streak when she saw a pickup pass slowly by the house—one she'd never seen in their neighborhood before. Her hand stopped moving but the truck kept rolling, down the street and out of sight. The windows were tinted and the truck was dark, but didn't really look black. Maybe blue, maybe green. Near dark, when she went out to feed Winston, she saw it again, stopped a block or so down the street headed in the opposite direction. When she looked up, the brake lights faded, and the truck disappeared around the curve. She hurried into the house.

Fifteen minutes later the phone rang. She expected to hear Dan's voice after she said hello, but heard no one. She listened silently and the breathing began, soft and low, throaty. Then the music—*Under the Boardwalk*—barely audible, but definitely there. Emily placed the receiver back in the cradle gently, trying not to make a sound.

She checked the locks on the doors, closed and locked all the windows. Emily had always loved letting the late summer breezes into the house, but not now. Before she went to bed, she opened the safe in the closet, took out the .38 revolver, made sure it was loaded, and placed it under Dan's pillow. She tried to remember the last time they had spent an afternoon at target practice.

§ § §

Dan called at least twice a day while he was gone, but never at the same time of day. Emily stayed home the rest of the week, barely even went in the yard so she would be there to answer his calls. She did not want another argument with him. The voiceless calls came daily, and the jitters they produced were long lasting. Emily found herself constantly nervous—not just at night when darkness masked the serenity of her neighborhood. Unsettling thoughts also kept her home during the day. What if she came back and found someone in her house?

And scariest of all—the heart palpations were back, the difficulty breathing, the pressure like an elephant walking on her chest. The symptoms swept over her like a sudden summer storm—nowhere to hide. Emily knew what came next—the crying for no reason, the yelling at people she loved. She had fought so hard years ago, after she lost her daughter, to overcome the depression, the anxiety attacks. She endured the electric shock treatments, took the medications that made her feel like a zombie. And she won. She had been off her meds since the day eight years earlier when the doctor said, "Congratulations, you're pregnant." She'd been such a good mother—everybody said so. She would not become that other person again—not with her boys. But they weren't there—no one was—so Emily crawled into bed and cried.

By mid-afternoon on Friday, Emily knew she needed to get up and get moving. She had been in bed all day. Dan would be home that evening and she had promised to prepare his favorite dinner. She didn't have any cubed steak in the freezer, no cheese in the fridge, no pears or potatoes in the pantry. Whether she wanted to or not, she had to leave the house, go to the grocery store, act like a normal person. And she hadn't picked up the mail all week. At least the house was clean—every nook and cranny. With her self-imposed confinement, she had spent every waking moment scrubbing and cleaning—anything she could do inside to keep busy, to make the hands of the clock move, the dates on the calendar pass. But no matter how hard she worked physically, no amount of housework required enough mental stimulation to keep her mind occupied.

She had no idea who was making the calls or who drove the truck that made daily slow passes by her house. She'd never seen windows so dark. She knew she should tell Dan, but she knew instinctively that it would become her fault. She hadn't done anything wrong. When Dan's truck was back in the driveway, when her boys were home, everything would be fine. The calls would stop and her life would return to normal. Everything would be okay.

Determined to be optimistic, Emily dressed and headed into the garage to get Winston's food. Her newfound courage quickly dissipated at the sight of flowers—four roses in different colors and varying condition of wilt—placed under the wipers of her car. One for each day she had not left the house. Emily quickly slapped the button to open the garage door and it rattled up. Winston came bounding in, craving attention and food. With the sunlight pouring in, Winston obviously unconcerned, and no one standing there ready to attack, Emily found the courage to approach her car, remove the roses and throw them in the trash. As she lifted each one, she noticed that all the thorns had been removed. Did that mean anything?

Emily checked the door that opened to the back yard. She must have left it unlocked. She looked around the garage—saw the boys' bikes, Dan's hand tools, her gardening supplies, the balls and bats, scooters and pogo sticks—nothing seemed to be disturbed or missing, but Emily flinched at the sight of the ax. Someone had been inside her garage—as close to the inside of her house as a simple wooden door—and the very tool he needed to break down the door, come in and kill her was leaning up in the corner, waiting. She looked around for a place to hide it, to make it less conspicuous, less inviting. She saw none. So she opened the rear hatch on her station wagon and placed the ax inside.

"Wanna go for a ride, ole buddy?" she said to Winston. He had never been in the car. When he went to the vet, he rode in the back of the truck, tied in to keep him from bounding over the side at the first sight of another animal or humans, especially kids. But Emily didn't care. With a little convincing, the bribery of a chew bone, and a bit of shoving, she loaded him into the back seat and slammed the door. Emily backed the car out, comforted by Winston's big head hanging over the front seat right next to her face.

She went to the post office first, looking around at all the vehicles parked along the street and in the small lot. No trucks with dark windows.

"I'll be right back," she told Winston.

Emily turned the combination lock on her mailbox, but it wouldn't open. She tried again with no luck. She couldn't have forgotten the combination—her brain was not totally incapacitated—so she went to the counter and stood in line.

"My lock doesn't seem to be working today," she told the postal clerk. "Box 576."

"Well, it's good to finally see you, Emily. We've been wondering where you were. Is everything okay?"

"It would be if I could get to my mail." Emily didn't mean to sound rude, but sometimes small towns really bugged her. You couldn't even miss picking up your mail for a few days without people gossiping about you.

"Probably just jammed. You haven't been by and the box is so full it's probably caught on the latch. Wait right here and I'll get it for you. We have some behind the counter that wouldn't fit in the box. Have you been on vacation?"

"No," Emily said.

"Well, when you go on vacation, you need to give us a call. We can hold your mail for you, and we won't keep trying to stuff it in the box thinking you're going to pick it up."

"I'll remember that," Emily said.

"You won't believe how many people don't remember. They just leave town and we keep trying to stick the mail in their box and it won't fit and we have to start piles on the outside. Sometimes people aren't on vacation. They just moved away without leaving a forwarding address or changing their address and then we don't know what to do with their mail. We don't know they're really gone until they don't pay the rent on their box. You're not moving away and leaving us now are you?"

"No. But I do need to run to the grocery store. Could I get my mail, please?"

"Oh yeah, sorry. Just rambling on and holding you up. I am glad to see you. Everyone will be relieved to know you've been by."

Emily took the armful of mail with a quick "thank you" and hurried out the door. She would have to do some fast work to take care of all that mail and cook dinner before Dan got home. She glanced around again on her way back to the car. No trucks. The stack of mail was hard to handle with one hand and when she tried to open the car door, the envelopes tucked inside *The State* magazine slid out onto the pavement.

"Shit," she whispered under her breath as she knelt down to scoop up the mail she had dropped. Someone tapped her on the shoulder and she jumped, releasing all the mail. It flew in every direction, under her car, on the sidewalk, under the car next to her. Winston started barking, a loud excited series of yelps. Emily was scared to look up.

"Why so jumpy, little sister?" Norma stood over Emily with her hands on her hips, a big smile on her face. "Nobody's gonna getcha."

"You just startled me, that's all. How about a little help."

"Sure. Where've you been? Mama and I thought you might call us and take us out to lunch or something while you were all alone this week. You have better things to do? You obviously didn't come to the post office."

"I've just been busy."

"A little action on the side?" Norma winked at Emily and shook her hips. She was wearing tight hip hugging bell-bottoms and a form-fitting sweater that didn't cover her midriff. Even in her thirties with five children, Norma was still a looker. But that was her priority, after all. Her goal in life, as she put it, was to have "six-pack abs."

"That's your style, not mine. I've been cleaning house, catching up on things I let go during the summer when I was spending time with my boys. Being a mom."

"Sorry, I forgot. Emily, the perfect. Anyway, I just thought you should know that Mama is feeling hurt. She thought you'd spend some time with her while your husband and boys were away. You haven't even called. Well, gotta go. I'm taking my kids to the movies—one last big hurrah before school starts. Being a good mom. You don't have the monopoly on that, you know."

"I didn't mean it that way, Norma, and you know it." Emily was exasperated. No matter what she did or said, her sister-in-law could twist it to suit her needs. "I'm going to the grocery store now. I'll call Mama when I get home."

"She won't be there. Daddy's taking her out to dinner. It's Friday night, or did you forget?"

"I know what happens on Friday nights." For as long as Emily could remember, Daddy had taken Mama on a Friday night date. How could she have forgotten that? "But it's not that late."

"They're going out to eat early tonight." Norma smirked at her. "So they can go to the movies with me and the kids. We don't neglect them." She turned and walked away.

It was true. Norma and her children spent a lot more time out at the farm. Emily had always hated that Norma called her in-laws Mama and Daddy. The one time she let that slip in front of Dan, he told her she was being petty and selfish. Norma had been married to Emily's brother Charles for less than two years when he was killed in an accident. Their daughter Elizabeth was just a baby. But Mama

33

considered Norma her daughter from the very beginning and even after she kept getting married and divorced and having more children, Mama kept including them all as part of the family. Maybe I am selfish, Emily thought.

She knew that Norma called Mama every day. She took her children out to the farm for supper two or three times a week and for Sunday dinner. Mama always put on a big spread, hoping the whole family would be there. Emily tried to go on Sundays as much as possible, but if Dan had plans, he wanted Emily and the boys with him. But she couldn't blame her absence all on Dan. She had plenty of opportunity during the week, during the summer, and she did other things. It was just so incredibly hard to sit and listen to Mama singing Norma's praises every time she managed to get something right, no matter how briefly. If she only knew. But Emily would never tell. Mama thought of Norma as her daughter, and it would break her heart to know the truth.

At the grocery store, Emily struggled to remember what she went to buy. She walked up and down the aisles without putting anything in her grocery cart. *Think*, she commanded herself. *Concentrate.* She never made lists, had never needed to, but maybe now, maybe she would be more in control with a list. She rummaged through her purse for a pen and a scrap of paper. Finding nothing but an old grocery store receipt and one of Bobby's crayons, she started to scrawl down what she needed to buy for dinner, and breakfast. Heck, while she was there she might as well get what she needed for the week. The boys were coming home on Sunday. She would buy them a treat. Discarding the list, she pushed her cart to the produce section on the far right side of the store and began again— one aisle at a time.

The boys loved grapes, so she bought red seedless ones, then added a bag of white seedless, too. They were on sale. Strawberries with chocolate sauce for a romantic evening with her husband. Oranges, apples, onions, cucumbers, cabbage, salad fixin's, green pepper for fried rice, bananas, potatoes. Emily was on a roll. She had shopped weekly for groceries so many years, knew what her family loved to eat, knew what she needed for each recipe, knew exactly how much it would cost. All she had to do was make a mental note of menus for the week and the rest was easy. She felt good getting back into a normal routine. She could do this. The return of her symptoms was just a temporary setback. Everything would get back to normal tonight. She would take care of her husband, her boys, go visit her parents more often, go walking in the woods with her daddy, shopping with her mama. She would go back to church.

"May I have your attention please?" The store's announcements of specials—some things you can always count on, Emily thought. Expecting the young lady's voice to announce a special on peanut butter, Emily listened as she continued putting items in her basket. "Would an Emily Gillespie please come to the customer service desk." Emily stopped. What now?

She pushed her half-filled buggy to the front of the store. "I'm Emily Gillespie," she told the teenaged clerk. "You called me."

"Yes, ma'am. You have a phone call. We don't usually do that, call you on the loudspeaker, I mean, but the person said it was an emergency. Sounded like they were crying. You can come around here and take it."

Emily rushed through the swinging half door and up two steps to the customer service area that overlooked the store. She picked up the receiver lying on the counter.

"Hello?"

No answer. No sound.

"Hello!"

Breathing. The music, the words—*now I've finally found my candy girl, candy girl.* A click. Dial tone.

"Was it a man?" Emily asked frantically. "Did he give you his name?"

"I don't know. The voice was muffled. Sounded funny. I don't know if it was a man or a woman. I couldn't tell. Nobody gave me no name." The young girl was obviously flustered by Emily's reaction.

"I'm sorry. It's not your fault. I have to go."

Emily hurried out into the parking lot, leaving her groceries in the cart and what little sense of normalcy she had managed to muster in the store. She just wanted to get home. Tears began to well up and spill over, running down her cheeks despite her constant self-reprimand to walk not run, just get home, hold it together, just get home. Lock the door. She stepped on the tiny pile of red rosebud heads lying beside her car door before she saw them. A small handful, easily dropped while walking between cars.

Emily looked frantically around the parking lot. *He's here. I know he's here.* She saw no one she knew, no truck with dark windows, nothing. Winston's bark was continuous, but it was a happy bark, an *I'm glad to see* you bark. Emily opened the car door and sat down on the edge of her seat. The crushed rosebuds clung to the bottoms of her shoes and she bumped her feet together to shake them loose—tiny red buds falling to the pavement like drops of blood.

Winston stuck his head over the back seat and licked her in the face, big slobbery tongue wiping away the tears that fell freely. "Who'd you see, ole buddy?" Emily sniffled. "Who?" She pulled her feet up into the car, slid around, slammed and locked the door, put the key into the ignition, but couldn't turn it. The trembling in her hands radiated like lightening to the rest of her body. She fought to control the shaking, the pounding in her chest, the ragged breaths, the tears, but she lost. She sat in her car in the middle of the Wilson's parking lot and sobbed.

Emily wasn't sure how long she sat there. Time became inconsequential. Armies of self-reproach questions marched through her brain, taking her back to childhood then forward, tormenting her, laughing at her—*Why did I steal my daddy's dime? Why did I throw a fit over a hoodless jacket? Why did I tell my brother to leave me alone? Why did I lie about breaking that flower pot? Why did I play sick to miss church? Why did I drink that beer? Why did I yell at my mama? Why did I ignore Daddy's warning? Why did I have sex before marriage? Why did I marry Dan? Why did I lose my baby? My little girl. Why? Why the note, why the plane, why the phone calls, why the roses, why me? Why is somebody trying to drive me crazy? Again. Why?*

Emily pounded her hands on the steering wheel until they hurt. Cried until no more tears would come. Winston whimpered and nudged her shoulder. Then he began a low guttural growl that erupted into huge harrowing barks. Emily turned her head to look at him and someone tapped the car window behind her. She jumped.

"Lady, hey lady, you alright?" A teenage boy with shaggy brown curls and a bag boy apron peered through the car window. Dusk was settling in and streaks of the setting sun glared around his head causing an ethereal glow. He tapped on the window again. "You okay, lady?"

Emily rolled down the window slightly and tried to smile. "I'm fine," she said.

"Well, okay, if you say so. You been sitting here a long time and you didn't look so fine to me."

"I'm fine," Emily repeated. "Thank you for asking." She rolled the window back up, cranked her car and drove home. She drove slowly, scanning the neighborhood, looking down side streets, in driveways. When the garage door rattled up, she pulled the car in carefully, scouring every corner for signs of anything amiss, someone waiting. She saw nothing, no one, and quickly closed the garage door behind her. She opened the back car door for Winston, knelt down and hugged him; his soft chocolate fur tickled her nose and she tried to smile. He whimpered.

"You been cooped up a while. Bet you gotta go bad."

She walked to the door leading out the back of the garage and let Winston out. Her eyes scanned the edge of the back yard and the woods beyond. She closed the door, made sure the lock was secure, and hurried into the house.

Chapter 4

Dan's plane was scheduled to land at 8 p.m. at RDU, so with the two-hour drive home, he wouldn't be there before 10 p.m. at the earliest. Still, Emily had promised him dinner. She couldn't bring herself to go out in the impending dark, return to the grocery store, even though it was just 7:30. She checked all the window locks, the doors, turned on the television, the volume up loud, but she didn't sit down to watch it. She rummaged through the cabinets and the freezer for anything she could throw together for dinner. She found frozen chicken breasts, salmon, brussel sprouts, broccoli, lima beans. The pantry still held one can of cream of chicken soup, a few crackers left in the box, some chips, some garden peas. If she could find enough mayonnaise and some cheese, she could make chicken divan. Opening the refrigerator, she pushed around the Tupperware containers of leftovers from the week before. In all her cleaning, she hadn't made it to the refrigerator.

Emily started pulling out the leftovers, stacking the storage containers on the counter. She knew none of it would be any good; she had not cooked for herself or stored leftovers all week. She could hardly remember what she had eaten or when, and was suddenly hungry. Maybe because Dan was on his way home and the children would be home soon. Life could return to normal.

The Duke's mayonnaise jar in the door had several tablespoons left, maybe not a cup like the recipe called for, but it would work. Way in the back on the second shelf, Emily found a hunk of cheddar cheese lodged in the corner. She opened the plastic bag to find mold growing on the edges, but she could trim that off. She laid it on the counter to be grated and combined with crumbled crackers to make the topping for the casserole. Molded cheese didn't mean it had to be thrown away. Not as much could be said for what was in the containers, mold masking most of what had once been meatloaf, macaroni and cheese, tuna salad, roast beef, lasagna.

The crisper drawer hid remnants of carrots, shriveled with saggy, slimy leaves on one end and shrunken black tips on the other; half a head of lettuce with curled brown edges; grapes growing gray fungus at the stems; cucumbers succumbing to rot, sagging vertically down the center, hollowing out a vegetable canoe. Nothing Emily wanted to touch, so she pulled the drawer all the way out and sat it in the sink. The meat drawer revealed nothing salvageable—bologna blossoming white bumps, sandwich ham emitting a hideous odor, sandwich cheese slices curling brittle edges.

Emily pulled the trashcan from under the sink and started dumping drawers. Slime slithered down the edges, so she filled the drawers with hot soapy water and began emptying the Tupperware containers in the trash as well. Worried that the plastic bag might leak, causing even more problems to clean, Emily pulled another white plastic trash bag from the box under the sink, lifted the bag from the trashcan and slipped it into the new one. Freed from the confinement of the can, the bag offered more room. Emily set the double-bagged mess on the floor and finished dumping food, thinking about starving children and berating herself for being so wasteful.

She tied the bags and set them by the back door, needing a little more courage to actually unlock it and take them to the garage. Picking a pot from under the cabinet, she covered the frozen chicken breasts with water and turned the burner on medium high. She dumped the frozen broccoli into another pot and barely covered it with water, then turned the burner on medium to cook just long enough to become tender and stay green, but not long enough to make it mushy and dark. After it cooked, she would drain it in the colander, then dump it on a clean dish towel to remove all the excess water. Dan hated runny chicken divan. Placing a new trash bag into the can, she shoved it back under the sink, then on second thought, pulled it back out so she could let the molded trimmings from the cheese drop straight into the bag.

Emily was busily grating cheese when the phone rang. Her hand slipped, slicing her knuckle against the grater. Blood trickled into the sink as she rinsed her hands, postponing the inevitable. She had to answer it.

"Hello?"

No one spoke. Music played in the background, but Emily didn't recognize it.

"Hello?" Emily spoke loudly, trying to mask her fear.

"I was about to think you weren't there. What took you so long to answer? You know I expect you to answer the phone."

"Dan. It's you."

"You expecting somebody else?"

"No, of course not. I was cooking, getting supper ready for you."

"Well, unless you're hungry, you might as well stop. We're delayed, got a layover in Dallas, won't be in RDU until after midnight. I talked to my parents. I'm just going to their house when I get in. Mother wants me to stay and go to the circus with the boys tomorrow night, then I'll bring them home on Sunday. That'll save my parents a trip down."

"That makes sense." Emily tried not to let the disappointment show in her voice. "Maybe I could come, meet you there."

"No point in that. We'll be home Sunday. Gotta go. They're calling my flight now."

Emily said goodbye to the click of the phone. Both pots boiled over, sizzling on the stove. Emily lifted and tilted the lids, turned the burners to low, and continued grating the cheese. Tears leaked over her lower lids and trickled down her face while she crumbled crackers into the grated cheese, drained the broccoli, chopped the chicken, mixed the mayonnaise with the cream of chicken soup, layered everything into the casserole dish and placed it in the oven. While it baked, she showered with the curtain open, wrapped herself in the warmth of flannel pajamas, then made a pitcher of tea. She ate alone in front of the television, watching reruns of *The Andy Griffith Show* until she fell asleep on the couch.

Sun streaking through the blind slats woke Emily early on Saturday just as the television station resumed programming for the day—one more day without her boys, one more day without her husband, one more day without her sense of security. Emily summoned all the strength she could muster and began to plan her day, just one more day. And one more night. She couldn't let her family come home to an empty refrigerator, empty pantry—what kind of mother would do that? Whether she liked it or not, she had to return to the grocery store. But not the one in Burgaw. People knew her there, probably saw her leave her half full cart, sit in her car and cry. In a town this size, half of the population probably already knew. Emily could hear them now. In the parking lot. In the store.

Wasn't that Emily Gillespie?

Was she crying?

Yeah, she just sat in her car and cried.

At the post office.

Emily Gillespie sure was acting weird when she came for her mail. Hadn't been here in almost a week.

That yesterday? Somebody said she went to Wilson's Supermarket and cried in her car. Had to be right after she left here.

I heard her husband's been out of town. The boys, too.

Hell, that's no reason to cry. I'd be celebrating.

Yeah, me too. Time to myself. Never get enough of that.

On the phone this very morning. Jane and Marie.

Did you hear about Emily?

Emily Gillespie? No, what? Tell me.

Yesterday. She ran out of the grocery store. Left all her food. Sat in her car at Wilson's for over an hour. Little Jimmy saw her every time he took out somebody's groceries.

She always was a little weird.

Or Susan and Nancy.

I think Emily may be losing it again.

What do you mean?

41

You don't know?

Know what?

She was in the hospital one time, long time ago and it wasn't because she was having babies.

Yeah, so? She had a miscarriage, didn't she?

Yeah, but that's not why she was in the hospital. You really don't know, do you.

Know what? Tell me.

Maybe I shouldn't gossip.

It's not gossip. We're her friends, right? I should know what you know.

She lost it big time.

What do you mean lost it?

Looney. She went looney. Shock treatments and all. When they let her out, she was on medication for a long time.

You're kidding me. Why do you think it's happening again?

Kathy's son works at Wilson's. Saw Emily running out to her car crying. Said she sat there two or three hours, just crying.

That is crazy. Wonder what's wrong with her.

I have no idea. But you don't say a word to her, now, you promise.

Sure, no, I won't say anything.

No, she wouldn't go back to that store today. But she had to get groceries. Maybe she'd just drive to Wilmington. Maybe she'd see if Mama wanted to go shopping downtown then ride out to lunch at her favorite restaurant on the waterway—fried oysters at Faircloth's. Yeah, she'd call. She should have called her earlier in the week. Rode out to the farm. Spent some time with her mama. And her daddy. On second thought, maybe she'd just ride on out there. No phone call.

Emily put on an A-line skirt and matching peach toned pullover sweater. Hers was more conservative than Norma's and fully covered her midsection. She clasped her hair back in a barrette and grabbed her purse. She picked up the bag of trash on the way out the door and headed into the garage, reminding herself to buy some room deodorizer or scented candles. All that rotten food made the house stink.

Emily placed the trash bag into the garbage can, and started to get into the car. But she had second thoughts about leaving, or maybe more about returning to an empty house by herself. She went back inside, double checked the locks on each window, glancing outside toward the street from the front, the neighbor's house from the side, the woods from the back windows, the sliding door in the dining room, the kitchen window. Lantana bloomed bright gold along the perimeter of the yard, where grass gave way to trees and thick undergrowth—woods where anything or anyone could hide unseen, close but concealed. Emily rubbed her hands up and down her arms to ward off the chill, to force the goosebumps back below the surface. She felt warm tears well up in the corners of her eyes and squeezed them tight to dam the flow. When she could stop the tears, she felt at least a slight sense of self-control.

Driving out to the country, she passed the house where she grew up three doors down from Rob, in a neighborhood where kids rode their bikes on the street, parents walked the sidewalks late on summer afternoons, waving to older neighbors sitting in porch swings and sipping sweet tea. Gargantuan oaks shaded the yards on either side, reaching their powerful limbs over the sidewalks, forming an archway above the streets where branch tips met in the middle. Her childhood home was a large two-story white clapboard house with a porch that wrapped around all four sides. She remembered riding her tricycle round and round the house when she was small, skating across the bumpy boards as an adolescent, sitting in the porch swing as a teenager hoping to see and be seen by the older boys driving by.

She couldn't help but feel the strain of nostalgia every time she rode by and saw how much it had changed. The new owners painted it pink, tore off the side porch to add a two-car garage, cut down the apple trees she and Charles planted as children, lined the walkway with bushes that didn't bloom.

After her grandfather died, Emily's grandmother had deeded her parents the farm outside of town, reserving a life estate in the old house and an acre of land. When her grandmother became too feeble to be out there all alone, Emily's parents opted to build a smaller house out in the country, close to her grandmother who eventually moved in with them until she died. Emily felt that her parents were giving up too much, but her daddy reassured her.

"I've always wanted to live in the country," he said. "And think how much fun the grandchildren will have."

None of the grandchildren were born then, but Norma was pregnant with Charles's baby. Emily's mama hadn't said much about the decision except that her own mama needed her now. She had grown up in the country, but was adamant that she wanted to raise her children in town where they would have friends to play with, a neighborhood to grow up in. But she seemed happy, creating flower beds and vegetable gardens, feeding the wildlife.

Emily passed the house where Rob's parents lived. She hadn't talked to him since that one phone call. Didn't go to the wedding. She missed her friend.

Leaving the town limits, Emily struggled to concentrate, to truly see sights that normally filled her with wonder. Pender County might be flat, but it could still be beautiful in late summer, with flowers blooming everywhere, corn fields ready for harvest, horses in pastures lush and green, hay fields full of bales rolled and ready. In a few weeks, the pallet would change to red maple leaves against a canvas of evergreens, oak foliage yellowing, wild flowers blooming in purples and pinks, and a sky as blue as tropical waters. The farm wasn't far from town and Emily arrived in less than half an hour. Her mama's flowers radiated love and care—impatiens in whites and reds bordering the drive, lantana in rich gold, petunia petals fluttering like purple butterflies. Some of them would thrive under her mama's tender touch until the first heavy frost, maybe beyond—sometimes as late as Thanksgiving. The window boxes paid homage to fall with mums in yellow and orange—candy corn colors.

Emily saw her dad on the tractor and waved. He tipped his big straw hat and kept on driving—plowing in sweet corn stalks to plant wheat later. The grapevines hung heavy with ripening fruit—scuppernongs, juicy sweet jewels that Daddy called health food. "Listen to me now," he would say. "I know what I'm talking about." He was so obviously happy in the country—tan and lean—spending his days plowing or fishing or just walking in the woods. He built a tree stand and climbed it every day during hunting season. But he never armed himself with a gun—only a camera.

Emily mounted the steps to the porch and knocked on the screen door.

"Who is it?" Mama called from the kitchen. Emily saw her walking toward the front of the house, wiping her hands on her apron.

Emily opened the door and stepped inside. "It's me, Mama."

"Well, Lordy be aren't you a sight for sore eyes. I thought you'd forgot the way out here." She hugged Emily tightly, then held her at arm's length, her hands resting gently on her shoulders while she gave Emily the Mama's once over. "You look drained, child. What's wrong? I thought with that husband of yours gone for a week and the boys at the Gillespies', you'd be rested up and beaming. You're not getting sick are you?"

"I'm fine. Thought you might want to ride to town, go shopping, out to eat. I'll buy you a new dress for your birthday. That's coming up soon, you know."

"Don't remind me. On second thought, I guess it's a good thing. Better than the alternative, that's for sure. I reckon being a Christian I shouldn't say things like that, but the good Lord knows I'm not ready to go yet. I'm hoping He'll let me stay down here a spell longer and watch my grandkids grow up."

"I'm sure of it. You and Daddy are still young, not even true retirement age yet, and you're healthy and hardworking. No reason you won't see great-grandchildren some day."

"Now wouldn't that be something. Elizabeth's only twelve, though, so we don't want to rush that part just yet. You want some tea? I just made a fresh pitcher full. And there's biscuits left from breakfast. I can heat some up and pull out the molasses. You look like you could use a little meat on your bones. You're looking mighty thin, Emily. You're not sick are you?"

"No ma'am, I'm just fine. But some biscuits and molasses sound great—butter, too." Emily followed her mama into the kitchen. "I remember the first time we tried to get Danny to taste mixed up molasses and butter. He cried because he didn't like the way it looked. But once he tasted it, he loved it. I guess I should make biscuits more often at home. The boys do love them."

They sat at the little kitchen table, sopping up molasses and butter with fluffy hot biscuits. "This is great, Mama, thanks." Emily had forgotten to eat breakfast before she left home.

"You sure you want to go shopping today? Aren't the boys coming home?"

"Actually, they're not coming until tomorrow. Their grandparents are taking them to the circus tonight. And Dan's plane got in late last night at RDU, so he just went to his parents' house. He's going to bring the boys home and save his parents a trip."

"In that case, I'll take you up on your offer. I'd love to go shopping. Let me just get cleaned up a bit."

"Okay, I'll walk out to the field and give Daddy a hug. If I can get him off that tractor."

"Good luck. You know that's like his Tonka toy." Mama laughed, shaking her head as she walked to her room. Emily envied her parents' relationship. She always thought, and hoped, that she and Dan would develop that kind of bond. But they seemed to grow more distant with time, not closer. Sometimes she felt like she didn't know him at all—he could be so sweet sometimes, but those times seemed fewer and farther between. He could also be short-tempered, with her and the boys. Occasionally, when he was really angry, she feared he might hit the boys, but he never had done more than spank them. Maybe it was her fault. She'd just have to try harder, give more.

Daddy was coming up to the end of a row when Emily neared the field. He acknowledged her presence, stopped the tractor, set the brake, but left it running. Hopping off the side, he strode over to Emily and wrapped his strong arms around her in a big bear hug. She loved the way he smelled—a combination of sweat and Old Spice mingled with Tide and Clorox from his work clothes.

"Good to see you girl. Sure have missed you."

"I missed you, too, Daddy. The field looks good. Everything

does. I love the smell of freshly plowed dirt."

"You'd of made a great country girl, Emily. Maybe your Mama and me should have moved out here a long time ago. Brought you and your brother up in God's country, tilling the earth instead of playing in the streets."

"I loved where we lived. We had a great childhood."

"I know, I know. And you turned out just fine—smart, hardworking, good marriage, great kids. I sure do miss Charles, though, and worry about that Norma. Them kids."

"You and Mama did a great job raising Charles and me. It's not your fault about Norma, and you don't need to worry about it. She'll do just fine."

"Well, speak of the devil. There she is now. I know she'll be fine; I just worry about your Mama 'cause she worries about Norma and the younguns. Thinks she needs to fix it all. Worrying'll kill you, you know."

"I know. That's why neither one of you needs to worry. I'm taking Mama shopping. I know you don't want to go, but do you want us to bring you anything?"

"Can't think of a thing in the world I need but another hug from my baby girl."

Emily hugged her daddy again, kissed him on the cheek and turned to walk back toward the house. Over her shoulder, she heard him say, "I'll have a big bucket of grapes picked for you when you get back." She turned to see him boost himself back up into the black seat of his Massey Ferguson, the red paint gleaming in the sunlight like a sports car.

When Emily entered the house, her mother exclaimed. "Look who's here Emily. I invited your sister to go shopping with us. I knew you wouldn't mind. It'll be great, just us girls."

Emily cringed. The last thing she wanted today was to deal with Norma. She was not her sister, and she hated that her Mama and Daddy kept calling her that. But what choice did she have?

"Sure, that's great." Then she looked at Norma and asked. "Where are your children?"

"It's weekend with daddy, or should I say daddies." Norma laughed. "They don't really want anything to do with the kids, but since I make 'em pay child support, they insist on visitation. Sometimes all the visitations fall on the same weekend. Works for me, and as long as I get the money, who cares."

Elizabeth emerged from the hall bathroom. Her eyes were swollen, obviously from crying. She'd never had a chance to know her own daddy. Emily's brother died in a car wreck before Elizabeth's first birthday, but Norma seemed oblivious to how that affected Elizabeth when she talked so much and so badly about the boys' daddies.

"Hi sweetie," Emily said. "I didn't know you were here." Emily stared at Norma—the 'how could you be so cruel' look that never did any good. "I sure hope you can go shopping with me."

"Sure," Elizabeth said with no enthusiasm. Emily's heart wrenched. She wanted to hug her niece and slap Norma, but she did neither, just simply said, "Let's get going."

"We can drive my station wagon," Mama said.

"That's ok, I'll drive," Emily said. "I need to get groceries while we're out, and that way I won't have to move them twice."

"I thought you got groceries yesterday," Norma said, "after I saw you at the post office."

"I changed my mind."

"That's not what I heard."

Emily stared, daring her to say more. The gossip wheel was alive and well.

"What are you talking about?" Mama asked.

"Oh nothing," Norma said, then turned and smiled at Emily. "I surely don't want to wander around a grocery store with you. You'll just have to drop us off somewhere."

"That's fine, but you know you don't have to go at all if you don't want to. Elizabeth can go with me and Mama, and you can have some time to yourself."

"Nonsense," Mama said. "How often do we girls get to spend the day together, just us?"

"I wouldn't miss it for the world," Norma said.

Shopping actually turned out great, much to Emily's surprise. They went from store to store searching for just the right dress for her mama, who feigned disgust at having to try on so many, but couldn't really hide her pleasure each time she came out of the dressing room and twirled in front of her girls. Emily found a fall outfit for each of her boys and bought a new pair of bell-bottoms and a sweater for Elizabeth, who finally smiled. Norma complained about not having any money, and Mama slipped her some folded bills when they were at soda fountain in the drug store. Emily saw, but still savored the double chocolate macadamia nut crunch mouthful by mouthful. Oh, the powers of chocolate.

They drove to Wrightsville Beach for lunch at Faircloth Seafood Restaurant near the bridge. They followed the young waitress outside to the deck. The late summer days were still warm, the sun shining, and Emily wanted an unencumbered view of the docks, the Intracoastal Waterway, and the colorful cottages lining its shoreline on the other side. The restaurant was close enough to the inlet that diners could watch the boats maneuvering toward the ocean—sailboats gliding with the wind, fishing boats laden with gear, yachts claiming first rights of passage.

"I need me one of those," Norma said.

"A yacht?"

"No, one of those," she emphasized, pointing to a tanned, muscular man walking down the docks, wearing an open white button-up with long sleeves rolled up just below his elbows, khaki shorts and dock shoes—wealth written in the way he walked. "And if he owns one of the yachts, all the better."

"You're incorrigible," Mama said, closing her menu. "Let's order. I'm ready for some fried oysters."

After lunch, they rode across the bridge and down the beach to the southernmost end of the island and parked. They left their shoes in the car and walked across the sand to the ocean. A young woman in a wedding dress was in the middle of a photo shoot—first in the white gazebo next to the walkway, then in the dunes amongst the sea oats, then at the edge of the water.

"She's ruining her dress!" Mama exclaimed as the bride-to-be lifted the full skirt of her gown above her knees, waded into the remnants of a wave descending on the hardened sand and kicked delightedly with her bare feet. The photographer moved expertly, catching her from every angle, as the waves swelled then abated. Soft breezes lifted her veil, floating it wispily behind her like angels' wings.

"Oh, but look how happy she is," Emily sighed.

"Wonder how long that will last."

"Oh Norma, don't be such a pessimist," Mama said. "Happy ever after happens. Just look at your sister."

They walked along the shoreline; watched long-legged birds chase the water back out to sea, picking up tiny creatures delivered by the waves for their dinner; saw the pelicans flying low, swooping down to scoop up fish, then lifting on heavy wings and flying out of sight; laughed at frenzied gulls circling above a trio of children, the birds dipping down to catch the scraps of food the kids tossed into the air.

"This is really nice girls, but I better be getting back home to fix your daddy some supper. He fares alright by himself for lunch, but I sure don't want him trying to do any real cooking."

"And Emily still needs to get groceries," Norma reminded them. "There's a nice Harris Teeter on the way home from here without having to go back into town. You could drop us off next door at that strip mall with the surf shop in it. There's a little café where we could sit and have dessert while we wait for you."

"I couldn't eat another bite," Mama said. "But sitting sounds good."

The store was clean and bright with wide aisles and bountiful produce—exotic items Emily had never seen before. The meat counters were burgeoning with beef and pork and chicken and lamb. The selection of name brands for every item she needed to buy boggled her brain and so did the prices. Emily decided to purchase only what she needed to get by for a few days. The boys would be going back to school on Monday, Dan would be at work, and she could ride to the Piggly-Wiggly in Wallace to stock up on everything else. It had good meats and low prices—and no one there would know her.

She found the basics and pushed her cart to the checkout line, then remembered she wanted to buy molasses so she could make the boys some biscuits. She left her cart in line behind a woman whose cart was overflowing and hurried halfway across the store to find the aisle where the molasses sat next to pancake syrup. She chose a small jar with the familiar bright yellow label—Grandma's Molasses—and headed back to her cart to check out. In the child's seat atop her eggs, a single red rose lay encased in a clear cellophane wrapper just like the ones she had seen in the flower department of the Harris Teeter.

"Did you see who put this in my cart?" she almost yelled to the checkout clerk who was busy counting back change. "Did you see?"

"Excuse me ma'am, but I'm busy. I'll be right with you."

"Did you see who did it? My cart was sitting here, right here."

"I'll be right with you, ma'am."

"Did you see?" Emily touched the arm of the woman checking out ahead of her.

"No," she answered briskly. "I wasn't watching your cart." She took her change and walked away behind the bag boy pushing her groceries.

Emily asked the woman standing in line behind her, but she only shook her head.

"Now, ma'am," the clerk said. "What can I do for you? Is something wrong with the rose?"

"I don't want it. I didn't put it in my cart."

"No problem, ma'am, I'll just lay it right here and have Jason put it back. It's okay to change your mind."

"No, you don't understand. I didn't change my mind. I didn't put it in my cart. I didn't put it there."

"Please calm down. I'm sure it was just a mistake. May I check you out now; others are waiting behind you."

Emily struggled to regain her composure, placing her items

carefully on the slow moving black conveyor belt. She concentrated on each item as she lifted it with shaking hands, afraid she would drop something, make a scene. Cry.

"Here you are ma'am. Nine dollars and twenty-three cents change. And here's your receipt. Thank you for shopping at your friendly Harris Teeter."

Emily stuffed her change into the top of her purse, anxious to leave the store, find her family and just go home.

"May I have your attention please." At the sound of the loudspeaker, Emily's pulse quickened. "Phone call for Emily Gillespie. Phone call for Emily Gillespie."

Emily ignored the announcement, focused on the newfangled door that slid open and shut with shoppers coming and going. *Just get to the door. Get to the door. Don't cry.* Her chest tightened and she struggled to breath—in, out, in, out. She concentrated on every breath, every step. People around her seemed to glide in slow motion. Their mouths moved but she heard nothing. She consciously put one foot in front of the other, but the door seemed to move farther and farther away. A black tunnel formed around it, closing in from the edges, growing smaller.

"Hey lady, are you okay?"

Emily looked up into the eyes of a young man with huge blue eyes.

"You okay lady? Let me help you over here to the bench."

From a sitting position on the floor, she looked around trying to get her bearings. A few people stood looking at her, but others just walked by, the doors sliding open to let them in or out. "What happened?"

"I think you must have fainted ma'am," the young man said. "Good thing I caught you or you would have hit your head. That floor's pretty hard."

"What's your name?"

"Simon, ma'am."

"Thank you, Simon. I think I will just sit on the bench for a minute." He held her elbow and helped her to the bench.

"When you're ready, I'll help you get your groceries to the car."

"I'm ready. But Simon, please don't say anything about this if my family is there, ok?"

"Whatever you say, ma'am."

Emily reached into her purse for the change she had stuffed there and handed it to Simon. "Thank you," she said.

When they reached her station wagon, Emily started the car and rolled down the back window. When she walked to the back and let the door down, she was surprised to see the ax still lying there.

"Had to get it fixed at the hardware store," she answered to Simon's questioning expression. "Just put the bags on top. They'll be fine."

By the time Simon finished loading the groceries in the back, Emily saw her family walking across the parking lot.

"Are you sure you're not getting sick, Emily," Mama said. "You look awfully pale."

"You do look a bit green around the gills," Norma chimed in.

"I'm fine. I just want to go home."

Chapter 5

Emily sat on the porch steps rubbing Winston's head. Any minute she expected to see Dan's truck coming down the street. He had called two hours before to let her know they were almost ready to leave Raleigh. Emily just knew that once her boys were home, everything would be fine. She could, would, will herself to overcome the fear, the anxiety, the overwhelming urge to cry because nothing was more important in her world than her boys.

Winston's ears perked up and he whined, a low guttural noise that made the hair stand up on Emily's arms. "What is it boy?" Then his big tail started swishing back and forth on the concrete. He leapt up and began barking, turning in circles, almost knocking Emily off the steps. Winston sprinted off the porch and down the drive just as Dan's truck came into view a couple of blocks down the street.

"It's them, they're home!" Emily ran out into the yard with Winston, waving both hands above her head in unabashed delight.

"Mommy, you should have seen it," Bobby said, jumping off the truck seat onto the grass. He grabbed Emily around her legs and hugged her tight. "There were elephants and lions and tigers and people flying through the air!"

Emily loosened his arms and knelt down to eye level. "I missed you so much."

"Me, too. But the circus...I had popcorn and cotton candy and peanuts and I fed the elephants, and the clown was funny!"

Danny slid off the truck seat and headed straight to Winston, grabbing him around the neck and wrestling him to the ground in a hug. Winston licked his face and neck and hair. "What about me?" Emily said.

"Hey, Mom." Danny grinned up at her. She reached down and tousled his hair. He was growing up so fast.

Dan emerged from the far side of the truck with a smile on his face and his right hand behind his back.

"Oh, yeah! We brought you a surprise," Bobby said, running toward his daddy. "Let me show her, let me." Bobby ran around behind his daddy and brought out a huge bouquet—at least two dozen roses in yellow, pink, red and white.

Emily could not control her response. Tears welled up and spilled down her cheeks, she began to shake and dropped to her knees in the grass.

"Don't you like them?" Danny asked. "I wanted to buy chocolate, but Daddy said you liked roses better." He sat up, stood up, leaving Winston for Emily's side.

Bobby dropped the bouquet and ran to his mother, put his little arms around her neck. She let her head rest on his bony shoulder and took Danny by the hand. "I do love them. I just missed you so much. I'm glad you're home." She pulled both boys close to her and stood up. "I bought you a surprise, too. And I made cookies. You want some?"

"What about me?" Dan said, sounding a bit disgusted. He picked the roses up off the ground and shook off the dirt. "These weren't cheap, you know."

"I know, I love them, I really do. And you. Bring them in and we'll find a vase." She stood up to peck him on the cheek as he walked by.

"Guess I know where I fit in the order of things," he mumbled.

§ § §

Although the boys' homecoming wasn't exactly how Emily had planned, life did fall back into a normal routine for a while. Dan earned a promotion and raise at work, the boys went back to school, Bobby in the second grade, Danny in third. The phone calls stopped—except for Dr. Z who still called at least every two weeks.

"Just checking to see if you're ready to come to work, Emily. No one can do the job as well as you could. It's yours anytime you want it. Please at least think about it, ok?"

She did actually think about going to work—not with Dr. Z, of course, but maybe something part-time so she could be home when the boys got out of school. But then what about summers and holidays? Even though her boys were getting older, she didn't want anybody else taking care of them. That was her job and she intended to do it well. Besides, they really didn't need the money. And, more importantly, Dan would never allow her to do it. She wasn't into that women's lib stuff anyhow.

They weren't rich, but they lived in a nice neighborhood; their vehicles were paid for; they had the boat and enough money to eat well; she could buy the boys what they needed, even little extras now and then. She had her own checking account for taking care of paying the bills, living expenses, buying groceries, but Dan knew how every dime was spent—he insisted on doing the bookkeeping and giving her a monthly housekeeping allowance. The only good thing about having a job would be earning a little money of her own, something more than her weekly personal cash allowance from Dan.

Dan seemed less anxious and angry most of the time. Less jealous even. He allowed her to help out at school occasionally, but she never went back to being a pink lady at the hospital. She made a special effort to go out and visit her parents at least once a week, have lunch, help with whatever project her mama was working on. Daddy taught her how to drive the tractor. No matter that she was almost thirty with a family of her own, he still called her his "baby girl" and Emily didn't mind.

And though the urge to cry for no reason at all still surfaced occasionally, Emily had willed herself to be in control. When her chest felt tight, she breathed deep and slow, counting, concentrating. When she started worrying about past decisions she couldn't change—the ones that no matter how small they were caused deep anxiety, she forced herself to concentrate on the present, the future, her boys. When she lost her battle with the tears, she just made sure no one saw.

The first Saturday in October, Emily and the boys spent the day at the farm. Poppy hooked the trailer to the back of the tractor, threw on a couple of bales of hay and told Emily and the boys to hop on. He rode them down to the edge of the woods where he had stacked the sturdiest corn stalks before plowing in the field.

"Pick the ones you want and throw them in the trailer," he said. "You'll have the best decorations in the neighborhood." Then he took them to the pumpkin patch to pick out a few for decoration and one big one to carve for their jack-o-lantern. He didn't grow many, just enough to supply what the kids wanted and some for holiday pies.

"Watch for black widow spiders," he warned. "They like to hide out around the stems."

Emily loved watching her daddy with the boys. His love for them was so obvious, simple, pure.

Their Granny supplied the boys with a basket full of colorful squash and gourds, plus a patchwork shirt she had sewn for the scarecrow they would stuff with fresh new pine needles.

"You can have this old pair of your Poppy's pants, too," she said. "Just don't let him see 'em. They were his favorite, but he's worn holes plum through the seat."

"We need a straw hat," Bobby said. "You got one of those Granny?"

"And a red scarf," Danny added. "Scarecrows always have a red scarf."

"Maybe. I've got a box of old stuff up in the loft over the tractor shed. And I think there might be a hat hanging on a nail up there. Why don't you boys run up and see what you can find while your mama and me take a little rest."

"Be careful on the ladder," Emily said to the backs of her boys as they ran out of the kitchen, letting the screen door slam shut. Even in October, the days were warm, the windows open, with clean country air wafting through the house. "I really love it out here, Mama."

"Me, too. I had my doubts, now mind you, when your daddy said we'd just build a house and move out here. I didn't know if either one of us would be happy. But it's been good, Emily, real good. And I'm glad I was able to take care of my mama those last few years."

"It couldn't have been easy."

"No, not easy. You know my older brothers and sisters weren't real happy when they found out Mama and Papa gave us the land. And after everything that's happened, they still resent me. But I guess my parents knew we'd take care of it—and them. Your daddy has surely been a blessing."

"I don't think I've ever seen him happier."

"Me either. I was a little worried about money when he retired so early, but the good Lord provides. We don't have much extra, but we sure don't go hungry. And we've got the health insurance for emergencies. Thank God we've been healthy, haven't needed it. Knock on wood." Mama tapped her knuckles on the edge of the table.

"You know if you ever need anything, ever get in a bind, you just let me know, ok?" Even as she said the words, Emily prayed that Dan would agree if her parents ever needed financial help.

"Naw, I don't worry about us. But I do worry about Norma, about her kids. She might need some help, Emily. But she might be too proud to ask."

Emily wanted to say that no, Norma was definitely not too proud to ask. She'd asked over and over again—a little here, a little there. She seemed to think she was entitled—even though she wasn't even kin. Norma had made bad decisions—lots of them—but she never seemed to own up to the fact that she caused a lot of her own problems. She was always the victim—and she used her children as a means to an end when it came to money. Emily had done without herself, even bought less for her own boys, to make sure Norma's kids had new clothes for the first day of school, or a new mitt for baseball, ballet slippers for dance. She'd paid for it out of her little bit of cash allowance so Dan wouldn't know.

"Norma's a grown woman, Mama, and talented. She could do just fine if she would."

"Now, Emily, I never expected you to be so harsh. She's your sister."

No, she's not my sister, Emily wanted to say. The sting of her mother's words set the elephant in motion. Emily's chest began to tighten and tears threatened to tumble. She stood up and walked to the back door.

"I better check on the boys, make sure they haven't fallen out of the loft." She walked onto the back porch, letting the screen door shut softly behind her.

"I'll be back," she said without turning around. Emily wiped her sleeve across her face, erasing the tears that escaped before she regained control. The aroma of oak coals filled the air, and she followed the scent and the small pillar of smoke behind the tractor shed where she found her boys and her daddy standing around a bed of coals with a large black cast iron pot perched on cinder blocks, steaming.

"Poppy's boiling peanuts," Bobby said. "They're not ready yet. Can we stay, please, can we?"

"How long before they're ready, Daddy?" Emily asked. "You know how I love 'em, but Dan's expecting us by four."

"Oh, I expect they'll be tender in about fifteen minutes or so. That should get you home in time."

"Sounds good. I'd love to sit around the fire and eat them with you, drink a Pepsi, too, but I guess we'll have to put them in a bag and take them with us this time."

"Ah, Mama," Bobby said. "Do we have to?" Emily was sure her youngest son could become a country boy and be happy as a pig in a mud puddle.

"Yes, we have to. Your daddy's expecting us, and you know he doesn't like for us to be late."

"I found a hat," Danny said, "and a scarf just where Granny said it would be."

"Let's get everything loaded up while the peanuts finish boiling. Run on in and tell your Granny goodbye."

The boys bounded off toward the house, Danny wearing the

straw hat and scarf. He leapt onto the porch skipping all three steps, but Bobby fell trying. Emily started to run toward the house, but Daddy stopped her. "Let your Mama take care of it, Baby Girl. I'm sure it's just a scratch."

Emily looked back at him, tears threatening again.

"Are you alright Emily? I didn't want to say anything in front of your boys, but you seem a little edgy lately."

She considered telling her Daddy about the phone calls, the roses. Confiding in somebody might help assuage her fears. But what could he do? He would just worry and she didn't want that. Besides, they had stopped. She'd get past it. She was doing better every day. Really, she was.

"I'm fine. Just a little tired, I guess. Don't worry about me."

"Okay, if you say so. But you know you can come to me with anything, don't you? I know I didn't help a lot back when you were sick. Didn't understand, I guess. Not being a woman and all. But I love you, Emily. You know that, right?"

"I do, Daddy, I do."

§ § §

On the night before Halloween, Dan helped the boys bring their prize pumpkin into the kitchen. They spread newspapers on the floor and began their annual tradition of carving a jack-o-lantern. The boys had spent the previous week with markers and paper every day after school designing faces. Since they couldn't make a unanimous decision, Emily folded up their favorites—two of Danny's and two of Bobby's and placed them in a paper bag. When Dan finished cutting a hole in the top of the pumpkin and scooped out the seeds and soft flesh inside, the grand drawing took place.

"Danny can shake and Bobby can pull out the winner," Emily said. She handed the big brown grocery bag to Danny who shook it up and down and back and forth and tilted it over and over before opening the top and holding it out to his little brother. Bobby reached in with his eyes squinted shut, pulled out a folded sheet of paper and handed it to his mother.

Emily began unfolding it, hoping in her heart that it was one of

Bobby's. A three-eyed monster with an upside down grin stared back at them.

"Yay!" Danny yelled. "My favorite. I win!" He danced around the kitchen.

Emily's heart ached when she saw the dejected look on Bobby's face. He was such a sensitive child. His eyes brimmed with tears, and she could see him fighting to hold them back.

"Don't be a crybaby," Dan admonished. "This happens every stupid year that you don't win."

Emily stared at Dan, hoping he would feel the darts she tried to sling, that they would pin the harsh words in his throat. "Here Bobby," she said. "Take this marker and draw the mouth. Then Danny can draw the eyes."

"Quit babying him, Emily." Dan said. "He'll be a sissy forever if you don't."

Bobby ran to his room and shut the door behind him. Danny looked at his mother, then his father, and followed his brother to their room. Dan took the marker, drew the face on the pumpkin and finished carving it as though his boys were beside him helping. Emily dared not say a word. She was always amazed at how quickly family fun could turn to disaster. Maybe the promotion was causing more stress than Dan could handle.

Emily carried the plastic bowl full of pumpkin guts out the back door and to the edge of the woods. She slung it as far as she could, holding tight to the bowl, and listened to seeds and flesh splat against the tree trunks in the dark. She wondered how in the world she could fix her family. Just as she turned to go back in the house, Emily heard a rustle in the woods. Then a whimper. She realized she had not seen Winston since Danny fed him earlier that afternoon. He usually met her at the door every time she went out.

"Winston," she called. "Here boy. Here Winston."

She listened carefully, heard a rustle, a whimper. Too scared to enter the woods alone, Emily ran back to the house, shouting for Dan.

"What the hell's wrong with you?" he asked, then his demeanor changed when he turned in his recliner and saw her face. "What's wrong, Emily, what is it?"

"Something in the woods. I think it might be Winston. He sounds hurt."

"Grab the flashlight. Don't say anything to the boys. They love that dog."

Emily followed Dan through the back yard and into the edge of the woods, brushing against bramble and scratching her legs on briers. The small beam of light swung back and forth searching. All sounds had ceased.

"There he is," Dan said, pointing. They pressed twenty feet through the scraggly undergrowth to where Winston lay, a brown pile slumped against the trunk of a pine tree. He was completely still, his eyes staring blankly, his head soaking in a pool of yellow vomit, whitish foam floating from his lips.

"Oh, Winston," Dan said. "Winston."

He handed the flashlight to Emily and scooped the dog up in his arms, burying his face in Winston's fur. It was the rawest emotion Emily had seen from Dan in years.

She followed him silently back toward the house, shining the light so he could see where to step. Dan laid Winston on the ground behind the garage. "I'll get the shovel."

"No," Emily said. "I'll call the vet. We need to take him to the vet."

"He's gone, Emily. Dead. The vet can't do anything for him."

"He can tell us what killed him."

"What good would that do? He's dead. No damn vet can bring him back."

"But don't you want to know why?"

"It won't bring him back, Emily. It's a waste of money. I'll just bury him. He's gone."

"What about the boys?"

"Look at him, Emily. The boys don't need to see him like this. They'll have nightmares. I'll bury him. You go tell them."

"By myself?"

"Okay, you bury him. I'll tell them."

Emily thought how harsh Dan could be, even when he didn't mean to. "No, I'll tell them."

She walked into the house and down the hall toward her boys' bedroom. Winston had always been a part of the family—longer, even, than Danny. Their light was on and she stood outside the door wondering how she could possibly tell them. The night—meant to be so much fun—had spiraled out of control, lower than Emily could have ever imagined. She turned the doorknob and slowly pushed the door open. They were asleep, both in Bobby's bed. The boys had changed into their pajamas—Bobby's with fish and Danny's with dogs. Bobby curled around his big brown stuffed monkey, and Danny snuggled up behind him, an arm thrown protectively across his little brother. Emily turned out the light and gently closed the door. Maybe it would be easier in the morning.

She walked back outside. Dan was still digging at the edge of the woods. "If I don't bury him deep, something will dig him up," Dan said. Emily stood beside her husband and watched him shovel and toss spade after spade full of dirt. Whatever emotion had surfaced earlier, Dan successfully buried deep behind those dark blue eyes. She longed for the easy-going, tender-hearted man she thought she had married, hoped he was somewhere beneath the calloused stranger who now shared her life. She vowed to find him again.

"The boys were asleep. I couldn't bear to wake them."

"Don't guess it matters. The dog will be just as dead in the morning." Dan dropped the shovel, grabbed Winston's back legs, and slid him into the hole. Emily felt the thud deep in the pit of her stomach when Winston's body hit bottom. Dan methodically picked up the shovel, scooped and pitched until he had replaced all the dirt, then stomped around on the top, packing the loose soil as tightly as possible. He pulled a few stray limbs from the edge of the woods across the top of the grave. "Maybe that'll help keep the scavengers away."

"What do I tell the boys?" Emily asked, hoping for help.

"How the hell do I know? He's dead. Not much you can say."

Chapter 6

Kids are so resilient. Emily watched her boys eating breakfast, smiling, laughing. They were so excited about wearing their Halloween costumes to school, they seemed to have forgotten all about the scene in the kitchen the night before. She hadn't told them about Winston, couldn't bring herself to spoil their mood. Maybe after school—if she could get them there without noticing he was gone.

"Joey Beluga said he was going to be a pirate, too," Bobby said, "but I bet my costume's better than his. Don't you bet it, too, Danny?"

"Yeah, I bet nobody's got as good a pirate suit as you."

"I got the bestest eye patch ever. And a wooden leg."

"You take that patch off if you can't see how to do your schoolwork," Emily said, placing another plate of pancakes on the table. "You guys sure are hungry this morning."

"I'm done," Danny said. "Can I take the extras out to Winston? He loves pancakes."

"No, I'll do it," Emily said quickly. "You better get started if you're going to get fixed up with hobo dirt on your face. You need some help?"

"Nah, I can do it. You help Bobby. He's little," Danny said.

"I'm not little. I'm a pirate."

"Go on and get started," Emily said. "I'll check on you in a few minutes."

Emily was relieved when the boys headed off to their bedroom. She opened the back door, then closed it loudly, dumped the extra pancakes into the trashcan under the sink, and started making sandwiches for the boys' lunch boxes.

Emily barely made it back into the house after taking the boys to school when the phone started ringing. She dropped her purse and keys on the kitchen table and answered it without a second thought.

"Hello?"

Nothing.

"Hello-o," she said, still thinking how cute her boys looked walking into school.

"Woof, woof." The voice was coarse, low.

"Who are you? What do you want from me?" Emily screamed. She started to hang up the phone when she heard the music—loud, cheerful. *How much is that doggie in the window, the one with the waggily tail...* Emily slammed the phone down—more angry than scared.

She ran out the back door, across the yard to Winston's grave, pulling the limbs away with both hands, throwing them left and right. Underneath it all, a single long-stemmed rose lay dead and shriveled, black. Emily ran to the garage and grabbed the shovel. She started digging, slinging dirt left and right. It took her almost two hours to reach him, the hole deeper than she remembered, her arms weaker than she wished. She dug a while, then rested a while, dug, then rested. The deeper she dug, the harder it became to bring the shovel up.

When she finally uncovered Winston's body, she lay on the ground and tried to reach him, to pull him up, but her arms weren't long enough. She slid down into the hole, careful to step beside him, not on him. Emily tried to lift her dog, push him up out of the hole, but he was too heavy, the hole too deep. She climbed back out, mud stuck to her clothes, her shoes, in her hair. She didn't care. She went in the house, dirt shedding onto the kitchen floor, grabbed her purse and her keys, then put them back down and went to the linen closet in the hall. She pulled down an old blanket from the top shelf, picked her keys and purse up on her way through the kitchen and locked the door behind her.

Emily went into the garage, searching for rope, anything to tie on the dog. She saw the bright blue and white ski rope wound up in the corner—the one they used to ride the inner tube. She threw it in the car with the blanket and her purse. She opened the garage door and backed her car out, pulled slowly around the edge of the garage, close to the ditch, into the back yard, backing up to the hole. Emily took the blanket and threw it on the ground.

Emily's station wagon had no trailer hitch. The wooden handles of the rope kept her from being able to wrap it around the middle of the bumper, so she tried tying it on the end, but it kept slipping off. Emily jumped back in the car, cranked it up and rolled down the window to the back hatch that opened down like a tailgate on a truck. She threw the rope handles into the back of the car, holding the rope off to the side while she slammed the tailgate closed. She pulled hard on the rope; it felt snug.

Holding tight to the rope, Emily worked her way slowly into the hole. She tied the other end around Winston's hind legs and knotted it over and over again. She tugged on the rope to make sure it was secure, then used it to help her scramble back out of the hole. With every move, she shifted more dirt back on top of the dog, but kept climbing.

Emily drove the car slowly across her back yard, dragging Winston up out of the hole. Watching in the rear view mirror, she stopped when she saw his body lying fully on the ground. Emily backed up to release the pressure on the rope, then got out. She tried to untie the rope from Winston's legs, but the pressure had pulled the knots tight. Emily spread the blanket out beside her dog and slid him on it. She wrapped it around him as best she could, then drug him the few feet to the back of the car. Every move was a struggle. Letting the tailgate down, she sat on it a few minutes to rest.

Emily looked up to see lights flashing through the windows of her house. She heard the whoop whoop of a cop's car. Two policemen came striding toward her, right hands poised just above their weapons.

"We got a call from your neighbor. What's going on here?"

Emily started to put her hands down to hoist herself off the tailgate.

"Don't move," the young cop said. He looked like a kid, and Emily didn't recognize him.

"Keep your hands where we can see them, Emily." It was Frank, a couple of years ahead of her in school. He'd been with the town police department for years.

"What?" Emily couldn't believe the police were in her back yard.

"Your neighbor saw you digging, Emily, wrapping something up in a blanket. Where's Dan?"

"At work."

"The boys?"

"School."

"Okay, I'm going to walk over to the blanket now. Just stay where you are. Keep your hands where I can see them."

"Are you crazy Frank? It's my dog. My dead dog!"

"Okay, no need to get excited."

"No? You drive up in my yard, lights and sirens, threatening to shoot me and you say don't get excited. Are you crazy?" She jumped off the tailgate.

"Calm down, Emily. Stay where you are," Frank said. "Don't move another inch." Then to the young kid, he said, "Joe, walk over there real slow and see what's in that blanket."

"It's my dog, Frank. I think somebody poisoned him."

"She's right, detective. It's a dog."

"Why don't you tell me what's going on, Emily."

"Why don't you go turn off those stupid lights. The whole neighborhood's probably watching. Every gossip in town will know before you get back to the station."

"You go ahead, Joe. I'm sure Emily will drop me off after we have a little chat."

"I need to get to the vet, Frank. Help me get the dog in the car, please."

"I don't think a vet's going to do old Winston much good now, Emily. Do you?"

"I'm not crazy, Frank, not yet. But somebody's trying to make me that way. Winston died last night. I think somebody poisoned him. But Dan wouldn't let me take him to the vet. He buried him. But then I got another phone call today and there was a dead rose on his grave. I gotta get him to the vet, have him tested. See what killed him."

"Another phone call?"

"Yeah, I've been getting them for a while. Breathing, music, no words. Not until today. He barked at me, Frank, barked. Then played a dog song. That's when I knew he'd done it, killed Winston. That's when I found the rose, when I knew he'd been murdered. Will you help me or not?"

"Why didn't you tell us sooner, Emily? What if he'd hurt you instead of the dog? This may be a warning. You need to come clean, tell me everything."

"Help me get Winston to the vet, and I'll tell you on the way."

"Okay, okay. Let's load him up."

Frank put Winston in the back of the station wagon and quickly filled the hole with dirt. Emily drug the limbs and leaves back over the top of the grave so it looked as much the same as possible.

"You don't want anybody to know you dug him up, do you? Not even Dan."

"No, I don't."

They rode in silence for a block or two, then Frank prodded for information. "Why don't you start at the beginning, Emily. Tell me what's been going on."

"I've been getting phone calls since the week before Labor Day. Dan was gone on a business trip and the boys were gone to stay with their grandparents in Raleigh. I was alone for a whole week. The calls came every day. I was scared, didn't leave the house for three days. Then I had to go to the grocery store because Dan was coming home. There were roses on my windshield—one for every day I hadn't left the house."

She turned into the vet's driveway, parked, turned off the car. "Keep talking," Frank said. "A few more minutes won't matter for Winston."

"I threw them away. They wilted, some worse than others, but still sort of alive, not like the one on Winston's grave—dead and black. And all the thorns had been plucked off. I remember that. When I was in the grocery store, somebody had me paged—a phone call, but no one was there. I was scared. I left the store, left my food. I stepped in a pile of little rosebud heads next to my car door. I couldn't drive. I sat there and cried. I don't know how long."

"So that's what that was all about."

"Yeah. The whole town knows. They probably think I'm crazy."

"Go on."

"So the next day, that was Saturday, I went to see my mother. She and Norma, my sister-in-law, and her daughter, Elizabeth, went to Wilmington with me. We went to the beach for lunch. I still needed groceries so we stopped at Harris Teeter, there near the beach. He was watching me. All that time. He had to be. I left my cart for just a few minutes and when I got back there was a rose lying on my eggs. Then they paged me. A phone call. I didn't answer it. I just left."

"That's eight weeks ago or more, Emily. Why didn't you call the police? Did you at least tell Dan?"

"No, I didn't tell anyone. The calls stopped. Dan and the boys came home and the phone calls stopped and everything was better. I thought it was over."

"Tell me about Winston."

"He was fine yesterday. Fine when the boys fed him his supper. He eats early. Feeding him is Danny's job when he gets home from school." Emily began to cry. "How will I tell my boys?"

"They don't know?"

"No, they were asleep when we found him. I walked out to throw pumpkin guts in the woods, and I heard him whimper. I got Dan and a flashlight and by the time we found him in the woods, he was dead. I wanted to bring him to the vet and Dan wouldn't let me. He said it didn't matter how he died. He was just as dead, it didn't matter." Emily stopped.

"And then you got the phone call today?"

Emily nodded, wordless.

"I'll take him in and tell the vet to do a necropsy. We probably won't know for several days."

§ § §

The results came back a week later. Winston may have been poisoned, but toxicology reports were inconclusive—too much time had passed, the vet said. Frank insisted that Emily come into the station and file a report about the dog, about the phone calls, the roses. She told him she didn't want anyone to know, not even Dan. But she did file the report, promised to let him know the next time she got a phone call.

Emily had dropped Frank off at the police station that day he helped her, then went home and started cleaning—the back yard, the car, the garage, the house—trying to erase any sign of what she had done. She took a shower, but not a long hot one like she loved. She cleansed her hair and body as quickly as she could, with the curtain open, then sopped up the water from the floor.

Telling the boys had been as traumatic as she feared, but they held a funeral for Winston and invited their friends. That seemed to help a little. No one knew his body wasn't in the grave. The vet had disposed of it after he was done, cremated, Emily thought. Every night, the boys added Winston to their prayers, asking God to play with him so he wouldn't be lonely.

Weeks passed with the phone calls came sporadically, never the same time, never the same day, but always when Dan and the boys were gone. Same thing every time—quiet, then breathing, then some song Emily loved, or once had, songs popular when she was in high school. Frank said the caller must be someone who knew her well. Emily could have figured that much out on her own. Having Frank to talk to about the calls helped a little, but Emily did not tell him everything. Some family secrets were meant to be kept. And she didn't tell Dan she was talking to Frank. She hoped that didn't blow up in her face.

Emily didn't feel much comforted by the fact the cops knew and were supposedly trying to help find out who it was. She knew that most of them whispered behind her back, called her crazy. She'd be damned lucky if they didn't tell Dan. Or maybe they did tell him, and they all had a good laugh about his crazy wife.

She quit volunteering, quit visiting her parents. She only left the house to take the boys to and from school. Emily felt safer just staying home unless she absolutely had to leave. She ran necessary errands only when the boys were with her, and so far, no calls had followed them. When she got back home after leaving the house, she checked in every closet, under every bed, before she could relax and feel the least bit comfortable inside her locked house. Without Winston, she felt totally vulnerable, even in her own yard.

§ § §

Six months had passed since the calls started, and Emily found herself sitting in her living room, thinking about that trip to the beach, wondering if it could have had anything to do with the phone calls that continued to come on a regular basis. It was such an innocent day, but she didn't tell Dan. She lied and everything started falling apart. She was still lying by omission.

Things with Dan had actually improved. He didn't ask why she stayed home all the time, but she could tell he was pleased. She stopped protesting when he wanted to watch the movies as foreplay. Emily was herself involuntarily aroused by them, but she knew child molesters and serial rapists were, too, so it did little for her self-esteem. But it made Dan happy, so that was something. And Emily wasn't sure if the two were related, but since he had his sexual fantasies fulfilled on a regular basis, Dan seemed more easy-going, less critical, more tolerant of the boys.

Emily tried to be productive, but most weekdays found herself on the couch in front of the television, not bathing or dressing or even combing her hair until just before the boys came home. She cooked breakfast, but rarely ate. Slept through lunch. The theme song for *Days of Our Lives* was her wake-up call. Two o'clock—time to get up, shower and dress, become just mom for her boys. From the time she picked the boys up until sleep granted release, Emily forced herself to be normal—cooking, cleaning, smiling, playing, loving.

Weekends brought some respite—true concentration on the people she loved most and knowing the calls wouldn't come—but by Monday morning, the enormous effort exerted over the weekend sent her in a downward spiral. Once she was alone, she walked around the house yelling and screaming, cursing and crying, releasing all the emotion that had built over the weekend until she was spent, then slept a deep, dreamless sleep. If the caller was trying to drive her crazy, it was working.

One rainy Monday in late March, Emily realized her life had become quicksand swallowing her whole. No one reached out a hand to save her. She didn't wake up when the soap opera hourglass turned. She dreamed Dan was building a cradle, tapping each little spindle into place. She sat next to him, crocheting a pink blanket. But the tapping grew louder, then she heard crying. "Mommy, Mommy!" She struggled through the darkness trying to find the nursery, but each door opened into an empty room with another door, then another. She stumbled across the room, following a new sound, tapping on glass. Rain pounded in her head. "Mama, let us in!" Emily forced her eyes open. She stood at the front window seeing her boys, banging on the glass, their clothes drenched, rain dripping from their hair. She ran to the front door, out into the yard, and cradled her boys against her, then led them inside to safety. They had been trying to wake her up for over an hour, knocking on the doors, then the windows, calling, crying, banging, waiting.

"Where were you?" Danny cried. "You didn't come and you didn't come and we waited and waited. All the kids were gone!"

She learned that Bobby's teacher had dropped them off, but didn't wait to see them into the house. Emily was thankful, embarrassed, frightened.

The next morning, Emily forced herself to shower and dress as soon as Dan left for work. She had convinced the boys not to say anything to their father about what had happened. Emily hated what she said—"You don't want Daddy to yell at Mommy, do you?" Such a heavy burden to place on small shoulders. She prepared their favorite breakfast—chocolate chip pancakes, small drops linked together to formed a caterpillar squirming across their plates on a bacon roadway. Then she dropped them off at school with a promise to be waiting when the bell rang in the afternoon. Emily drove out to the farm, stayed just long enough to have a cup of coffee, some homemade cinnamon rolls, ask about the flower beds, the garden, plans for Easter dinner.

"Is everything okay, Baby Girl?" Daddy asked as he walked her to her car.

"No," Emily answered honestly, "but I can't talk about it right now." She reached up and brushed her hand across the stubble of his beard, smiled and left.

She drove to Wilmington, down Market Street where ancient oaks arched across, sheltering travelers on the skinny street. Tulips and daffodils swayed in the medians, dogwoods and azaleas ready to burst brilliant blooms. The Azalea Festival would be held soon; the boys would love the parade, the circus, the horse shows. Emily turned right on 16th Street and headed toward the hospital. She would try the doctor's office first, the emergency room as a last resort.

She walked into the office and told the receptionist, "I need to see Dr. Shepard please."

"Do you have an appointment?"

"No, but I'm one of his patients." Emily could feel the tears rising like a tide, methodical, irrepressible. They cascaded down her face, a waterfall splashing dark splotches across the front of her soft pink blouse.

"Let me get the nurse."

Emily placed her hands on the counter to steady herself. A nurse came through the door with a wheelchair and guided her into it. "The doctor is really busy," she said. "I'm not sure he'll be able to see you, but let's get you back here and have a little chat." She wheeled Emily into a small room, asked her name, apologized for not knowing it.

"Emily Gillespie."

"Stay right here and I'll go get your chart. How long ago did you last see Dr. Shepard?"

"Nine years." The flow had stopped, but Emily had the snubs.

"Oh child, no wonder I don't know you. I've been here seven years, pride myself in knowing our patients by name and face. I didn't recognize either of yours. You'll have to fill out some paperwork for me. The charts are purged every five years. Yours would be in the storage unit down the road there." She spoke in a low monotone, soothing, quieting.

Emily finished the paperwork and handed it to the nurse, who then checked her vitals. Emily's heart was racing, head pounding, hands shaking. "Let me see how Dr. Shepard's coming along," the nurse said. Her name was Nancy, white letters on a dark tag. "You stay right here, okay?"

Emily opened her purse and began counting the bills she had hidden in the zipper pocket on the inside—allowance she had not spent in all the months of her self-confinement. She would pay with cash, no paper trail. She did not want Dan to know, not now, not ever. The tears came again.

"Well now, Emily, what can I do for you today?" Dr. Shepard's soft voice drew her attention away from the money, but gave her tears permission to flow.

"This," she said, pointing to her face. "Can't stop them."

"It's been a long time, Emily. I assumed you've been doing well since I haven't seen you. I appreciated the pictures you sent of your boys when they were born. Two, right? Why don't you tell me what's changed."

He listened attentively as Emily talked, as though he had no other patients waiting. She told him about the calls, the roses, Winston. She didn't tell him about Dan. She told him about the crying, the anxiety, the pressure on her chest, her fear, the cops. The people who thought she was crazy. Maybe they were right, she said. She told him about her boys.

"I need to take care of them," Emily said. "But sometimes I can't even take care of myself."

"Well you know I can give you something to help. Medications are even better now. But, I think it best that we watch you for a little while first, run some tests, treatments maybe."

"I can't go to the hospital," Emily said, standing. "No treatments. I won't go."

"What are you afraid of, Emily? Please sit back down. You would be safe there—no phone calls, no roses. No one would be brazen enough to come into a hospital, now would he?"

"But I don't want Dan to know." She said it softly, her head bowed. "He might leave this time. Take my boys. I'd just as soon die."

Dr. Shepard took her right hand in both of his, "Look at me, Emily, look at me." She lifted her head, met his gaze. "I'm going to get the nurse now. She'll draw some blood, run some tests. I need you to come back on Thursday, after we get the results. Can you do that, Emily?"

She nodded.

"Good," he said. "I'll see you then."

§ § §

Emily waited outside the school for her boys, watching other parents, wondering what they knew. She saw Jay Kane and remembered the extraordinary anger he directed toward her at the PTA meeting when she expressed support for the new principal. Could it be him? Or Ben Stocks, the Boy Scout leader, who called her a stuck-up bitch when she refused his advances in high school. Could he hold a grudge that long? Or Sue Beverly, whose husband, Tim, made drunken passes at Emily at their last class reunion. Dan threatened to kill him. Could they be retaliating? But why at her and not Dan?

"Hey, Mom," Danny said, opening the car door before Emily even saw him. "Can we get ice cream?"

Bobby bounded up behind him. "Mommy! Can we get ice cream?"

"You guys ganging up on me? Two against one, I guess you win."

"You like ice cream, too," Bobby said, hopping into the back seat.

"You're right, I do." They detoured by way of the drug store soda shop and each chose their favorite flavors—two scoops in cones—walked across the street to the courthouse square and sat on a bench under the towering oak trees while they ate.

When they arrived home, Emily sent the boys out in the back yard to play. She didn't want them to see her checking closets and under the beds. Standing at the kitchen sink, she peeled potatoes and watched them, worried about them.

§ § §

Emily entered Dr. Shepard's office at 10 a.m. on Thursday.

"All your blood work and vitals look fine, Emily. I think we'll be safe putting you back on some medication. But remember, you must take it every day and it may take several weeks for it to really kick in. I'd feel better about you if we could do a few treatments, too."

The wheelchair squeaked as they rolled down the hallway. Through her drugged haze, Emily could see the silver chairs lined against the wall, people waiting. The doors swung open. Emily can you stand? Here let me help you. Swing right around here now. Just putting your feet up. Arms pressed down. One, then the other. Straps wrapped, buckles fastened. No, Emily could hear herself say. No, please. Then she couldn't talk, couldn't move her tongue. Something jammed between her teeth. Lights too bright. Cold metal on her head, here, here, there. Can't move arms. Searing pain. Body shaking. Darkness.

"Emily. Emily. I need you to listen carefully."

She was shaking, but she nodded and focused.

"You can't stop taking the medication when you start to feel better. It will help you control your emotions, but it can't change whatever is going on in your life. Only you can do that. Do you understand?"

Emily nodded.

"I want you back here in six weeks."

Chapter 7

The telephone rang. Emily winced at the sound, but knew it would not be him. It was Saturday after all, the last weekend in March. Dan was out in the driveway washing his truck, Bobby in the back yard playing. The calls never came when they were home, so she answered calmly, but always as a question.

"Hello?"

"Emily, Emily Gillespie?"

"Yes."

"This is Trooper Lewis of the Highway Patrol. I'm sorry to tell you this, but there's been an accident."

Emily's knees buckled. Danny was on a field trip with scouts. "The bus, tell me it wasn't the bus. Not Danny!"

"Calm down ma'am. I'm not sure what bus you're talking about, but it was a truck, one of those little foreign jobs, your father's truck. You are Paul Turner's daughter, aren't you?"

"Yes."

"Like I said, ma'am, there's been an accident out on Route 117. You need to come to the hospital as soon as you can."

"How bad is he hurt? Is he okay? Mama, did you call my mama?"

"She was with him, ma'am. Now please, just come to Pender Memorial."

Emily grabbed her keys, rushed outside and told Dan she was leaving and why.

"Not by yourself, you're not," he said. "You're a mess. I'm going with you. Just let me go inside and shower and change."

"I can't wait that long," Emily screamed, then tried to calm her voice. "I'll be fine. I'll call you when I know something. You need to pick Danny up at school—4 p.m. Don't forget." She left without giving him time to respond.

The hospital was only a few blocks from her house, so Emily arrived quickly, even before the ambulance did. She rushed in and asked for her parents, but the staff was just sitting around talking, the three beds in the small emergency room empty.

"Who are you looking for?" one nurse asked.

"Paul and Marie Turner. They were in a wreck. The wreck on Route 117."

"Yeah, we got a call about that," the orderly said. "Some truck with dark windows ran 'em off the road, somebody said. Didn't even stop. Nobody got no tag numbers."

Emily heard the sirens and thought briefly about Norma. She should call her. But she didn't have time to find a phone. The ambulance backed up to the emergency room door and the volunteers piled out, two from the front ran around and opened the back door. She saw two more inside performing CPR. Emily, being pushed aside by the hospital staff, could not see if it was her mama or her daddy, but she knew it was only one of them.

"Where's the other one?" Emily sobbed. "Where's the other one?"

No one paid any attention to her.

"We got a heartbeat. Let's move!"

They rolled the gurney out of the ambulance and into one of the partitioned areas. Emily tried to follow.

"Stay here ma'am. You'll be in the way."

"My mama, daddy? They need me." Emily tried again to follow.

"I said stay here ma'am. This man is alive, but barely. If you get in the way, he could die right here. Now move."

Emily acquiesced, fighting back every little voice that told her she needed to be close to her daddy. She focused on her mama—where was she? Emily walked back out the door to look for her ambulance. She saw one coming down the street slowly—no siren, no lights—obviously empty. She wondered why they were taking so long to bring her in. Emily began pacing, back and forth just outside the door, down the sloped drive, then back up.

The ambulance pulled up slowly beside her, past her, and backed up to the door. Emily ignored it and kept pacing. No other ambulance in sight. Emily felt her chest tighten. The elephant was back. She struggled to breath. Slow deep breaths, deep breaths, she reminded herself. You can't lose it now.

"Ma'am, hey ma'am. Emily?"

She looked up and saw someone she vaguely recognized. "Yes, I'm Emily."

"I knew it. Emily Turner. We were in Mrs. Tate's French class together. And Mrs. Rivenbark's algebra, and Miss Glisson's English."

Emily could not remember his name, but smiled slightly as though she did.

"You remember that time Julius brought the snake..."

"John, you coming? We gotta transport," one of the other paramedics yelled.

"Yeah, I'm coming," John replied, then turned back to Emily. "I gotta go. I'm real sorry about your folks, Emily. But it's good to see you. So good to see you. Man, it's been too long." He started to walk away, then stopped and turned back to face her. "Oh yeah, I think they need you in there to identify the body."

"What?" Emily screamed, but John was rushing off to help load a gurney on the ambulance, surrounded by people and machines. Emily heard words—hurry, let's go... BP's dropping again—but John's words reverberated in her ears—*identify the body, identify the body*. Emily walked slowly into the hospital.

"Ms. Gillespie," a nurse said, meeting her at the door. "I need you to come with me please."

Emily followed, feeling weightless except for the heavy pressure on her chest. She forced herself to take deep slow breaths, to concentrate on where they were going and what the nurse was saying. Emily had not really heard a word. They walked down the hall from the emergency room, turned right past the nurse's station, Emily vaguely aware of the smell of garlic as they passed the lunchroom.

They kept walking until they were headed out the door to the loading dock.

"We had to convert the storage room into a makeshift morgue," Emily heard the nurse say. "She's in here."

Emily stopped.

"Are you alright?" the nurse asked. "Do you have anyone with you, anyone at all?"

"No," Emily said, answering both questions with a single, barely audible syllable.

Emily followed the nurse into a small cold room and saw her mama lying on a stretcher.

"She didn't suffer," the nurse said.

Emily touched the fingers of the hand closest to her, the skin thinning, blue veins mapping it just below the surface. She touched her mother's face, ran her fingers across the soft skin. Marie Turner had never worn make-up, never needed it. Emily combed her fingers through her mother's short curly auburn hair, noticed the silver streaks as the curls bounced back into place. Her eyelids were thin, blue veins prominent, hiding the eyes that Emily loved, eyes the color of coal—or molasses. She thought about the last time she sat at the kitchen table, sopping molasses with homemade biscuits. Thought about her mama's appeal that she help Norma. It was the least she could do now.

Emily scanned her mama's body—her dress still intact, peach cotton with an eyelet collar, white flowers embroidered around the hem. Her hose were torn and her shoes gone, but otherwise she looked normal.

"How?" Emily queried.

"Head trauma," the nurse said. "We cleaned her up as best we could." She walked to the end of the gurney and pointed.

Emily gently turned her mama's head. Much of the back was missing.

"She's in a better place," the nurse said. "Gone home. God has her now, you don't need to worry."

Emily jerked her head around and stared. That's what she'd

been taught all her life—she knew it to be true—but she didn't want to hear it now. Platitudes, just platitudes.

"I want to see my father now," Emily said. "Take me to the emergency room and make them let me in."

"But he's gone," the nurse answered. "Didn't they tell you?"

Emily's knees failed her and she fell to the floor, hyperventilating, shivering. "No, not both of them, not now, not the same day."

"Oh no, not gone that way," the nurse replied. "Gone to New Hanover Hospital. They transported him. His injuries were more than we could handle here, but he was still alive when they left. I'm sorry child, I didn't mean to..."

Emily was on her feet, through the doors and down the hall, ignoring the nurse, ignoring the people who stared at her as she ran. New Hanover Hospital was in Wilmington, almost thirty miles away. *Hold on Daddy, I'm coming, hold on, hold on, hold on, hold on.* Emily repeated that two-word mantra in her head, using the rhythm to pace her breath, steady her heart rate—*hold on, hold on, hold on.*

Emily didn't call Dan. She didn't call Norma. With singleness of intent, she drove without thinking of anyone but her daddy, hurt and alone, in a strange place with doctors he didn't know. Within forty-five minutes, Emily pulled into the emergency room parking lot. Fifteen minutes more passed before she stood beside her father's bed, or at least they said it was him. Heavily bandaged and attached to a multitude of machines, a slim man lay still beneath the sheets.

"Are you the next of kin?"

Emily looked toward the soft-spoken man in a white coat, a stethoscope around his neck, blue cloth booties covering his shoes. "I'm his daughter."

"I'm Dr. Wilson," he said. Emily shook his extended hand. "I'm not going to lie to you. Your father is seriously injured. I don't know if I can save him, but I'll do everything I can. He has definite head injuries, but we don't know how serious they are yet. His immediate threat is from the internal bleeding. I need your permission to operate, exploratory surgery to find where the bleeding is. Will you give that to me?"

"Yes. Anything."

"Thank you. I'll send the nurse right in with the forms. I don't know what I'll find when I get in there, but I'll do everything I can to save your father. That's all I can promise."

"Thank you."

Emily signed the papers and followed her daddy's rolling bed as far as she could. At the double doors to the operating room, the nurse gently said, "This is as far as you can go. Someone will let you know when it's over."

Emily stood motionless with no regard for time, staring down the hospital hallway. *Think, think, move,* she commanded herself. *Do something. Call. Dan. Norma. Phone. Find a phone. Mama's dead. Find a phone. Daddy cannot die. Find a phone.* Emily conjured up the words her therapist had told her many years before. One step at a time. Baby steps. Just move forward one step at a time.

In the surgical waiting area, Emily found a courtesy phone. She called home first.

"Hello." Dan's voice was stern, edgy. Emily could hear her boys arguing in the background. "Hello," Dan repeated.

"Dan, it's me."

"Where the hell are you? I've been worried sick. The boys are fighting over some stupid game. I didn't know where you were. There's nothing for supper."

"I'm at the hospital."

"No you're not. I called there. They said nobody's in the emergency room or the waiting room. I had them look for you, Emily. I called your parents' house to see if they were already home. I called Norma. She didn't know anything about a wreck. Are you lying to me?"

"Mama's dead. Daddy's in surgery. I'm in Wilmington, Dan, the new hospital. Mama's dead."

"Oh, Emily, I'm sorry. I'm sorry," Dan's voice changed instantly. "I didn't mean it. You should have called me sooner. How did you get there? You know you shouldn't drive when you're upset.

Did you drive yourself? Who's with you?"

"I'm alone. Just me. Mama's dead. She's in the morgue at the hospital, at Pender. I left. I didn't tell them where to take her. I left her alone. Oh god, Dan. She's alone. I left her alone."

"What do you want me to do? I'm stuck here. What do I do with the boys?"

Emily said nothing. She couldn't think.

"Never mind. Don't worry. I'll call Ms. Reid next door. Maybe she'll keep them. I'll call Quinn-McGowen and get them to pick up your mother. Is that what you want, where you want her? Have you talked to Norma about it?"

"I haven't talked to Norma."

"Not at all? She doesn't know?"

"No. I don't know."

"Damn, Emily, she's your sister. You didn't call her?"

"No, she's not. And I didn't have time. I didn't think."

"Okay, look, I'll try to get up with Norma. I'll call Ms. Reid. I'll call the funeral home. You just sit there, and I'll come as soon as I can, okay? I'm coming, Emily, just sit there, okay?"

"Okay."

Emily hung up the phone and tried to sit in the empty surgical waiting area, tried to obey Dan. She could not. She stood, walked back and forth, twelve steps from the couch at one end to the loveseat at the other. Not enough. She walked out in the hall, two hundred thirty-nine steps to the end, past two corridor crossings, CVICU, SICU, people leaning against the walls, waiting. Everybody waiting. Red phones. She turned and started counting again. At step seventy-nine, she crossed another corridor and almost ran head on into Norma.

"Where is he?" Norma demanded.

"Surgery."

"Why didn't you call me?"

"No time."

"What do you mean no time, they're just like my parents, too, Emily. I've been part of this family for 13 years. You should have called me. Why didn't they call me? The cops should have called me."

"No, they should have called me."

"I would have taken the time to call you, not made you call all over the place trying to find out. Did you ever call Dan? He was looking for you, called me. That's how I found out, Emily. I had to call the hospital, track you down. You should have called me."

"I know. I'm sorry. Mama's dead. She's dead, Norma. Dead. Mama's dead and Daddy's dying." Emily started walking again, counting in her head. Daddy helped her count tadpoles in the edge of the river, fireflies in her jar. One, two, three... *That's good, Emily. My good, smart baby girl.*

"Don't walk away from me, Emily. You know this is your fault, don't you. Don't you? If you hadn't been so stingy, so money grubbing. If you had loaned me the money I needed to fix my car, they wouldn't have been driving that little truck. I wouldn't have had to borrow the station wagon. Mama wasn't supposed to be with him. Not in that truck."

"What?"

"Dan makes good money, Emily. You could have shared just a little bit of it. If you weren't always seeing dollar signs. Boy, you've got everybody fooled, you self-righteous bitch. Everybody says you're just like Mama, but you're not. Nowhere near. You should have given me some money when I asked for it, needed it."

"Which time? You are not blaming this on me. This is not my fault, not anybody's fault. It was an accident, Norma, an accident." Emily turned and started walking.

"Don't you walk away from me."

Emily kept walking, all the way to the end, then back past the surgical waiting area, past the double doors to the surgical unit, down the hall to the windows that overlooked the city. She saw the sun glinting off vehicles, people rushing from place to place, always rushing, life in a hurry. Accidents should happen on rainy days.

"Ms. Gillespie." Emily heard the soft voice of the doctor, felt his hand on her shoulder. She didn't know how much time had passed. "We need to talk. There's a room right over here where we'll have some privacy. Do you have other family members with you?"

Emily turned from the darkened window. "My sister-in-law. In the waiting room, I think."

"We'll get her on the way by."

When Emily walked into the waiting room, she saw not only Norma, but Dan, too, sitting on the couch, close, talking softly, holding hands. They stopped abruptly when she walked in.

"The doctor needs to talk to us."

"Emily, honey," Dan said. "Are you alright? You've been staring out that window for hours."

"He said to come this way," Emily said. "Privacy."

Norma and Dan followed Emily and the doctor to the next room—small with brown leather chairs lined around the walls, enough to hold a big family. Dan sat between the women, holding both their hands. The doctor sat on the arm of the chair directly across the room. The air was stifling. Emily struggled to breathe.

"We found several sources of bleeding," the doctor began, "and we were able to stop it for now. I believe that problem is stable. But I will not lie to you. He appears to have major head trauma."

"I want to see him," Norma said.

"When he comes out of recovery, he'll be in surgical ICU. You'll be able to go in one at a time for just a few minutes."

"Is he in a lot of pain?" Emily asked.

"I wish I could tell you no. He's going to be in some pain, but we'll keep him heavily sedated to alleviate as much as possible. He was in a coma when he came in, and the medicine will keep him in one for a while."

§ § §

Several days passed in a blur. Sitting in her daddy's hospital room, listening to the whoosh and whir of the machines, Emily became edgy, needed to move, do something. She walked to the window, saw the cars far below. She lifted each item on the nightstand, read the ingredients before putting them back down. She opened the drawers to find them empty. She walked to the closet, opened the door and saw a white plastic bag overflowing on the floor. She took it out and started pulling the items from within. She found her daddy's jeans and chambray shirt—the same thing he wore everyday whether he was going out to mow the lawn or driving Mama to town to buy groceries—jeans and a chambray shirt, just like he wore in the Navy. But they were covered in dark splotches, one of his pant legs ripped from the groin to the knee. Both his white socks were there, but one black shoe was missing, the other still tied neatly. She replaced the items, closed the closet, and walked back to the bedside.

She let her gaze creep up the length of his body. His arms lay prone to his sides, outside the sheets, his huge hands unblemished. Emily stared at the mass of hair graying on the backs of his hands and the first section of his fingers. Childhood memories flooded her senses—her first trout flopping on the hook before Daddy's hands wrapped firmly around it and wriggled the hook from its mouth; those hands giving her a boost before she could reach the first step of the treehouse; those hands pointing to a whitetail doe and her fawn when Emily and her Daddy and brother took their Sunday afternoon walks in the woods at her grandparents' home; those hands spanking her bottom the day she ran out in the street after a ball. Daddy had been so scared.

She remembered climbing into bed with him on Sunday mornings while Mama cooked breakfast. She and Charles would snuggle up under the covers while he read to them. When she was very young and he read *Little Red Riding Hood*, Emily looked at his hands and thought he might really be the wolf in her daddy's flannel pajamas.

But his hands didn't move, so Emily forced her eyes to continue slowly up the length of his body. She had always been proud of her daddy's physique, how he kept in shape with hard work and walking. Her boys could never keep up when they went for walks in the woods. She smiled when she thought of the boys calling, "Poppy, slow down."

His eyes were closed, but Emily could see them clearly—sparkling dark pools like the tannin stained water of the Black River he loved so much. His hair, graying heavily, peeked from beneath the edges of the bandages. She heard the door open.

"He's going to be a coma for quite some time, I'm afraid," Dr. Wilson said.

Emily turned and looked at him.

"I understand you lost your mother."

"Yes."

"And her funeral is when?"

"We haven't planned it yet. I can't leave Daddy. I just can't."

"He doesn't know you're here right now, and I'm not sure when he will. We can't find much brain activity. The machines are keeping him alive, will keep him alive while you take care of your mother. Be with the rest of your family. Mourn your mother. Go to her funeral."

"I can't leave him."

"I haven't known you very long, but I do know this. You will never forgive yourself if you don't go to your mother's funeral. Even if your father woke up—and I'm telling you he won't—he would understand, wouldn't he? What would he expect you to do?"

"He would want me to take care of her."

"Then do that. I'll take care of him."

Chapter 8

The driveway to Emily's parents' home was long, but straight, cutting right through the middle of the thirty acres handed down from her granddaddy on her mother's side. The two-room house where her grandparents had lived—also on the property—was long since abandoned. Emily's grandmother had spent her last ten years living in the "big" house with the Turners. She'd been gone barely a year when the wreck happened. That was a blessing, Emily thought, as she passed the little clapboard siding cabin with its rusted tin roof nestled under gargantuan oak trees. Granny never would have survived the news—parents shouldn't have to bury their children. Then Emily felt a twinge of guilt. She loved her granny fiercely, but she would not want the responsibility of taking care of her now that her own mother was gone. And she couldn't expect Daddy to do it by himself.

Emily's car glided smoothly along the dirt drive and she thought about Daddy, about how proud he was of his home and his land, how he spent hours with the tractor grading the drive so there was never a mud hole or bump. How he tended the towering long leaf pine trees and picked up the pinecones each year, leaving a soft bed of clean new straw. He gathered a little to mulch Mama's flowers and let the neighbor rake a bit once in a while, but otherwise it just fell softly to the ground like chocolate snow. He probably could have sold the straw and made a fortune, but he didn't like disturbing the land or anything on it.

"I'm just God's caretaker," he would say. "Gonna leave the land be, except to grow crops."

So it was that most of the thirty acres remained wooded, a haven for deer and bear and turkey, foxes and rabbits, squirrel and birds—

and snakes. Only about ten acres had been cleared—one around the old house, a couple for the new house and garden where Daddy raised vegetables for the family, two for grapes and melons—Daddy's little side business to supplement his early retirement income from his shift-work job at the textile plant—and two as a field of corn for the deer, which, of course, was always raided by the black bear.

When Granddaddy died and Granny couldn't live by herself anymore, Emily's parents had chosen to build their home near the back of the property next to the creek—Moore's Creek that fed into the Black River, then the Cape Fear River that flowed into the Atlantic Ocean. Emily had always loved to hear Daddy explain the way the waters ran, and her boys would sit and listen to Poppy for hours. If he died, they would miss him so much. Emily already did. In a split second, her whole world had been decimated by someone in a big black truck who didn't even have the decency to stop.

Emily hadn't wanted to go to the house alone, but Dan said he needed to go back to work and Emily didn't argue. And Norma—anybody's guess where she was—probably being consoled by the latest boyfriend, Emily imagined. The funeral home needed clothes. Her mother-in-law had offered to go with her, but Emily asked her to stay with the boys and forced herself to go alone.

The driveway ended in the side yard of her parents' home. Even though they often referred to it as the "new" house or the "big" house—relative to the first house on the property—it was twelve years old and had only four rooms, plus a sun porch. The house was white with a black-shingled roof that slanted off on two sides to cover a wide porch. Mama had recently asked for a red front door, so the fresh paint gleamed in contrast to the age-dulled black shutters that had yet to be re-painted. Emily parked between the beds of azaleas bursting crimson with blooms. The limbs of the dogwoods appeared to hang heavy, seemingly burdened by the weight of their delicate white blossoms. Emily sat for a few moments, gathering her strength and courage, controlling her breath, commanding her heart to slow down.

When she opened the car door and stepped out, all her senses were flooded. The wisteria bloomed profusely, its syrupy sweet aroma silently filling the air. A cacophony of frog song celebrated the previous evening's spring rain, droplets clinging to leaves and flower petals, glistening in the morning sun. In the distance, a woodpecker tapped rhythmically, searching for food. The swing chains creaked and Emily swung her attention toward the front porch. The swing barely moved—only the wind, Emily convinced herself. But she felt none, and shivered.

Pansies lined the brick walk to the front porch. Her mother changed the color combination every year—this year purple and gold. Mama always replaced the pansies with petunias when the heat began to scorch their petals and wilt their leaves. Since the pansies were purple this year, the petunias would be, too—a solid purple bed of beauties dotted randomly with purple and white striped ones.

Emily placed her foot carefully on the first wooden step, trying unsuccessfully not to make it creak. She stopped. Listened. Stepped again. Creaked. Stopped. Listened. Just the woodpecker in the distance. She hurried up the last two steps and across the porch to the front door. Her parents never locked the house, so she slowly turned the knob, pushed, and let the door swing open. Sunlight filtered through the sheers, glanced across the dark pine floor, revealing a few days of dust settling. Dust mites danced in the sun's rays. Mama would be so embarrassed.

Emily let her eyes slowly rove the living room with its eclectic furnishings—new soft overstuffed furniture balanced by antique tables, a desk, a brocade upholstered rocker. Lace doilies sat beneath the lamps and the cookie dish filled with M&Ms; crocheted afghans draped the back of the couch and loveseat. Daddy's newest copy of *Field and Stream* lay on the table by his recliner, his reading glasses folded neatly on top. Mama's knitting basket sat beside her chair, a partially completed baby blanket in soft pastels peaking from inside with needles stuck up like porcupine quills. Someone at church must be having a baby.

As Emily looked around the room and onto the sun porch, she

became increasingly angry at the person who had stolen her family. Mama and Daddy loved their plants—his African violets and her houseplants of every shape and color. They were all so full of life, so lovingly tended, so artistically displayed. Her parents didn't deserve to die.

Returning to the singular mission for her trip to the house, Emily entered her parents' bedroom. It was as neat and clean as she expected it to be—the bed made and pillows fluffed, no stray clothes lying around, no shoes out of the closet, a Bible on each nightstand. She wasn't sure where her mother stored the things she needed to find—socks, underwear, a gown, or would Mama prefer one of her nice Sunday dresses? Should she take her mother's favorite pearls?

She started opening drawers, going through her parents' things, felt guilty for plundering. She decided against jewelry. Her mother was, after all, a simple Christian woman, and Elizabeth would treasure anything that belonged to her grandmother. Almost a teenager, she would soon begin to look like a young woman instead of a little girl. She'd save the jewelry for Elizabeth. Emily searched in the smaller drawers first because that's where she would have kept her own underwear, but found instead a stack of receipts, a ledger of notes, and a rubberbanded pile of credit card bills. She didn't know her mother even owned a credit card. Her parents had never been extravagant and always paid cash. Even the one big thing they had purchased—a navy blue station wagon for their 40th wedding anniversary—had been paid for in cash. Daddy had saved for years and years to give Mama that surprise. He wanted her to be able to haul all the grandchildren around and be safer on the roads.

"Crazy fools driving the roads, these days," he had said.

Emily pulled the small drawer from the nightstand and placed it on the bed. The credit card bills were in just her mother's name and many of the charges were cash advances at exorbitant interest rates. The statements showed monthly minimum payments since the first withdrawal two years earlier. Emily flipped through the bills, becoming more and more confused. Why would her mother need so much cash, and why would she hide it from her husband?

Then Emily picked up the ledger and began to understand. The first date coincided perfectly with Norma's third, and so far last, divorce. The first entry—attorney's fees. Then Elizabeth's ballet lessons, Isaac's and Peter's coats, shoes for James and John, food, electric bill, rent—smaller increments itemized to tally up the large advances. Emily had no idea. Norma had come to her for money again and again—so many times that she finally said no—had to say no when she wanted so much more than Emily had to give. She knew Norma cried on her mother's shoulder all the time, but she never dreamed she would have the audacity to go that far.

Norma was smart, talented, able, but she couldn't or wouldn't hold down a job. She would start a new job, good jobs—and Mama would brag on her endlessly—then after a few months, sometimes as little as a week or two, she would quit for one reason or another. Always some excuse. But she was receiving child support from two different men. That new government program paid the children's medical bills, and sometimes she even worked long enough to draw unemployment. She knew how to milk the system. Why did she have to milk Mama, too?

Emily thought she heard the screen door creak open. She held her breath and waited for a knock. Nothing. Norma, she thought, and hurriedly replaced the paperwork in the drawer and the drawer in the nightstand. She would deal with that later. She stood up, smoothed the quilt where she had sat on the edge of the bed and walked to the kitchen. No one was there, no cars in the drive other than hers, no sign of anyone at all. Just her imagination.

Not surprisingly, the sink was void of dirty dishes, the dish cloth hung perfectly folded across the stove handle; pictures of all seven grandchildren clung to the refrigerator door along with cards and pictures they had drawn. Everything was waiting, just as they left it, waiting for them to return home. But Mama wasn't coming, not ever. She prayed that her Daddy would.

In a strange way, Emily felt comforted by being among her parents' things, in their house—even though it wasn't where she grew up. Everything that made them who they were had been transported to that house and reminded Emily of a time and place where she didn't have to make the big decisions, where she knew she would be loved unconditionally and taken care of. But reality kept creeping in, shattering the past with shards of the present, so she returned to her mission—find what she needed to bury Mama.

When Emily walked back into the bedroom, she focused on the tall chest of drawers next to the closet, hoping to find what she needed. The top drawer held the jewelry she had decided not to take. In the second drawer she found underwear and socks. She chose white, then slid the drawer closed. She opened the closet door. Sliding the hangers one by one, she perused her mother's Sunday dresses. Mama always looked so beautiful when she went to church or celebrations or other people's funerals, but she preferred dressing comfortably, working in the yard, getting dirt under her fingernails, tending to her flowers, vegetables, children. Emily couldn't imagine making her lie for eternity dressed up.

On the floor of the closet, she spotted yellow satin slippers and picked them up. They looked like daffodil petals, and Emily made her decision. She remembered the gown and robe her boys had picked out for their granny last Christmas—soft yellow nylon with flowers embroidered on the yoke of the gown and collar of the robe. She just had to find it. She saw a white gift box on the closet shelf with strips of Christmas wrapping still taped to the edges. She recognized the blue and silver striped paper as what she had used the previous Christmas. Emily reached up and brought the box down, opened it to find the gown and robe carefully refolded with the boys' Christmas card on top. Just like Mama to save it for a special occasion. She placed the underwear and socks inside the box and set the slippers on top. Mission accomplished, she was anxious to get home to her boys.

Emily closed the closet door and turned toward the bed. She stopped cold. Lying across her mother's pillow was a long-stemmed yellow rose, red tinges tickling the petals' edges like it had been dipped in blood. She looked around the room and saw no one, nothing else to indicate that anyone had been there. She heard nothing but her own breath coming in ragged gasps. She forced her feet to move, walked slowly to the bed, hoping it was a mirage—that she wasn't really seeing her mother's favorite of all the roses in her garden. They weren't blooming now, not this early in the spring. Emily touched the rose. It was freshly cut, firm, alive; droplets of dew nestled inside the tight bud. Emily began to shake, to cry.

Even the loud jangling of the phone on Daddy's nightstand did not register at first. Emily feared she would lose it now—all the composure she had struggled to contain through the last few days with her parents, the last few months with the phone calls, the secrets. The box tilted in her hand and the slippers fell to the floor, a soft thump, but enough to startle her to recognition of the noise, the phone. *Answer it. It might be Dan. Might be Norma. Something might be wrong with the boys. Answer it.*

She walked around the end of the bed to her Daddy's side, lifted the receiver and said hello.

No one answered.

"Hello," she repeated.

The breathing began, then a soft chuckle. Then the music. Her grandma's favorite hymn. *I come to the garden alone, while the dew is still on the roses...*

Emily dropped the receiver, grabbed the box and the slippers and ran to her car. She fumbled with her keys, dropped them in the floorboard, her head up, eyes darting around as she tried to find them. She rolled up her window, locked the doors, found the keys and cranked the car. She cut the steering wheel too sharply and backed into her mother's bed of daffodils, breaking the tiny white fencing, crushing the flowers before spinning off down the drive.

A large limb lay across the road and Emily slammed on brakes right in front of her grandparents' abandoned cabin. She had to get out and move it. Her eyes darted back and forth. She looked toward her granny's cabin and gasped. Had it come to this, was she so paranoid, so messed up that she was seeing things? The chairs on the porch rocked slightly, and dozens of roses lay scattered on the porch—yellow tinged in pink just like the one on her mother's pillow.

Emily didn't mention the roses when she got home. How could she? No one knew about the phone calls, the flowers that had appeared from nowhere. She hadn't told anyone but Frank, didn't trust anyone, especially after the police brushed it off as just some kid's prank. They had been flowers after all, and mostly live ones at that—one dead flower, a dead dog that probably just found something in the woods, no real threats—just music and flowers. *Maybe you have a secret admirer,* one deputy had the nerve to say with a smirk and a wink. She quit reporting the incidents after that. But she still listened when the phone rang, when the music played. She couldn't help herself. Frank called once to check on her, and she told him everything was fine.

Fine—a word so easily said without meaning. Certainly not a word that described any part of Emily's life. Not now, maybe not for years in the past, maybe never again in the future.

§ § §

Her mother's funeral was scheduled for Wednesday morning, April 3, 1968. It was a nondescript Carolina spring day—a little overcast, not much sun, no rain, a slight breeze. Norma had insisted that the casket spray be prominently roses. Emily's chest tightened and her heart quickened every time she looked at them. Her parents had been loved and respected in the community and the chapel looked like a garden—so many lively colors for a room full of death.

Following the chapel service, the funeral procession headed out into the country to the small family cemetery within walking distance of the farm. The boys sat quietly in the back seat. Emily's heart ached every time she glanced back at them. She could easily see Danny, seated on the driver's side, obviously trying to be stoic, looking out the side window where trees, pastures, cows, horses, and corn fields blurred by. As Emily watched, he leaned his forehead against the window, his eyes cast on the gray nothing of the highway. He needs a haircut, she thought, seeing wisps of chocolate brown hair touching the collar of his new white shirt, the cowlick at the crown of his head sending unruly sprigs in circular motion.

Emily twisted in her seat so she could look straight back at

Bobby behind her. She could see only the top of his head, his face bowed toward his shoes, his feet scissoring up and down one by one almost hitting the back of Emily's seat. He twisted his red tie round and round with his finger, flicked at the buttons on his sport coat. Fidgeting. That's the word Mama would have used to describe him. Stationary but not still.

Not trusting herself to speak, Emily turned back around and settled into her seat.

"Did your parents have any insurance?" Dan asked.

"Huh?" She turned her head to look at him. He continued to watch the road.

"Life insurance. Did your parents have any?"

"I don't know."

"Funerals aren't cheap. And if your daddy dies, too…"

"Can this conversation wait, please?" Emily looked back at the boys; both now faced their daddy.

"Yeah, sorry. I was just thinking. It's a lot of money I wasn't expecting to have to spend."

"I got money," Bobby said. "Twelve dollars and twenty-three cents. I counted it."

Emily stared at Dan but spoke to her son. "That's a lot of money, Bobby."

"Grandma G gave me it. Most of it, anyway. For my birthday. I found some in the couch cushions and a dollar on the playground."

Emily looked at her son, so innocent, sincere.

"That's stealing," Danny said.

"No, it ain't," Bobby argued.

"Is, too."

"You boys hush," Dan said, his voice short, sharp.

"Money's not something for you to worry about," Emily said to her boys. "And today is a day to remember all the fun times you had with Granny." She gave Dan that *don't mention it again* look that sometimes worked, but was usually just ignored.

Emily cast her eyes forward, Norma directly ahead driving her parents' car, the white flower van in front of her following the hearse.

Cars meeting the procession pulled off on the side of the road, a display of respect that swelled Emily's emotions. She thought about the food overflowing at her home, her parents' home, a Southern tradition of death—*I'm sorry your mother died, here's a pie.*

Emily chastised herself for those ungrateful thoughts. The food was important, a tangible way people could help in a situation no one could change. Her boys had been fed without her having to do anything, and no matter what had happened, growing boys needed food. She knew at that very moment, women from the church who would like to attend the service were at her parents' home, preparing lunch for the family following the funeral. She would be able to walk into the house, emotionally and physically drained, and feast on meats, vegetables, and desserts prepared by people who loved her mother.

A chain link fence surrounded the cemetery, yellow bells climbing its sides and bursting into bloom. Her parents had purchased a double headstone years earlier, their names and birth dates already engraved. Mama's death date would be added soon, but Emily prayed that her daddy's would not be needed for years to come. The funeral tent sheltered the grave and rows of chairs for family, a tethered bouquet of balloons bouncing from its corner in the breeze.

Exiting the car, Emily clasped the hands of her sons on either side and walked toward the chairs lined up for family. Sitting in the front row, she sobbed softly, not really hearing the words of the minister, nor the notes of the music. At the last amen, Elizabeth cut the ribbons of the balloons, releasing them into the heavens, but they snagged on a tree limb and hovered overhead, not yet ready to go.

People filed by offering condolences. Emily looked up at each one, whispered thank you until it held no meaning. In a brief break between people, Emily glimpsed a tall, slender man beyond the fence, standing at the edge of the crowd. He met her gaze and nodded slightly. He looked familiar. When Emily chanced to look again, he was gone.

Chapter 9

Immediately after the funeral, Emily returned to the hospital to be with her daddy. Just as the doctor promised, nothing had changed. She slumped onto the edge of her daddy's bed, dozing fitfully. A gentle knock on the door awakened her. She looked up, slightly lifting her head, her arms still folded on the sheets. The room was dark, the lights out, blinds closed. Emily saw the door open slowly, light from the hallway spilling in through the crack, illuminating the head of a single red rose. Someone was holding it, she was sure. Her heart began to race, her breathing became ragged. She grabbed her daddy's hand as if he could save her. Slowly, the door opened further, the entire rose in view, held by a hand with bronze toned skin, a white lab coat covering the arm. Then dark curly hair, and a large white smile.

"May I come in, Emily?" Dr. Z eased into the room. "I was afraid you might be resting. Such a hard day, I'm sure."

"Yes." She had no strength to say more.

"I checked earlier after my rounds, but the nurse said you had left for your mother's funeral. I am so sorry, Emily, so very, very sorry." As he talked, he walked toward her, around the end of her father's bed until he was standing directly above her, looking down. Emily stood and backed away, bumping into the recliner that was her bed at night.

"I brought a little something, Emily. Something beautiful to help ease the pain." He offered the rose. She hesitated, then accepted it. She had nowhere to turn, nowhere to go, nothing else she could do. The thorns had been removed, but their very absence pained her.

"I'll ask the nurse to find a vase," he offered.

Emily nodded. He reached out to touch her shoulder and she flinched. He stopped his hand in mid-air.

"You've had a hard day. I moved my practice to Wilmington, so I'm here every day. I'll check on you tomorrow after my morning rounds."

His words registered as a threat in Emily's tortured mind.

§ § §

The hours passed slowly, Emily slept little. She turned on the television Thursday morning and half-heartedly watched it all day long. She knew that when the news came on, she would simply turn it off. She didn't want to hear the same sad stories from Vietnam— young Americans dying in a land so far away, fighting for a cause few understood. News of war protestors, news of Negroes marching for human rights they should have already had, violence breaking out in the streets, always news of somebody dying somewhere, news of a world that seemed to be coming apart at the seams. News that she, in her self-acknowledged fragile state, did not want to hear. Even through the guilt of knowing she should care more, she would turn off the news. She was tired, just plain bone tired.

Emily awoke to the sound of Walter Cronkite's voice. "Good evening. Dr. Martin Luther King, the apostle of non-violence in the Civil Rights movement, has been shot to death in Memphis, Tennessee. Police have issued an all-points bulletin for a well-dressed young white man seen running from the scene. Officers also reportedly chased and fired on a radio-equipped car containing two white men. Dr. King was standing on the balcony of a second floor hotel room tonight when, according to a companion, a shot was fired from across the street. In a friend's words, 'the bullet exploded in his face.'"

As the news anchor continued talking, Emily softly sobbed. Was everyone going crazy? She couldn't control the tears anymore, so she just let them fall at will. Her mind wandered to the day she stood in the makeshift morgue and saw half her mother's head gone. It seemed like a lifetime ago, although only a few days had passed. When President Johnson came on talking about shock and sorrow, she saw a little boy, years earlier, saluting his father's casket. She held her father's hand, laid her head on his bed, and cried.

§ § §

Whether meant as threat or as a promise, Dr. Z was true to his word. Every morning he stopped in, bearing the gift of single long-stemmed rose. The colors varied, but Emily's response did not. She accepted each one without emotion and deposited it in the trash as soon as he left the room. She convinced herself that it was just a coincidence—the roses—that Dr. Z couldn't know. It couldn't be him. Otherwise, he'd never give himself away like that. No phone calls came.

Two weeks passed and the coma lingered. Two weeks and Emily never left the hospital. Despite Dan's constant reprimands to take care of herself, Emily never even left her daddy's bedside except for a few minutes when Dan or his parents brought the boys by to see her, or occasionally to run downstairs long enough to bring a hot meal back up. Mostly, she ate whatever anyone thought to bring for her. Norma, being her usual "woe is me" self, had no one to take care of her children, she said, so she couldn't stay at night.

"You're so lucky to have a husband," she had told Emily, "and in-laws who'll just drop everything and come take care of your kids."

Emily wasn't sure why Norma couldn't stay during the day when her children were in school, even the baby was in kindergarten now. If she'd stay just long enough for Emily to go home and take a shower in her own bathroom, that would be nice—but she knew she probably wouldn't leave anyway, so it didn't make much difference. There were many things she had never understood about her sister-in-law. Norma was being Norma, regardless of the tumultuous changes in their family.

She flitted in and out at will, coddling her children, or strolling in with the latest boyfriend, or tearfully accompanying her pastor—the one she worshipped from the church that Daddy called a cult. She dressed according to who accompanied her—bell bottoms and peasant tops with the kids, short-shorts and halter tops with the boyfriend, or a modest Sunday dress with the pastor. She changed her demeanor as easily and drastically as she changed her clothes, and Emily never knew what to expect.

Norma wore her religion like a cloak, wrapping herself tightly with a self-righteous smugness when it fit her needs, slinging it off to the side when she felt invincible on her own. It was the holier-than-thou Norma who stood across the bed from Emily that day.

"I know that Daddy can hear us," Norma said, "and being the Christian man he is would want you to know he forgives you for all these horrible things caused by your selfishness. Mama is in a better place waiting for him, longing for him to be with her. And I choose to forgive you for the pain you've caused me and my children all these years."

Emily stared at Norma and whispered, "This is neither the time nor the place. Not now, Norma." She knew Norma wouldn't be saying those things if she really believed Daddy could hear. Mama maybe, but not Daddy.

"Leave," Emily whispered. "Now."

Norma smiled and left.

Emily slumped into the recliner that had been her bed for two weeks and wept softly. She and Norma had never been close, but she never hurt those children—always did what she could to stabilize their lives, protect all five of them from a chaotic family with three different daddies, Charles's death followed by three failed marriages, countless boyfriends, and only God knew what else.

§ § §

Emily remembered one of the worst days, about two years earlier, when ten-year-old Elizabeth called.

"Aunt Emily, Mommy isn't home. The boys are hungry. It's getting dark."

"Was she there when you got off the bus?" Emily asked.

"No, ma'am."

"How did you get in?"

"The door wasn't locked."

"Did she leave a note?"

"No."

Emily tried to think where her sister-in-law could be. Norma was unpredictable, but Emily had never known her to neglect her children. Despite everything else, she had always tried to be her version of a good mother.

"Okay, sweetie, I'll come over. She probably got tied up at the store and will be back before I even get there. Lock the door and Aunt Emily will be there soon, okay?"

"Okay."

Emily loaded up her boys and drove across town to Norma's rental. She found the children huddled on the couch, Elizabeth trying to calm her crying brothers—stairsteps, Isaac eight, Peter seven, James five, and John three. Four husbands, five children. Still no sign of their mother.

"Run upstairs and pack your suitcases," Emily told them. "You can spend the night with Danny and Bobby. Would you like that?"

All six boys dashed off, little John trying his best to keep up, tears suddenly forgotten in the thrill of new adventure, but Elizabeth held back.

"Where is she?" the child asked, her huge brown eyes full of fear.

Emily's heart sank and anger seethed, replaced too quickly by fear of her own.

"I don't know sweetheart, but I'm sure she's fine. Go check on the boys for Aunt Emily, okay? And pack your clothes, too. I could use some help with that bunch, you know. Everything will be fine. I'll call Granny and Poppy and see if she's there. Run on upstairs now, okay?"

Emily had second thoughts about calling her parents. Her mother, especially, saw only the good in people. Norma could do nothing wrong in her eyes. Besides, she didn't want to worry them unnecessarily. She looked around for anything that might tell her where her sister-in-law was. Norma's fourth marriage had ended six months earlier. She'd had a string of boyfriends, but no one serious. At least Emily didn't think so. And they all seemed harmless enough. Emily looked around the room at the pictures Norma had painted, the curtains she'd made, the pottery she'd thrown, afghans she'd crocheted. So much talent for one person to waste. Nothing to indicate where she'd gone.

The phone rang and Emily answered quickly before Elizabeth could.

"Hello?"

"Oh hi, Emily, I'm glad you're there. I meant to call earlier, but I couldn't get to a phone. Are the kids okay? Can you watch them for me a while?"

"Norma, where are you?"

"On a bus, Emily, a bus to California."

"What?"

"I was going to call you earlier so you'd go get the kids but we didn't get to a bus stop until now. I just knew you'd let them stay."

"Your children were home alone, scared to death. Where in the hell are you going?"

"Now Emily, do not curse in my house. You know I don't allow that. I'm on my way to California. Phillip sent me a bus ticket. He said he needed me back and everything was going to be fine. I love him, Emily. My kids need a daddy, and Phillip will be a great daddy just as soon as he comes back with me. He has a plan."

Phillip was Norma's last husband but did not father any of her children. He was a dreamer and schemer.

"How long will you be gone?"

"I don't know yet. A week, maybe two. You'll take care of the children; they'll be fine. God bless you, Emily. I've gotta run. The bus is loaded, pulling out any minute."

That trip had lasted a month. Norma called twice, maybe three times while she was gone. Emily did her best to give the kids a stable environment, making excuses for Norma to her children, never saying one thing to make them think badly of their mother. She never let Mama and Daddy know that Norma deserted her children without warning. She came back home alone.

§ § §

Emily looked at her father, attached to so many machines and tubes—he could not breathe or eat or drink on his own; his heart would not beat without the machine; he did not move—not even his fingers when Emily held his hand, or his eyelids when she kissed his scruffy cheek. Her daddy was not there— Emily knew it even before Dr. Martin entered his room that day.

"Hello, Emily," he said. "Are you alone?"

"Yes."

"We need to talk. Do you want to call your husband, your sister?"

"He's going to die, isn't he?"

"I told you I wouldn't lie to you. I've done everything I can do. Tests show no brain activity at all. The machines are the only thing keeping his organs working. We can keep them on and make his heart and lungs work indefinitely. Or we can turn them off and let him go. But you have to tell me what you want."

"I can't make that decision by myself."

"No, you don't have to decide on your own, but you do have the authority to make that decision."

"I don't understand."

"Your parents' attorney contacted me, Emily. They have wills, and they also prepared a document that made you their power of attorney, gave you the right to make decisions regarding everything, including medical care. You didn't know?"

"I had no idea. We never talked about it."

"Like I said, you don't have to make this decision on your own and you don't have to make it now. Sleep on it, talk to your sister, your husband, your pastor, the attorney, whatever you need to do to make it easier. But I can't do anything else to help him. As much as you might want to keep him here for yourself, you need to think of what he would want. Obviously, your parents trusted you to make the right decisions."

After Dr. Martin left, Emily could do nothing but stare out the window at the tiny headlights of cars six stories below, a steady stream, people with somewhere to go, someone to see, something to do. At least her parents never thought she was insane. They trusted her. The next day was Saturday. She called home and left a message for Dan, asking him to come early. She called Norma and did the same. She knew what had to be done, but would wait until they were there to tell the doctor. The rhythmic beeps, whooshes, and whirs of the machines attached to her daddy oddly calmed her.

§ § §

A loud knock on the hospital room door awakened Emily. She was surprised how soundly she had slept through the night. No nurses had come in and turned on the lights, taken vital signs, checked the machines. It's over, Emily thought, even the nurses know it's over.

Dan's head appeared around the door. "You awake? Decent?"

"Uh-huh, come on in."

He pushed the door open and Norma immediately followed him in the room. That was odd.

"Are your parents with the boys?"

"Yes, they're still here. Will be as long as we need them. They're taking the boys to the park today, then a movie. The kids will be so spoiled by the time this is over we won't be able to do a thing with them."

"They need a little spoiling right now. Nothing wrong with that." She looked at Norma, tried to make inconsequential conversation before the serious discussion began. "Who has your children today?"

"Daddies' weekend. All the boys were picked up after school yesterday, and Elizabeth went home with a friend."

Even with her request, Emily was surprised Norma woke up that early if she were home alone. Maybe she wasn't. Emily tried to push a sudden unsettling thought from her mind.

"Did you come together?"

"Of course not," Norma said, almost defiantly. "I ran into him in the parking lot."

"Yeah, okay," Emily said. She walked over to the window and looked out. "Is it hot outside?"

"You ought to leave this room for ten minutes and find out yourself," Dan said. "You're not doing anybody any good cooped up in here all the time."

"I'll probably leave today." Emily walked back to her daddy's beside.

"What do you mean?" Norma asked. "You know I can't stay with him."

"Daddy isn't here anymore." Emily's voice broke. She paced back to the window and looked out again. Traffic had picked up.

"Have you lost it again?" Norma rebuked her. "He's right there where he's been for three weeks."

"The doctor said there's no sign of brain activity at all," Emily said, still looking at the traffic far below. "Never was much. Hasn't been any for at least a week." She turned slowly back toward Norma and Dan. "He said it's time to let him go. We have to tell them to turn off the machines."

"Well, it's about time," Dan said. "They probably only put those machines on him in the first place so they could run up his hospital bill. Or harvest his organs."

Emily stared at her husband, the man she was supposed to love.

"He's too damaged for transplants. Doctor already told us that." Norma pressed the nurse call button.

"What are you doing?" Emily asked, moving close to her daddy's side and taking his hand in hers.

"No point in prolonging the inevitable," Norma said. "Let's just do it and get it over with."

"May I help you?" The voice came through the intercom.

"We need the doctor. Dr. Wilson." Norma was right, however brazen.

"Should I tell him you've made the decision?"

"Yes." Emily spoke this time, softly, reverently.

"I'll let him know when he gets here."

"Thank you."

"I haven't had breakfast," Dan said. "I'm going down to the cafeteria. You coming with me, Emily?"

"No. I can't leave. You know I can't leave."

"Fine." He started toward the door, then stopped and looked

back. "Norma?"

"Yeah, I'll go. The doctor probably isn't even out of bed yet. I'm not sure why we're up at this ungodly hour on a Saturday." She turned to Emily. "Oh yeah, it was you. Have us paged if he shows up sooner."

Norma's callousness wasn't lost on Emily. She just added it to the list of things she didn't understand about her. But soon she and her kids would be the only family Emily had left other than her own children, and Dan. She wasn't going to say or do anything to alienate Norma and chance being ostracized from the children. With their grandparents gone, they would need Aunt Emily more than ever, and she needed them.

Emily sat close to the bedside, rubbing her daddy's arm and talking to him like she had done for weeks, hoping he might feel or hear something. She didn't believe that doctors knew everything. She watched for any sign that the doctor was wrong. Some last minute ray of hope. She had lost track of time when the phone rang. It wasn't an unusual sound, hadn't made her jump in a while. Neighbors and friends called often, asking how he was, how she was holding up. Could they do anything to help. Emily appreciated the offers, but always declined. She tried to answer as pleasantly as possible.

"Paul Turner's room."

Nothing.

"Hello?"

Organ music began in the background—funeral music—soft at first, then growing louder and louder until Emily slammed the receiver down. A few seconds later, someone knocked on the door. Emily started shaking and did not answer. She watched the door open slowly, her heart pounding, waiting to see who would appear, glancing around her for anything she could use as a weapon. A perky blonde teen poked her head in. "I have a delivery," she said, backing into the room, her red and white apron identifying her as a candy-striper. She held the door with her foot and pulled her cart through. At first, Emily could not see what was on it, but then the young girl turned and flashed a big smile at her, moving to the side of the cart.

"Get them out of here," Emily screamed. "Now!"

"But they're beautiful. A whole dozen." The girl was almost in tears, but Emily couldn't care, she just wanted them gone.

"Get them out. Out. Get out!"

"Alright, already." The girl became huffy, defiant. "I never heard of anybody in their right mind turning down a dozen red roses. What do you want me to do with them?"

"I don't care, just get them out of my sight. Leave, now."

"Don't worry lady, I'm out of here." She pulled the door hard so it swung open wide and she could push the cart through in one easy motion. "Crazy woman," she breathed as she left.

"I am not crazy. I am not crazy. I am not crazy." Emily paced from her daddy's bedside to the window, repeating the words over and over again. Out loud.

"That might be up for interpretation."

At the sound of Norma's voice, Emily spun from the window to see her holding the door open with Dan standing behind her.

"Doc back yet?"

"No, not yet."

"Told you we had plenty of time." Norma's words were directed at Dan and delivered with a smile. She walked to the bedside and pressed the nurse call button again.

"What are you doing?" Emily asked.

"What you should have already done."

"May I help you?"

"We've been waiting for Dr. Wilson for almost two hours."

"He's making his rounds now. He should be there any minute."

The doctor was not wrong. When he turned off the machines, silence filled the room. Paul Turner did not gasp for breath, did not move, did not make a sound. His heart did not beat, not once. Dan and Norma left immediately, but Emily lingered, sitting by his bedside listening to the silence, watching the color drain from her father's face, feeling the warmth leave his body. Then she gathered up her strength and his belongings, told the nurses she was ready, and left him to be picked up by the funeral home.

Emily sent Dan to the farm to get her daddy's clothes. The choice was easy—blue chambray shirt and denim jeans, white socks, no shoes. The funeral was the same as her mother's—same chapel, same songs, same preacher, same words, same cemetery, same scene—or so it seemed to Emily. Three weeks had extinguished the yellowbell blossoms and nothing but green leaves lay on the vines when Emily looked up and saw the same tall man standing by the fence—same spot, same acknowledging nod, same disappearing act. Same shivering response from Emily.

Chapter 10

"Your parents named you as executrix of both their wills," Ryan Simone said, looking straight at Emily, "and trustee."

"What exactly does that mean?" Emily asked.

"I'll tell you what it means," Norma said, almost under her breath. "They screwed me."

They had arrived at the attorney's office early that Monday morning, just a few days after Daddy's funeral. Sitting behind an oversized mahogany desk, Ryan appeared anxious. He held a pen loosely between his thumb and first finger, rocking it back and forth like a seesaw, tapping first one end then the other on the documents spread out before him.

"It means, Emily," Ryan continued, "that you are responsible for taking care of all the legal matters with their estate. You'll pay off any outstanding debts, collect money from the insurance policies, and disperse assets according to the directions they specified."

"But I don't even know what they had." Emily felt uncomfortable in Ryan's office. He had been their parents' attorney for a long time, but Norma had dated him recently, broke up his marriage.

"Everything's here in the file except their bank statements, savings bonds, and CDs. Those are in their safe."

"They had a safe?" Norma asked, flashing a questioning look at the attorney. "Do you know where it is Emily?"

"No, I have no idea."

"Don't worry," Ryan said. "I have instructions for finding it, and I have the combination, but I can only give it to Emily."

"That's bullshit," Norma said.

"Those are Mr. Turner's explicit instructions."

"Daddy's rules. I should have known."

"While you're both here, I'll read the wills. Then I'll have to ask you to leave, Norma, while I talk to Emily." Ryan looked directly at Norma as he spoke. Emily sensed an uneasiness that intensified the longer Norma stared back at him. An agitation fueled by familiarity. Emily had never met Ryan Simone before she walked into his office that day. She had talked to him on the phone after her mother died while her father lay dying. He explained the rights granted her by the power of attorney, told her waiting a few weeks on her mother's estate wouldn't hurt anything since her will directed that everything go to her husband if she died first.

But the unspoken exchange between the attorney and Norma was palpable. He rested his elbow on his desk, ran his hand front to back through his thick black hair, strain showing on his face, fear faintly reflected in his ice blue eyes. Norma was seething. Emily knew the look well. Seconds passed like hours.

"Their wills were identical in some respects. Everything to the other, depending on who died first. But your father's will places all money into trusts for the grandchildren with Emily as the sole trustee."

"Mama's will did not say that. I know it and you know it, too. I sat right here and heard her tell you what to do."

"But she died first, Norma. Everything went to Mr. Turner, and his will takes precedence now. You were secondary beneficiary. If he had died first, the estate would have been in your hands when your mother died. But she died first." His voice was softer, almost apologetic.

Emily felt like an eavesdropper on a private conversation, as though she were invisible, forgotten. She didn't know why her Mama would have chosen Norma over her. She wanted to slip out the door and forget it all, did not want to be privy to anything being said. She certainly did not want to be in charge. If not for the pills the doctor had prescribed, she would barely be functioning. How could she be responsible?

"What about the insurance policies?" Norma asked.

"Mr. Turner had one insurance policy, a half million face value, but double indemnity in case of an accident. So there's a million to go in the trust from that policy."

Emily could not believe what she was hearing.

"Mrs. Turner had two policies—the one she'd had for years to cover funeral expenses. Face value five thousand. Then the new one, also a half million face value, also double indemnity, which means another million."

"And I share that with Emily. We're the only ones left to inherit it."

"I'm sorry Norma, that's not exactly how it works. Since Mrs. Turner died first, the money went to Mr. Turner. They both came to see me a couple of months ago. They wanted to set up a trust fund for the grandchildren, opened it with fifteen thousand from their savings."

"They had fifteen thousand in savings?" Emily's surprise broke her silence.

"Much more, I think," Ryan said. "You'll find those documents in the safe. But according to your father's will, the two of you each receive ten thousand cash to spend as you like. Whatever money is left after all the estate debts are paid will go into the trust fund for all seven present grandchildren and any future children you have, Emily. That includes your mother's insurance money. The grandchildren can each withdraw their percentage of the money at age twenty-one. In the meantime, Emily as trustee is the only one who can access the money for the benefit of the children if a legitimate need arises, including paying for college."

"What the hell good is ten thousand dollars going to do?" Norma's voice bordered on screaming.

"If you really think about it Norma, they were very generous," Ryan said. "They made sure I knew they meant all five of your children, even though Elizabeth is the only blood kin. They thought of you as their daughter, and your boys as their grandchildren."

Ryan looked at Emily, apologies appearing in his eyes again.

"They left the farm to Norma—all of it. Your mother said you had a home, Emily, but Norma didn't."

"Well, sell the damn thing," Norma said. "I sure as hell won't live in the sticks with the rattlers and the bears. And a measly ten thousand dollars wouldn't take care of the place if I did want to live there."

"You have that option, but I would advise you to wait a while until emotions have settled. You can't do anything for about six months anyway, until the wills are probated and the estate is settled."

"I won't change my mind."

§ § §

Two months had passed since that day in the attorney's office, and Emily had not seen nor talked to Norma. She just didn't feel like dealing with her, but she missed the children. School was out and summer activities kept her busy with her boys. She hadn't received any more phone calls since the one in her daddy's hospital room, so Emily was beginning to relax. Keeping the tears at bay was easier most days. She'd even started listening to the news again—not because it had become any less depressing, but because she felt stronger. She was also watching the stock reports trying to learn more since she was in charge of the children's monetary future. She began paying attention to the political reporting and was glad to see another Kennedy doing so well in the presidential primaries—a man who spoke of love and compassion and wisdom toward one another, a man who wanted to end the war in Vietnam.

But then he was murdered, too.

One day in late August, Emily called Norma and asked to take Elizabeth and the boys to the Fort Fisher Aquarium and the beach before the children had to go back to school.

"Do what you want," Norma said. "You always get your way."

Emily was surprised when Dan declined to go with them. He usually loved going to Fort Fisher, driving on the beach. The boys begged, but he said no. "Just take them out at the walk-over," he told Emily. "Seven screaming kids is not my idea of fun. Besides, I've got something else to do."

113

Their summer had been odd that way, Dan choosing to stay home, sending Emily and the boys to the beach without him. They went to Topsail Beach a few times a week, Emily sitting in the sun watching the boys build sand forts and play in the waves. It wasn't the same as taking the boat and going to Hutaff Island, but any day at the beach was a good day. And she didn't have to worry about making Dan mad. They had wonderful peaceful days, and late in the afternoons on their way home, they'd stop in Rocky Point at the Trading Post, which everybody just called Freddie's, for ice cream cones. The boys almost always got chocolate, but Emily's favorite flavor was pistachio.

Dan and Emily had grown distant in other ways as well. She refused a few times to watch the movies, trying to arouse her husband with her own sexual prowess. She had kept her body in shape, had a golden tan and bathing suit lines that Dan had always thought were sexy. She even tried a striptease one night. But when he wanted to take out the camera and film her, she refused.

She had to adjust what she wore to hide the bruises, but since it was summer, he was more careful with his aim.

Eventually, without the movies and the toys, he seemed to lose interest in her altogether. So she quit trying. She started going to bed before he did, leaving him watching television or in his office working. Sometimes he came to bed in the wee hours of the morning and took her with no passion, no foreplay, just urgent need. She'd awake from a sound sleep with him on top of her pumping furiously, grunting, often hurting her. Then he would roll over and go to sleep, snoring within seconds.

Emily tried to concentrate on other things. The boys would soon be going back to school. The phone calls had nearly stopped. Just one every now and then, almost like a reminder that he was out there, but that she wasn't really all that important to him right now. She had a small vegetable garden, a few flower beds, did some sewing, some reading. Summer had been spent with her boys—at the beach, the park, the library, an occasional movie. She did enjoy that newfound freedom Dan's lack of interest had given her. But she knew her limits of freedom and never, ever crossed them.

When school started, Emily was lost. She had to find something to fill her time. Dr. Z had continued to call at least once a month asking her to come to work for him. Over and over again, she had tried in her nicest voice to say no. It had been out of the question when his office was in Burgaw. She didn't understand why he would even think she'd want to work in Wilmington.

"I need you," he said more than once.

"I don't need you," Emily finally said in September, although that was the time when she was most vulnerable—the boys in school, Dan totally disinterested in her. She was lonely. With Dan's disinterest, she started volunteering again at the hospital, working with the PTA, doing fund-raisers for Pop Warner. Danny was going to play football, even though she said yes with much trepidation.

Dan left on a Sunday morning in mid-September for another business trip—a week long this time. He had been to regular weekend conferences since late spring and this was a culmination of those meetings, he said. Emily didn't know why the job had recently become so meeting intensive, but she really didn't care. The tension in the house when he was home was palpable. She preferred being alone, even lonely, to trying to keep peace, an even keel, no arguing in front of the boys. Dan seemed to want to pick fights whenever possible over the least little thing, but Emily refused to cooperate most of the time. She just agreed with him. She didn't even ask him where the meeting was.

Monday morning, Emily took the boys to school, then stopped by the post office on her way home. The lack of phone calls allowed her sense of security to return. She had reinstated her old routine and it felt good. She would make a grocery run next, go home and pay bills, clean house, wash clothes, then make brownies for the boys before she drove back to school to pick them up. Danny had football practice every afternoon at four, so they went home for a quick snack and homework before practice.

Emily had finished lunch and just slid a pan of brownies in the oven when she heard a knock at the front door. That was unusual.

She rarely had visitors, but when she did, they always came to the back door. She walked into the living room and peeked out the window before she even considered opening the door. A police car sat in the drive.

She pulled the curtains back further and looked toward the porch. Frank was standing there, hat in hand, his head down.

"Hello, Emily," he said, looking up at her when she opened the door. "May I come in?"

"Are my boys okay? What's wrong?"

"The boys are fine as far as I know. May I come in, Emily? I need to talk to you."

She stepped back and motioned him to come in. "Have a seat," she said.

"Like I said the boys are fine. Nothing's going on at the school. But I do have some bad news for you, Emily, and you've just had too much of that lately. Too much."

"What is it, Frank?"

"It's Dan. The Columbus County Sheriff's Department just called. They found his car in the swamp way off the side of Hwy. 211. Took out a few trees in the Green Swamp. He didn't make it, Emily. I'm so sorry."

"What happened?" Emily surprised herself by her lack of emotion. The pills were doing a very good job.

"Couldn't really tell for sure. He ran off the road for some reason. No brake marks. Could have been a deer. He might have fallen asleep. What time did he leave home?"

"Yesterday morning."

"Was he going anywhere else first?"

"Not that I know of."

"That's odd. He was only an hour or two from home and they think the wreck probably happened sometime late last night, maybe even after midnight. Been partially submerged in water for hours. Bled out pretty fast from the femoral artery. Don't think he suffered long. That's some consolation, I reckon. Ain't it?"

"Yes, it is, I guess."

"You alright, Emily? You're not in shock or anything, are you? Women usually cry."

"I'm fine, Frank, thank you. I'll be fine. I just need to go pick my boys up from school now before they hear it from someone else. You'll excuse me, won't you?"

"Where do you want the body?"

"Quinn-McGowen, please."

§ § §

Telling the boys their father died was one of the most difficult things Emily had ever done. Despite the last few months, he had been a good daddy over the years, spent time with his boys, took them fishing, played ball with them. They would miss him. Emily, on the other hand, was conflicted by her own feelings. Beneath the surface, sorrow came with losing someone who had stolen her heart when she was a teenager, gave her two beautiful boys, and made a good life for their family. But strangely, she felt an underlying relief— relief that she didn't have to pretend to be happy, relief that she wouldn't be asked to watch the movies, relief that she could sleep without being manhandled awake. Relief.

Telling Dan's parents was a different matter altogether. He was their only son, their only child, and his mother was inconsolable. Emily had to wait several days to make funeral arrangements—Dan's mother was too distraught to participate any sooner. But they weren't too overcome to let Emily know at once that they would handle matters. They had Dan's body moved from Quinn-McGowen to a funeral home in Raleigh. When the funeral took place, it would be in their church, and he would be buried in the Gillespie family cemetery. Emily didn't mind. Dan had never liked the country anyway.

In the meantime, she held a visitation in the chapel of Quinn-McGowen so local family and friends would not feel obligated to travel—the boys' classmates and parents, teachers, PTA, coaches. Norma came and brought her children. Emily had not seen her in weeks, and she looked withdrawn, pale, skittish. But she said something to Emily that seemed out of place even for Norma. "You always were the lucky one."

§ § §

The funeral was held a week later in Raleigh on a drizzly fall day. The leaves in the cemetery wore their best fall foliage and the service was fit for an heir of Raleigh royalty—old money families. Emily didn't want to feel the way she did, but from the visitation to the church service to the cemetery display, it seemed to her more like a production of putting on airs. But the Gillespies' grief was far too real, and Emily ached for them. She could not imagine burying one of her boys. She would rather die.

She stood under a black umbrella by the graveside with the boys flanking her. They clung tightly to the skirt of her black dress. Mrs. Gillespie had insisted Emily and the boys go shopping for the "proper" attire—she a new black dress and pumps, they black suits, neckties, and wingtips. Their navy blazers and khaki pants weren't good enough. Emily wanted to argue that they were just small boys who had lost their daddy and making them physically uncomfortable would only make it harder on them, but she knew better. So, she kept her silence and just obeyed.

When the crowd began to disperse, Emily saw the same tall slender man who had been at the other funerals standing off to the side. When she made eye contact, he nodded just like he had at her mother's funeral and her father's. She shivered involuntarily and led her boys in the opposite direction. He looked so familiar.

Chapter 11

Two weeks had passed since Dan's funeral and the phone calls escalated rapidly. They came at all times day or night; no hour was sacred, no minute serene. Emily feared for her boys, for herself. She trusted no one, confided in no one. She needed to get the boys away from it all, get herself away somewhere safe, try to get one good night's sleep so she could figure out what to do next.

"Mother Gillespie?" Emily said softly into the receiver as she stood in the hallway peering into the moonlit room where her boys slept.

"Are you alright, Emily? The boys—please tell me nothing's wrong with the boys."

"No, they're fine, we're fine."

"But it's almost midnight. You scared me to death."

"I'm sorry. I didn't realize. Truly, I never meant to scare you."

"It's okay. What do you want, dear?"

"There's something I need to do. I'll be gone for a few days, and I was wondering if I could drop the boys off at your house."

"What about school?"

"They can miss a few days. Their daddy just died for god's sake."

"Emily!"

"I'm sorry, I'm sorry. I didn't mean to raise my voice. I didn't mean to swear."

"Well, it's been hard on us all. Of course the boys can stay as long as you need them to. But I have to ask, Emily. Where are you going?"

"I can't answer that. I just need you to take care of my boys. Promise me you'll take care of my boys. No matter what happens, take care of my boys." Emily was near tears and her voice cracked.

"Of course, dear, of course we will."

"We'll be there tomorrow."

"Get some sleep, Emily. Get a good night's sleep before you drive. Promise me."

"Okay, I will."

"And Emily?"

"Yes, ma'am?"

"I have to ask. Have you been taking your medications? What you've been through this year…"

"Yes, I'm taking the pills." Emily's voice was edgy, raw.

"Get some sleep, we'll be watching for you tomorrow. After noon?"

"Probably earlier. Goodnight."

"Drive safely. You have precious cargo. Goodnight, dear."

Emily walked back into her bedroom, trailing the stretched phone cord behind her, laid the receiver gently in the cradle, then changed her mind. She lifted it again and tucked it under her pillow so she couldn't hear the dial tone wailing. No phone calls tonight, she had work to do.

She tiptoed back into her boys' room and began scooping up the piles of dirty clothes strewn across the floor. She hadn't the heart to ask anything of them since their daddy died, and their room was a mess. So was everything else—dirty dishes in the sink, garbage stacked in the garage, dust on the furniture, empty snack bags in front of the television, leaves and tree limbs in the yard—that yard Dan used to groom so carefully it made "Yard of the Year" two times running. She pitched the boys' dirty clothes into the hallway, then followed them out, easing the door closed behind her.

Returning to her room, she sighed at the sight—her piles were as bad as the boys' had been. She caught a glimpse of herself in the dresser mirror—disheveled hair, baggy t-shirt, faded holey sweatpants. When had she become such a slob?

Emily began grabbing up her own clothes and tossing them into the laundry basket sitting empty in the bottom of her closet. She made three trips back and forth to the laundry room before all the dirty clothes were transferred. Sorting them into piles of whites and darks and bright colors, she lulled herself into a rhythm that carried her through into the wee hours of dawn. As the washer hummed and the dryer whirled, she washed the dishes, straightened up the living room, dusted the furniture, vacuumed the carpet, and carried more trash to the garage. But she couldn't bring herself to carry the can to the road, even though the sign over it proclaimed the impending arrival of the garbage truck. She'd remind Danny to do it before they left. Bobby could put the extra bags in his wagon and help, too. He'd like that.

By the time the sun sent slivers of light slanting through the backyard pines, Emily's house was clean and the laundry complete, folded neatly on her bed. She packed a bag for herself, then one for each of her boys. Then she stripped off her tattered clothing, tossed it in the trash, and climbed in the shower. As the almost scalding water washed over her body, she scrubbed her skin until it stung, scratched shampoo into her scalp, and sang.

"Purple haze all around; don't know if I'm comin' up or down; am I happy or in misery? Help me, help me..."

No, she wasn't asking for anyone's help. She was ready to take matters into her own hands. Take care of her boys and move forward. She had no choice.

Emily turned off the water, toweled dry and dressed—freshly ironed flowered bell-bottoms and a silky sky-blue sweater. She blew her hair dry and tied it back with a scarf, brushed on a little blush, eye shadow and mascara, then rummaged in the vanity drawer for the lipstick she used to love to wear. When she was satisfied with the reflection staring back at her in the mirror, she started out her bedroom door, then stopped in midstep. Returning to her nightstand, she took the .38 revolver from the drawer, unzipped her suitcase and tucked the gun under her clothes.

"Up and at 'em, boys," Emily said, bursting through the boys' bedroom door. "I have a surprise for you!"

"Aw, Mom," Danny said. "It's still dark."

"Not anymore," Emily said cheerfully, pulling up the shades and switching on the overhead light.

Bobby sat up rubbing his eyes, while Danny pulled the cover over his head.

"No school today, or tomorrow, or maybe even the next day."

"I got school," Bobby said, "and a spelling test."

"No matter, I'll call your teacher."

"But Mom…" Danny whined. "If I don't go to practice, I can't play on Saturday."

"No buts, no school, no practice. Now get dressed and let's go."

"Where?" Danny asked, his fearful response to his mother's stern tone so obvious it broke her heart.

"I'm sorry, guys. Mommy just needs to do something really important and it may take me a few days. You're going to Grandma and Grandpa Gillespie's. I promise I'll talk to your teachers and your coach. Everything will be alright. You know I never break a promise, right?"

"But I don't want you to leave me," Bobby cried softly.

"You'll be fine," Emily said, ruffling his hair. "I'll be back fast. And you'll take care of your little brother, right Danny? When we get back home, everything will be better. I promise."

"I'm hungry," Bobby whined.

"I made sausage biscuits for the road," Emily said. "And chocolate milk in your thermos."

The boys drifted off to sleep in the car as soon as they finished their breakfast, and Emily struggled to stay awake, the road stretching monotonously before her. Two hours to Raleigh. Four more to the mountains. That's where she thought she might go. Other than the beach—which was not far enough away—the mountains were the next best balm for her soul. In some strange way, they were calling her. She decided to listen.

The adrenaline that had fueled her all-night cleaning spree abandoned her body. She rolled down her window and turned up the radio. The cool October morning air whipped her hair out of the scarf and into her face. She brushed it away over and over until she became so frustrated, she rolled the window back up. She tried singing along with the radio, but couldn't remember the words. She turned the car fan on high, all vents aimed toward her face. That worked for a while.

"I'm cold," Danny said from the back seat.

"I gotta pee," Bobby piped up.

"Okay," Emily said, turning off the fan. "I'll stop at the next station. Can you hold it just a little while?"

"I gotta go bad."

"Well, help me look for a store, okay?"

"Okay."

"Grandma and Grandpa G have some fun things planned," Emily said, glad to have the boys awake so she could talk to them, making things up as she went. "They're going to take you to the museum, and to the Capitol, and to the park and the library."

"But where you gonna be?" Bobby asked.

"Mommy has to go somewhere to take care of some business. Oh, there's a store." Emily was relieved to be rescued by a bathroom. How could she ever explain where she was going when she didn't know herself?

§ § §

The Gillespies lived in an older residential section of Raleigh, stately brick homes with sloping manicured lawns stretching toward tree-lined streets, large landscape greenery grown full and thick with age. Dan's grandparents had lived in the house for years, and after a short stint in Pender County when Dan and Emily met and married, his parents moved back to the capital city to take care of aging parents. Emily had never felt comfortable there; she was simply small town and country, not big city and country club. Despite Dan's father's attempts to make her feel at home, she harbored a nagging feeling that she never quite lived up to her mother-in-law's expectations. She wasn't a debutante, after all, and she never even went to college.

But no one could question their love and devotion for Danny and Bobby, and Emily had no one else to trust, so she turned into the cement drive with little trepidation about the safety of her boys once she dropped them off there.

"Why Emily, it's barely nine a.m.," Mother Gillespie said, hurrying out onto the front stoop. "You couldn't have possibly gotten enough sleep, and the traffic this time of morning. You really should be more careful."

"We're here safe and sound," Emily said, pretending not to sting from the reprimand, remembering how dangerously sleepy she had become.

"Grandpa's having some breakfast. Why don't you boys run on in and grab a blueberry muffin. Mildred baked them fresh this morning."

"I'll get their bags," Emily said. "Thank you so much for watching them."

Grandma G followed her to the car.

"I must ask you again, Emily. Where are you going? You owe me that much."

"It's no big deal, really," Emily said, sure she wasn't convincing her mother-in-law. Neither was she convincing herself. "I just have some things to take care of, and I needed some time to myself. I just need some time to think. Really, it's no big deal."

"Well, where will you be? How will I reach you?"

"I don't know the number yet. I'll check in twice a day. I promise. You know I wouldn't ask if it wasn't important. You know my boys are my life. You know that, right? I can't leave them here if you don't know that. We'll just go."

She started to put the boys' bags back in the car.

"Nonsense, Emily. I may not have approved of a lot of things, but I have never questioned your devotion to your children. Just bring their things on in and rest a while before you head out to, to where ever."

Emily walked up the winding brick sidewalk lined with variegated monkey grass, still vibrant before the first hard freeze. Large potted mums bordered the steps leading up to the front door, creating a cascade of orange at the entrance. The slate floor in the foyer echoed under her mother-in-law's high heels. She was dressed and coiffed to perfection as usual, no hair out of place, no wrinkle nor speck of lint on her burnt orange dress.

"Hi Grandpa G," Emily said when she reached the kitchen. The boys sat on stools at the bar scoffing down muffins while their grandpa poured glasses of milk. "Looks like they have you busy already."

"My pleasure, child. I can't get enough of them, especially now with…you know." He turned his head, then walked toward the refrigerator. Emily saw him wipe his eyes on the sleeve of his madras plaid shirt before turning back around. She gave him a hug and a peck on the cheek.

"I know," she whispered. "I know." Then to her boys, "Come give mommy a hug. I really need to hit the road."

"I don't want you to go," Bobby whimpered.

"Nonsense," Grandpa G said. "We'll have us a guys' good time while she's gone. How'd you like to go to the country club and drive a few balls at the range?"

"We don't have any clubs," Danny said.

"Well, I can remedy that," Grandpa G replied. "It's time you boys picked up the sport."

Emily felt relief as Bobby and Danny excitedly quizzed their grandpa about shopping for clubs. "Hey guys, did you forget about me? I need big bear hugs."

Thoroughly hugged, Emily walked briskly through the den, casually tossing another 'thank you' at the boys' grandmother, who had already settled into her armchair and picked up her needlepoint.

Triangle traffic had begun to disperse into a steady stream by the time Emily merged back onto the highway, heading west toward Chapel Hill and Durham. She wondered what her life would have been like, how things would have been different if she had gone to college, spent four years, or maybe more, on the campus of Duke or UNC Chapel Hill. She had been smart in school, scored high on her SATs, had been accepted to Chapel Hill.

When she reached Hwy. 54, she almost unconsciously turned,

choosing the route toward downtown Chapel Hill. She drove slowly by the campus, tall oaks shading the lawn where students lay sprawled on their stomachs with books open before them. Others leaned against the trees, sat on benches, walked the sidewalks or rode bikes. She pictured herself there—years younger with no responsibilities but learning who she was and what she wanted to be, discovering different ideas and meeting new people, maybe even partying. Now, that would have been a switch—straight-laced Emily. She smiled.

She drove down the famous, sometimes infamous, Franklin Street where college kids and alumni hung out, shopped, ate, drank. The place where they all congregated in droves after the Tarheels beat Kansas for the 1957 National Championship in basketball. Emily had never been a fan, but she remembered searching the celebratory crowds on television wondering if she'd get a glimpse of Rob somewhere in the masses, knowing how ridiculously childish it was, but doing it nonetheless.

Rob. Thoughts of him sneaked in her mind. She wondered what he looked like now—more than eleven years since she had seen him. She thought back to that elusive phone call, how comforted she felt just to hear his voice. So much had happened since that day.

She found her way back to the highway, headed west. The minutes merged into miles; the tenseness in her muscles began to relax. Emily had never really been anywhere by herself and, despite the circumstances, felt a sense of freedom she began to enjoy. When she needed to go to the bathroom, she simply stopped at a station, didn't worry about having to ask and hearing that disgusted phrase, "You gotta go again?"

She turned in Winston-Salem to follow Hwy. 421 north and west. In the distance, she saw Pilot Mountain, stark, standing by itself in an otherwise rolling landscape. But that soon changed.

At the site of the Blue Ridge Mountain ranges in the distance and the increased hilliness of the highway, she could almost feel the lingering heaviness start to lift. Emily began to focus on finding a place to stop. Between Wilkesboro and Boone, she saw a sign for the

Blue Ridge Parkway and turned, knowing that couldn't be the most direct route to anywhere. But she didn't have a destination in mind anyway, so what did it matter? The few times they had vacationed in the mountains, Emily always asked to ride the Parkway, but Dan thought it was a waste of time—nothing to do but look or walk, he said. *Wasn't that the point*, Emily always thought.

She cruised for nearly two hours, pulling off on every overlook, sometimes getting out of her car to take in the view, other times just riding slowly along the edge. The autumn leaves that annually brought droves of people to the mountains were gone now, fall had come early and the trees were nearly bare. But Emily didn't care; it was beautiful anyway.

By mid-afternoon, she realized she was hungry. She needed to pee and the car was almost empty again, so she followed the arrows on a battered wooden sign that promised food and gas. Several miles down a winding back road, she spied a little store that looked like it had been there for a hundred years—white clapboard siding with peeling paint and a rusty tin roof that jutted out over a single round red gas pump. While the attendant filled the car, Emily went up the wooden steps, creaked open the screen door and peered into the dark interior. A drink box sat to the left with a Tru-Aide bottle painted on the front. Rows of rickety shelves held bags of chips and chocolate bars, pork rinds and potted meat. Wooden barrels filled with penny candy crowded the center.

"May I help you?"

Emily followed the sound of the woman's voice to the back of the store, a counter with stools, and a sign boasting burgers, hot dogs, and liver mush sandwiches.

Emily ordered the liver mush on white bread with a little mustard. "And a coke, please," she added. After finding the bathroom, she took a seat in one of two red vinyl booths, pulled out a map, and laid it on the white and grey speckled table. The lady from behind the counter brought the food, wiping her hands on a greasy white apron after placing the plate on the table.

"You lost?" she asked. "Not many strangers through here this time of year."

"I don't think so," Emily said. "Maybe. I'm not sure where I'm going."

"That sounds lost to me."

"I mean I don't know where I want to go. I know where I am now, I think."

The lady pointed at the map and said, "Well, this here's where you are. Raccoon Holler's that way," she said pointing out the front window, "and Jefferson's up the road a ways yonder. But if you go that way, you'll be in Tennessee. If you get back on the Parkway and go that way, you'll be in Virginia before long. Where you wanting to be, child?"

"I'm not sure. Just some place safe where I can rest."

The lady shook her head and smiled, her blue-grey curls jiggling around her face. "You young'uns these days," she said. "Looks like Sam's got your car filled up."

The screen door squeaked open and slammed shut.

"You were pert near empty. Put ten dollars' worth of gas in that car out there, washed the windshield, checked the air. She's good to go."

"You eat your food, missy, and then we'll talk about a safe place to stay. We might can help out with that. You look pretty worn out. Don't think you ought to be driving the mountain roads at night. It gets dark before you know it these days."

Emily was famished and the food disappeared quickly.

"I got some homemade grape hull pie, chocolate cake, or coconut macaroons. And I got an idea. Which you want?"

"Chocolate cake sounds nice," Emily responded, smiling at the delighted soul who obviously had something else she wanted to say. "And I'm open to ideas."

Placing the cake on the table, the waitress said, "My name's Faye. What would yours be?"

"Emily."

"Well, Emily, here's the thing. We got a room out back you're welcome to stay in 'til morning. Then I'll cook you up a good hot breakfast and you can be on your way. We don't rent it out regular or anything like that, but it's safe and it's comfy."

Emily had not planned ahead, didn't know where she wanted to go or how long it would take her to get there, hadn't thought about having to sleep along the way. Had not thought about where she'd sleep when she reached her ultimate destination, wherever that was. Now it all seemed suddenly immature and naïve to her—leaving home and her boys to traipse off to who knows where to do who knows what. A knot formed in her chest and tears welled up in her eyes. She looked up at Faye.

"Lordy be, child, what'd I say wrong?" Something in Faye's face reminded Emily of her mother, maybe the eyes—molasses dark with slight wrinkles at the edges. She appeared much younger than first impressions created by the white hair, but time and hard work were apparent. It was a kind face, though, trustworthy, real.

"No, it's not you," Emily sniffled. "The room would be nice. Thank you."

"Come on. You're too young and pretty to look so distraught. A good night's sleep will do you good and that bed back yonder—it was my grandpa's—nothing sleeps better than a mattress stuffed with goose down. Not no store bought mattress. He plucked every feather and stuffed every corner."

"I need to use a phone," Emily said. "Do you have one?"

"Use this one right behind the counter. There ain't another one around."

After Emily checked in with the Gillespies and knew her boys were fine, she followed Faye out the front door. Dusk was settling in and the mountains loomed dark all around.

"Where's my car?" Emily asked, seeing none.

"Oh, Sam's probably already moved it around back," Faye said as though that possibility made perfect sense to her. "This way."

Emily followed Faye around the corner of the store onto a narrow stone path barely splitting thick foliage. "Watch your step." The path became steep, the stones creating small jagged steps protruding from the side of the hill. "Here you are."

The room was actually in the basement under the store, its door and single window facing a small flat expanse of grass that rolled down to a rocky stream, the water cascading noisily downhill. Two wooden steps led up to a rickety porch just large enough to accommodate the rocker sitting there, formed by vines intertwined and looped and tucked. "How lovely," Emily whispered.

"Grandpa built the chair, too. Heck, Grandpa built it all—the store, the furniture, everything. Lived right here in this room 'til he died right there in that bed." Faye opened the door and motioned Emily inside, pointing toward the far right corner to a full size bed, the four posts made of tree trunks, bark scraped clean. "Right there, five years it's been now. He was a hundred and six. Outlived all his young'ns and some of his grandkids. I'm sure missing him still."

"I don't want to intrude." Emily hesitated.

"Nonsense. Go on in."

The room was not as small as Emily expected. Opposite the bed sat a small wooden table with two chairs similar to the porch rocker. A counter held a small sink and a hotplate. An old ice chest stood in the corner and a black potbelly stove stuck out in the center of the room, its flue directed out the wall between the window and the door. A round rag rug covered the center of the wooden floor and a patchwork quilt spread across the bed. The pillowcases were bright white, and the room was amazingly clean. Emily felt at ease.

"There's a toilet in that wash closet right through there," Faye said, pointing to a quilt hanging on the wall beside the bed. "It's a little cramped, but you can roll right out of bed into the bathroom. Beats the outhouse any day," she added, chuckling. "You need anything else?"

"My car, I need to get my bag out of my car."

"It's right there. At the foot of the bed. Sam brought it in for you."

Emily had not noticed her suitcase sitting there, but was not pleased by the gesture.

"My keys?"

"On the table, there, right by the lamp."

"Where is my car?" Emily's voice was tense, shrill.

"Oh, don't get your dander up, child, it's right out here. Come on, I'll show you."

Between the room and the rise of the hill opposite where the path led down, a cave-like opening jutted under the store, a shed of sorts with a tractor, lawnmower, hand tools. Emily saw her car tucked safely inside between the old green John Deere and a battered barely black Model-T Ford pick-up truck. Emily safely assumed it was Grandpa's.

"I'm sorry I was a bit snappy," Emily said. "You've been nothing but kind to me. It's just that I... I ..." Emily began to cry. She felt soft arms pull her in close. Faye even smelled like Mama. Guided along, Emily walked back toward her room, heard the screen door squeak as Faye pulled it open, then heard it slam behind them. She sat on the edge of the bed and sobbed into Faye's soft chest.

"Now, now, child, whatever it is, this too shall pass. God doesn't give us more than we can handle, even if we think he does. You wanna talk about it?"

Emily told Faye everything—about her parents' deaths, the phone calls, the roses, her boys, Dan. More about Dan that she had ever told anyone else. Totally spent, she crawled under the quilt and barely heard the door close when Faye left the room.

Chapter 12

A solid repetitive knock on the door woke her. Sun streamed through the sheer curtains on the small window. "Emily, are you awake?" She heard a man's voice at the door. "Faye sent me to get you. Lunch is ready."

"Sam, is that you?"

"Yes'm it's me, Sam. You done slept half the day away and Faye's got worried about you. I'll tell her you're alive. There's chicken and dumplins done when you want 'em."

Emily splashed water on her face, took off the clothes she'd slept in and pulled on jeans, a sweatshirt and sneakers. Lunch? She rifled through her suitcase to find her pills. Now was not the time to forget to take them. She straightened the quilt on the bed, picked up her keys and suitcase and walked out of the little room, letting the screen door slam just because she liked the way it sounded. She left her suitcase and keys on the porch, then walked down to the creek before starting up the stone path. Water rushing across rocks was a novel sound for a flatlander, but she loved it—soothing, cleansing. She sat down cross-legged on the grassy bank and just listened.

"I can't never get enough of that sound either." Emily looked back at Faye walking across the grass. "It'll soothe the soul for sure. I told you that mattress would give you some good sleeping, but I shore didn't expect you to sleep 'til noon!" Faye smiled broadly. "Come on up and get some lunch. You're welcome to stay here as long as you want, but you gotta eat."

Emily scrambled up and gave Faye a hug. "You remind me of my Mama. I am hungry, but then I've got to be going."

"Well, thank you. That's quite a compliment. I figure your Mama was a mighty special lady. You didn't say where you're headed or what you're looking for," Faye fished as they walked. "You need Sam or me to go with you?"

"No, you've done more than enough already. Thank you so much. For everything. I do need to use your phone again, though. To call my boys."

After talking to Grandma Gillespie and both the boys, Emily felt so alone. The restaurant was filled with a noisy lunch crowd. Everyone seemed to know each other, talking from table to table, booth to booth, stool to stool. She walked through the seating area where she had eaten the day before and into a back room Faye said they used for overflow and parties. The walls were covered with large black and white photographs of local historic sites and a few paintings of mountains and streams and gristmills.

As Emily ate her chicken and dumplins, turnip greens and hot cornbread, she kept glancing around the room at the paintings. One on the far wall seemed out of place, yet familiar. It was the ocean at daybreak, the pinks and oranges, blues and yellows blending in dramatic detail. A single seagull flew high in the top right corner.

Faye brought her fresh apple pie and ice cream for dessert. "Made the pie myself," she said. "With our own apples."

"I'd outgrow my clothes in no time if I stayed here long," Emily laughed. When she tried to pay for the food and the room, Faye refused.

"You just take care of yourself, and those boys. Bring 'em here to visit me. That'll be pay enough," she said.

"Can I ask you something?" Emily said. "Those paintings in the back room. Did the same person paint them all? The one from the beach reminds me of home."

"No. They were painted by several local artists. Mostly gifts 'cause they like our food. That beach one is from a mountain transplant who grew up down on the coast. It's right special since his granddaddy and my daddy were good friends. He pops in every now and then to get some lunch and see if we need anything. He's a good fellow, but stays to himself way too much if you ask me. That place that belonged to his granddaddy is a little bitty place up high on the mountain, straight up at the end of Laurel Lane about two, three miles that way. Can you find your way back to the main road?"

"I think so," Emily said. "It's just that way and two right turns?"

"That's right. You take care of yourself, you hear?"

"Yes, ma'am, I will, and thank you. More than you'll ever know, thank you."

As Emily started walking between tables to the front door, she saw an eerily familiar man sitting at a table in the far corner. Tall and lanky. The man from the funerals. Sweat beaded on her face and arms. Her heart started to race. With a sudden rush of adrenaline and bravery she never knew she possessed, she turned and marched toward the man.

"What are you doing here and why are you following me?" She screamed. The hum of conversation in the restaurant died to silence. He turned to face her full on, and she saw his eyes, knew those eyes.

"Rob?" she asked quietly.

"Emily, what are you doing here? How did you find me?"

"I didn't," she said, grabbing a chair before her legs betrayed her and she hit the floor. "Not on purpose, anyway."

Rob stood, towering over her. How could this be the short friend she knew and loved? He pulled out the chair and guided her to sit down next to him. "Growth spurt," he said, answering her unasked question. "First year of college. Who knew that could happen?" He smiled and she knew for certain this man really was her childhood friend.

Everyone around her seemed to relax, and the conversation hum picked up again. Emily saw Faye, halfway to their table, stop, shake her head, and turn to go back behind the counter.

Emily's mind was spinning. Her Rob? She sure could use a friend right now, but didn't know who she could trust.

"You've got to stop calling me," she said with quiet authority. "Just stop. And no more roses. Nothing. No calls, no music, no roses. Understand?"

"What are you talking about?"

"The wordless phone calls. The heavy breathing. My favorite songs. The flowers. My dead dog. Why would you do that, Rob, why? I thought you were my friend. Why would you scare me like that? Why would you kill Winston?" Emily lost the composure she struggled so hard to maintain, lost the strength she wanted to exert in her voice. She started to shake.

"Whoa, there," Rob said, sliding his chair back a bit. "Have you gone mad?"

His words cut through her façade and left her defenseless. Tears started rolling down her cheeks.

"I didn't mean that, Emily. I'm sorry. I shouldn't have said that." He wiped her cheeks with his thumbs and gently took her hand. "I just don't understand any of this. Come on, let's go outside where we can talk. Maybe walk down to the creek. It's beautiful down there. We'll talk, okay?"

He tossed some money on the table, took her hand, and led her out the front door, around the store and down the steps. She let him. When they reached the edge of the creek, he sat down on the grass and motioned for her to join him. She glanced back at the store, then sat on a rock several feet away from Rob.

"Now tell me about these phone calls. And Winston. Who is Winston and what happened to him? It wasn't me, Emily, I swear. What phone calls? I wanted to call you. After your parents. But I didn't want to cause problems with Dan. And after Dan died, I wanted to call, but I didn't want you to feel like I was pouncing at the first chance. I wanted to give you time, Emily. But I was there, all the funerals. I was there because I cared, and I couldn't stay away."

Emily heard him, but made no attempt to respond aloud. Just questioned herself in her mind. *How could I be such a fool? Maybe I am totally mad, over the edge, crazy.* She began to cry, uncontrolled shaking sobs.

Rob knelt down in front of her, held her face in his hands, once again tried to wipe the tears away with his thumbs. But they were falling fast. He took her hands and said, "Come sit with me." Emily stood and let him lead her to the swing on the porch. Rob sat down and guided Emily down beside him.

"I'm sorry you've had to go through all this death in your family, Emily. I don't know how you've been able to cope. It would be enough to drive anybody..." He stopped in mid-sentence.

"Crazy. You can say it."

"But..."

"It's okay, really. Sometimes I wonder if maybe I am. I sure acted like it a few minutes ago. I don't think I've ever screamed at anybody like that. I'm sorry I embarrassed you in front of all those people. People who know you."

"That was a bit scary, I'll have to admit. Didn't see that one coming. But I don't think you're crazy."

"I was, you know."

"I heard you had some problems back when you lost the baby. I was really worried about you, but I didn't want to make things worse by calling. Everybody knew how jealous Dan always was."

Emily saw the compassion in his eyes, but she just nodded.

"I understood that all your dreams had shifted focus. I remember the afternoon you told me you were getting married, that you weren't going to college after all. I knew you'd be a great mom, but you would have been an awesome doctor. I couldn't imagine having the responsibility of a family at that age."

"I couldn't imagine doing anything else."

"My little brother told me you were in the hospital. He thought you were physically sick. Mom told me why you stayed so long after you lost the baby. What happened?"

"I don't know. The baby was fine just a couple days before at my last doctor's appointment. I don't remember that morning at all, I just know that when the pain started, Dan was at work. The pain was awful, and I was bleeding so badly. I dream about that day all the time, but I can never remember that morning—what happened before," she said.

"I had a hard time after. It was a girl. Did you know that?" Emily paused. Rob nodded. "I finally decided to make the best of the situation. Dan really loved me. We made a good life together."

She wasn't sure if she were trying to convince Rob or herself.

"Tell me about these phone calls."

Emily started at the beginning, the day she returned from her only solitary beach trip, and recounted every phone call she could remember, every song that was played, every flower left, every strange feeling she had about being watched or followed, being paged at the grocery stores, their dog Winston.

"Oh, Emily, what do the police say?"

"They think I'm crazy. I know they do. At first Frank acted like he believed me. You remember Frank, I'm sure. But they couldn't get a trace on the phone calls, and I couldn't tell them what they needed to hear. The flowers were always live ones, so they think I'm crazy for not liking them. Frank helped me take Winston to the vet, but he didn't even believe that Winston was poisoned—the tests were supposedly inconclusive and they said he could of found something poisonous in the woods, but I know better. I know somebody killed him as a warning to me. I know it."

"Emily, why would you think it was me?"

"I don't. Not now that I know who you are. But when you were a stranger standing outside the funeral every single time, and then I saw you and thought you followed me. You don't look like you did. I had no idea it was you."

"Well, yeah, I sort of shot up and slimmed down. Surprised everybody. I would have loved to call you, but not to scare you. I wanted to hear your voice. I wanted to call you and console you, tell you how much I was thinking about you. I tried to keep tabs on you all these years through my family. I knew I could never actually talk to you because of Dan's jealousy. Did that get better with age?"

Emily visibly cringed. "No," she said. "Worse."

"Tell me."

Like she had the previous evening with Faye, Emily shared the sordid details of her life with Dan.

Rob reached out and laid his hand on hers. Squeezed. Electricity shot through her body and the muscles in her abdomen tightened. She gasped involuntarily.

"Emily?"

She looked up at him. With her free hand, she touched his cheek, rubbed the one-day stubble with the tips of her fingers. He stood and brought her up with him, then put both arms around her back and pulled her into him, holding her so tight she could feel his heart beating against her chest. He buried his face in her hair and held her as though he would never let go. But he did, placing his hands on her shoulders and holding her outward just far enough to look her in the eyes. His were piercing, determined, fierce. Almost to the point of scaring her.

"I will help you, Emily. If we can't get the police to do anything, we'll do it ourselves. I won't let anybody hurt you or your boys. I promise you that right here and right now. Nobody is going to hurt you ever again."

She wanted so much to believe that he could make the horror go away, but she was much too realistic. "If only you could," she whispered.

"I have to ask you something," Rob said hesitantly. "I don't want to scare you more, but I think it's something you need to consider."

"What is it?"

"Are you sure Dan's accident was an accident?"

"What do you mean? He ran off the road and into the swamp. Hit trees on the way."

"But do they know why? I mean, are they sure it was an accident? Have you had his truck checked out, Emily?"

"Checked for what?"

"I don't know, the tires, the brakes, the steering, anything somebody might have done to it."

"You think somebody killed him? Why?"

"I'm just speculating, but what if the person who's been calling you wanted him out of the way. You said the calls had gotten worse since he died."

"They have, but nothing else has happened."

"Are you sure? Anything at all different in the yard, the garage, anywhere you go. Are you sure nobody's following you? Have the boys mentioned seeing anybody hanging around school?"

"Now you are scaring me."

"I just want you to be careful. I have a couple of things to finish up, then I'm coming down there. I'll just stay at my grandpa's house on the lake until this whole thing blows over. I want to help you, and I can't do that this far away."

"Okay."

"Emily, I have to ask you another question. This one will be even harder. Are you sure your parents' wreck was an accident?"

"Somebody ran them off the road. But the cops never investigated it. Why would someone want to kill my parents?"

"We'll need those answers, too. I have a friend who's a PI. I'll talk to him. In the meantime when you get home, call Charlie Smothers. He's got a mechanics shop back home. You remember him from school? A couple of years behind you, I think. Can you get access to Dan's truck? How about your daddy's truck? I know that one's been a while, but do you know where it is?"

"I think so."

"Make that your first priority when you get home. Tell the authorities you need access to both vehicles and call Charlie to let him know where to pick them up."

"Now I have to ask you a question. You can tell me if it's none of my business, but if you're coming back east for an indefinite amount of time to help me, I have to know you're not going to get in trouble at work. How are you going to get away for so long? I don't even know where you work."

"I got lucky. I was teaching, living closer into town, but I sold a few of my paintings, commissioned a few big murals. Built a small following. It was enough to let me live comfortably. Not extravagant. But that's not me anyway. Then a few years ago when my grandfather died, he had a big life insurance policy with all the grandchildren as beneficiaries. Set us up for life if we're frugal. So I get to live here and draw and paint. Couldn't ask for anything more."

"But aren't you lonely?"

After a noticeable pause, he answered. "Sometimes, sure."

"Have you ever been in love? Wanted to get married?" Emily questioned. Another pause from Rob.

"I thought so, once. But it didn't work out and that was for the best. I know that now." He made direct eye contact before continuing. "I didn't really love her—not the never ending more than life itself kind of love. You can only have that once in your life. I really believe that."

"I used to believe it. But love isn't always what you think it is."

"Maybe you didn't marry the right person." This time Emily hesitated to answer, bouncing her foot and twisting her hands. Rob placed his hand on her knee to still the motion. "Maybe you didn't marry the right person," he repeated.

"I thought I did. Now I guess I'll never really know."

Faye came walking down the hill.

"It's going to be dark soon," she said to Emily. "Sam's just going to bring your car back around and park it under the shed. You can get an early start in the morning, but snow's moving in so you can't sleep 'til lunchtime like you did today."

Emily smiled at the sound of motherly advice in Faye's words. She didn't dare disagree with her.

"I need to call the boys again. Will that be ok?"

"Of course, child. And while you're up there, you might as well have some supper. You, too, Rob."

"How do you know each other?" Emily asked Faye.

"He's that transplant artist I was telling you about, the one who painted the ocean picture."

"Oh," Emily whispered, then looked at Rob. "I never knew."

"Now it's my turn," Faye said. "How do you two know each other, and don't try to make me think you don't. I don't know what that scene back there was about, but I'm sure glad you worked it out."

"We grew up together in the same little town," Rob answered. "But I wasn't smart enough to snatch her up way back then. She didn't recognize me at first because I had a crazy growth spurt in college. Grew up and slimmed down."

"Maybe you've grown some brains, too." Faye winked at Emily and patted Rob on the shoulder. "Come on in and eat."

§ § §

Emily was up at first light. A soft snow tickled her face as she walked around to the restaurant for breakfast. She was surprised to see Rob already sitting at a booth.

"Snow's going to be coming down hard soon," he said. "Since you're not used to driving in snow, I'm going to lead you down the worst part, then you're on your own for a little while. I'll be there soon, I promise."

Faye brought plates of bacon and eggs and grits and pancakes and biscuits and jelly. Then she shooed them out the door almost before they finished their breakfast. "It's really starting to come down now," she said.

Emily tried to concentrate as she followed Rob's taillights around the winding mountain road, but her mind was reeling. She hadn't thought about any of the things Rob had mentioned. If someone really was trying to kill everybody she loved, what about her boys? She had just talked to them right before she left that morning, so she knew they were safe for now. But how long? They were excited that she was coming home, but now she wasn't sure that was such a good idea. Maybe they'd be safer if they were far away from her. But if she didn't have her boys, she might as well be dead.

Rob led Emily down the mountain a ways, pulling into the parking lot of a service station. She could see a Parkway entrance sign close by. Emily got out of her car. She needed to go to the bathroom. Rob followed her into the store and out again.

"You can't watch my back forever," she said, reaching out to touch his cheek. "But it sure feels good."

"I know, but please be careful. It'll be easier and faster to stay off the Parkway."

Emily opened her car door and started to get in when Rob reached for her, pulling her toward him and wrapping both arms around her.

"I'm sorry," he whispered, "for everything you've been through—not just recently, but ever since I went to college."

"No," Emily said. "It's not your fault."

"And I didn't mean to scare you last night."

"You did scare me a little," she said, pushing away and looking up. "But, I'll be okay, Rob. I don't have a choice. I'll start working on all those things you said. And I'll go through Dan's papers and files, too. I haven't done that yet. Haven't even been to the lawyer. Maybe I'll find something that will help me understand. I'll see you soon, okay?"

"Soon, I promise."

Emily saw the entrance to the Parkway and turned. Her choice. She drove for almost two hours, replaying the last couple of days in her mind over and over again. When she left home, she really had no idea where she was going, and certainly not who she would find when she got there. But now that she had found Rob again, she had no reason not to let him help her. Not anymore.

Rob had suggested she make a list of any men she could think of that might have developed an infatuation for her. Any little thing, he said, could set it off, according to his PI buddy. Thinking back to when the phone calls began, she remembered the guy in the airplane on the beach. That was definitely odd, but she had never seen him again and there was no way he could know who she was. And the note in the restaurant, but she had his name and number, he didn't have hers. Could the waitress have mentioned her name, where she lived? Then there was Dr. Z. If anybody surprised her, he did. She never saw that one coming. And he had been persistent for a while, calling and asking her to come to work. All those visits and roses in the hospital. But he always talked to her. Had he changed his tactics? How would scaring her to death make her come to work for him? Killing her husband might.

Emily needed to pee—bad. She had been so deep in thought, she hadn't enjoyed the views at all, hadn't pulled into any overlooks, noticed any exits to towns. Now she needed a bathroom and every time she started thinking about it, it always made it worse. But the characteristics of the Parkway that made it so beautiful also made it inconvenient. It hung off the side of the mountains for miles, not close to any place in particular. Picnic tables were dispersed at the overlooks occasionally, but bathrooms were few and far between. The further she drove and the more she thought about it, the more desperate she became. She had not seen a car for miles and contemplated just pulling off the side of the road. But the rocks rose straight up on her right, and across the road at the guardrail, the mountain went straight down. She'd surely fall to her death if she tried squatting there.

No signs for towns materialized, but Emily finally saw a brown wooden sign with a picnic table drawn at the top and stick figures of a man and woman at the bottom—a picnic area with a bathroom, at last. A quarter of a mile later, Emily pulled off the Parkway onto a small paved drive that led into the woods, following the arrows that she hoped led to the bathroom. No one and no cars were in sight. The little road turned to gravel and wound around through the trees and up the side of the mountain. Picnic tables sat perched on small flat areas on either side. Emily pictured families enjoying summer lunches there, traveling families with no cares—mom, dad, children, normal people having fun. But they were empty now.

A smaller sign with bathroom figures and an arrow kept Emily driving to where the road stopped and a walking path began. Hesitantly, she left her car and started up the small rocky path through the trees. Leaves crunched under her feet. A scurrying chipmunk startled her and she jumped. Wind whistled through the nearly bare limbs that hung menacingly above her head. The path opened into a small flat clearing at the top of the mountain. A few picnic tables sat along the edge of the cliff. Emily heard the leaves crunch and spun around. She saw nothing. Her heart beat so fast she could feel it in her ears.

The bathroom was a grey wooden structure—the sign for men on one end and the one for women on the other. Emily pulled open the door and peered inside, fearful of what she might find, human or otherwise. The room housed a wall hung sink and two stalls with swinging doors. It was colder inside than the late October outdoors. Emily let the large door close behind her. She hurried into one of the stalls, not closing the door, preferring a view of the outside door in case it moved. She had visions of ax murderers or that strange creature haunting rest stops that she had read about in a novel. When she finished, she hurriedly washed her hands and dried them on her jeans. The paper towel holder was empty.

Emily stood at the outside door, hesitating to open it for fear of what might be on the other side. She would be helpless to save herself if anyone were there. Gathering up her courage, she placed her hands on the door and pushed. It wouldn't budge. She wrapped her fingers around the small metal handle and pulled. It didn't open. Emily was certain she had pulled it open when she came in and would need to push it to get out, then remembered the short piece of wood nailed to the outside that she had to turn before she could open the door. Maybe it had fallen down—or someone had turned it. She backed up as far as she could and half ran to the door, hitting it with her shoulder. It flew open and she landed on the ground. She jumped up quickly, turning in circles, looking around. Seeing no one and nothing to indicate anyone had been there, she walked briskly down the path, turning her head back and forth, watching, waiting.

By the time she was close enough to see her car, she was almost running, her foothold precarious on the rocks. Thankful she had not locked the driver's side door, Emily jerked it open, climbed in and locked her door. Trying to regain her composure was difficult. She envisioned someone knocking on her car window—a snaggle-toothed old man in rags—cold, hungry, wanting help and willing to kill for anything she had. Emily quickly turned around and checked behind the front seat to make sure he wasn't hiding there. Nothing. She could only hope he wasn't behind the back seat. Why did she have to be driving a station wagon?

Get a grip and go.

Emily cranked the car, thankful to hear the motor whine to life. She backed up, surveying the woods carefully for anyone or anything, promising herself she would never stop at a place like that by herself ever again. She kept glancing in the rearview mirror, afraid to see someone looking over the back seat.

Reaching the Parkway, she remembered that she had not taken her pill. She put the car in park and stretched to reach her bag in the back seat. She had nothing to drink, but didn't care. The small green pill slid down by itself.

At the first opportunity, Emily exited the Parkway and opted for driving regular roads that wound through towns where people lived and worked and shopped. She stopped for lunch at a bustling little restaurant. That seemed safe enough. Before she left, she found a pay phone and called her boys, telling them she'd be there in a few hours.

"You must plan to stay for dinner," Grandma Gillespie said. "I don't know where you've been or why, and it doesn't look like you're going to tell me, but if you've been driving all day, I want you to rest here for the night before putting these boys in your car."

"Yes, ma'am," Emily said. It was just so much easier to agree. She knew her mother-in-law would continue to pry, and she guessed she really owed her some kind of explanation, but it certainly couldn't be the truth.

Emily and the boys drove home on Friday. They had missed almost a week of school, so she stopped by on their way home to pick up their assignments. The teachers were understanding. Convincing the coach to let Danny play football the next day was a little harder, but she found that using the "his daddy just died" phrase was still working, so she'd play it as long as she could if it helped her boys.

Emily looked up the phone number for Charlie's garage and called him, asking for an appointment on Monday. With that done, she fed the boys and sent them out to play. She was just beginning to unpack their clothes when the phone rang. She answered without hesitation, feeling stronger now, ready to face whatever came. But that changed quickly. She heard not just his heavy breathing, but in the background her boys, laughing and playing, then the sound of brakes squealing, metal meeting, cars crashing. Then silence.

Emily rushed outside. The boys were fine, tossing the football back and forth, running and tackling each other. She looked around the yard for signs that anyone had been there, and she saw nothing. But she wouldn't let the boys out of her sight. Rather than do anything that would worry them, she simply sat down on the back steps and watched them play.

"Mommy," Bobby yelled when he saw her sitting there. "Watch me tackle Danny." He ran head first into his big brother, who faked a fall. The boys tumbled over and over, reeling with laughter. She would do anything to protect them. Anything.

When she put them to bed that night, she double-checked the locks on their windows. She rummaged through the attic and found the baby things she had stored there. She remembered thinking the monitor was such an extravagance when they bought it, since no one else she knew had one. But she was glad she had it now. Taking out the monitor, she carried it to their room and plugged it in, then slipped the base under the edge of the bed where they wouldn't see it. She clipped the speaker to her waistband so she could hear every sound from their room anywhere she went. Unpacking her suitcase, she made sure the gun was loaded and placed it on the top shelf of her closet, where she could get to it easily, but the boys couldn't reach it.

Emily went into Dan's office off the kitchen, just large enough for a small desk, a filing cabinet, and a safe. He had always kept a few hundred dollars there, and his collection of pistols, but he also used it to store the movies. He even set up the projector in his office after he stopped making Emily watch them. Sometimes he would spend a few hours "working" and come out ready for action. Emily had been more and more repulsed every time he touched her.

She wasn't sure where he bought them, and didn't want to know. Some had cases with titles and provocative pictures. Emily slid the trashcan in front of the safe and sat down in Dan's chair. She began pulling the movies out one by one, stripping the film from the reels before tossing them in the trash. He had managed to hoard a much larger collection than she realized, but she had quit asking, preferred not to know. Behind what she thought was a store-bought collection,

Emily found tapes with no names, no pictures. Obviously homemade. Fearful of what she would see, Emily forced herself to turn on the projector and run one of the movies. She saw herself in her most intimate moments, in the bathroom, taking off her clothes, sitting on the toilet, getting into the shower, toweling off. She saw her naked self take out her hair dryer and start drying her hair, flipping her head over and bending down to dry it from below, her breasts hanging, swaying with her movements.

The tape skipped, blank for a few seconds, then a dim light, two bodies, her bed. Emily wasn't sure which she feared most—seeing herself or another woman. When she saw her own face, she immediately stopped the reel and ripped it apart, pulling the film with a fury she'd never felt before. *If he wasn't dead, I'd kill him myself.*

As much as she wanted to just chunk them all, Emily felt an obligation and a surreal sense of curiosity to see what was on the other movies her husband had made, had sat in this room and watched while she read bedtime stories to their children. She took another from its case, then another and another. He had obviously been taping their lovemaking for a very long time. She felt dirty, abused, raped. How could he? How could she not know?

Five reels remained. Emily needed a break. She walked down the hall to check on the boys. They were sleeping soundly and nothing seemed amiss, but she checked the locks on the windows again. Then she went into her bedroom, and judging from the angle of the videos, started searching for a camera. She remembered the day more than a year earlier when Dan had brought home a mounted large-mouth bass. Despite her resistance, he insisted on hanging it over the closet. Emily pulled a chair from the corner of the room and climbed up, very carefully lifting the fish. A cord ran from the back into the wall. She looked inside the closet and could not see where it went. She'd save that search for later and the bathroom camera, too. But she did wonder how he operated it, how he turned it on without her knowing, how the close-ups were achieved. She thought about the close-ups and cringed. Something that should have been beautiful and sacred reduced to vulgarities.

Emily searched around her bed. As many times as she had stripped the bed, washed the sheets and remade it, something would have had to be hidden well for her not to find it. She thought about their times together, how they had changed, trying to recall anything Dan did differently in the past year. Then she remembered. Dan began wanting to start on his stomach with her lying beside him on her back. In fact, he insisted. But he wouldn't touch her at first. He always started with his hands between the mattress and the wall, pulling himself back and forth on the sheets. Emily thought he was just masturbating to get hard, that touching her wasn't enough for him anymore. She searched but found nothing between the headboard and the wall. Then she pulled the pillows away and threw them to the side, lying on her stomach on the bed, reaching between the box spring and the headboard. In a pocket on the box spring, she found a small handheld devise with buttons—some type of remote control. She put it back in its hiding place, another chore for later.

The movies would not go away unless she threw them away. She knew that. And as much as she dreaded seeing herself even one more time, she knew she couldn't just destroy them. Anything could hold a clue. She sat down in the chair again, turned on the projector and loaded another reel. Not her bedroom, but familiar nonetheless. She looked at the pale green walls, the quilted comforter, the pictures on the dresser. Norma, it was Norma's room. No sooner had Emily realized what she was seeing than Norma walked into the room, nearly naked, prancing, waving at the camera, throwing kisses, jiggling her breasts beneath a sheer silk gown. She threw the covers back on the bed and climbed in, sitting on her knees facing the camera. Then she wiggled her finger invitingly and in walked Dan.

That movie lasted more than an hour and Emily watched every minute—her husband and her sister-in-law in every sexual pose imaginable and some she could not have imagined had she not seen them. It was more like a tutorial than an encounter bred of love or even lust. But the next three tapes were different. They lost themselves in lovemaking, sometimes gentle, sometimes explosive, but obviously not an act for the camera. Emily wondered if Norma even knew the recorder was on during those times when she declared her love for Dan. It was a vulnerable Norma whom Emily saw, clinging to a man who was not hers, giving him whatever he asked. The camera watched them watching pornographic movies projected on the bedroom wall, Dan encouraging Norma to repeat what she saw. He used his handcuffs, the whip, other gadgets inside and outside her body, Norma supple and willing at first, then crying from the pain. Emily was repulsed, but some part of her felt pity for Norma, too.

Only one movie left. Emily was drained physically and emotionally. She walked into the kitchen for something to drink. 4 a.m. At least she was almost finished with the movies. The papers could wait for another day. She returned to the office determined to finish before she called it a night. The last one started out the same as the others—Dan and Norma in the throes of passion. Then it skipped. Blank for a few seconds. Then Dan's voice. "It's ok, you won't get into trouble." It was soothing and soft, coaxing.

"But I'm not supposed to be in Mommy's room."

Elizabeth. Oh, god, no.

"Now would Uncle Dan do anything to get you into trouble? The boys are asleep, and we can watch mommy's television without waking them up. Come on." They walked into the room with Dan holding Elizabeth's hand, then he lifted her up and tossed her on the bed. She giggled, but starting pulling on her t-shirt that had risen up, baring her midriff.

"See, that's not so bad. We'll have fun."

Elizabeth started to sit up, but Dan grabbed her around the waist and threw her back down playfully, tickling her relentlessly. At first she seemed to be laughing, then she started to cry.

"Please stop, Uncle Dan." Emily's heart ached. Elizabeth was immature for her age, despite her mother's constant parade of friends. Physically, she was just beginning to bud.

"Okay, enough of that." His voice was edgy, impatient. He propped several pillows up on the headboard and encouraged Elizabeth to lean back on them. "We'll watch some TV 'til your mom gets home. If you fall asleep, I'll carry you to bed, okay?"

"Okay." She was on the verge of tears but obviously scared and confused enough to do whatever he said.

They watched a re-run of *I Dream of Jeannie* and Elizabeth seemed to relax, her eyes heavy with sleep. Then Dan walked over to the television and turned it off. "You're just about grown up on us Elizabeth. Uncle Dan's got a special surprise for you."

He turned on the projector and the movie wasted no time—a secretary on a desk with her boss's face between her legs, his hands splayed across her naked breasts.

Elizabeth's eyes grew large, fearful, full of tears. She tried to get off the bed, but Dan grabbed her thigh, keeping his hand high up on her leg, his thumb grazing inside her shorts. He wrapped his other arm around shoulders. "Don't be a baby," he said. "Watch and learn. You'll get your turn at what she's doing." Dan pointed to the wall where the woman and man had switched places. "Don't turn your head, girl. I said watch it and learn." He held Elizabeth's face toward the action with his hand on her forehead.

"Let her go, you bastard." Norma's voice. "I'll kill you, I swear, I'll kill you." The tape went black. Emily could hardly breathe. Elizabeth, the poor baby. If Norma had killed Dan, she wouldn't blame her. But she didn't tear that tape apart. She put it back in the safe, spun the lock to make sure it was secure, and went to bed. If Norma had killed Dan, Emily decided, she would not tell.

Chapter 13

When Emily dropped the boys off at school on Monday morning, she reminded them never to talk to strangers and never to go anywhere with anyone they didn't know. "And don't go anywhere by yourself. I'll pick you up right here after school. I'll be early, ok?"

"Sure mom," Danny said. "I'll watch the squirt, too."

"I don't squirt," Bobby said. Emily couldn't help but laugh.

"I'll be here, right here, early." Emily tried so hard not to let the boys sense her fear, but she knew she wasn't doing a very good job of hiding it. She wanted, needed to talk to Norma, but she had some other things to take care of first. She had an 8:30 a.m. appointment with Charlie at his shop, but she wasn't sure she wanted to keep it. If Dan's truck was tampered with, if Norma had done it, she didn't want anyone else to know until she decided what to do. Besides, that wouldn't lead to learning anymore about the phone calls.

Fifteen minutes after she walked in the house, the phone started ringing. Always nervous about answering it, she lifted the receiver slowly and said nothing.

"Emily, are you there?"

"Oh, Rob, yes, I'm here. I was just expecting it to be, you know, not you."

"I know. I've been waiting until I knew the boys were back in school before I called. Are you okay? Have you talked to Charlie? Have you made a list of suspects?"

She had made a list of men she thought might be calling, but it was a very short list—the airplane guy, restaurant guy, Dr. Z, one of the PTA dads, and an assistant coach. The last two were really far-fetched, but Emily was grasping at straws to come up with that many.

"I've been working on it, but I have children to take care of, too, remember?"

"I know, I just want everything to be alright so you can put the past behind you and move forward." He paused. "Have you talked to Charlie yet?"

She had already called Charlie and canceled, using her impending appointment with the lawyer as an excuse, but that wasn't until 10 a.m. She had yet to do anything to settle Dan's legal matters, and she really didn't know what to expect. Dan had insisted on keeping most of the books himself since, as he put it, he was the one making the money.

"I talked to him, but I have to see the attorney today. I'm not sure what good it will do to check out the truck anyway."

"We talked about that Emily. You need to know if it was tampered with, if somebody killed Dan. You have to know if that has anything to do with the phone calls."

"I tell you what. When you come down, you can help sort some of this out. Right now, I've got to take care of my boys and go to the lawyer. I don't even know if I'm going to have enough money to live off of or if I'm going to have to find a job. I don't even know who would hire me." She did, but she didn't want to think about that.

"I'm sorry. I know you have to do this in your own way, your own time. I just want to help. I want it to be over."

"No more than I do."

"I don't like saying goodbye."

"Then don't. It's too final anyway. See you soon. That better?"

"See you soon."

Emily appreciated Rob's desire to help, but he was right. She did have to do this in her own way, her own time. She wasn't even sure if she would tell Rob about the movies. She went back to the safe and opened it again. The lone tape sat there taunting her, but it was the paperwork she needed to find—a manila folder that said life insurance, a folder with mortgage information, checkbooks, savings statements. Dan had been nothing if not organized, so Emily just boxed it all up to take with her. She looked for the cash and could not find any. She knew Dan had always kept close to a thousand dollars in hundred dollar bills in the safe. "Just in case," he always said. Emily wondered if he had other women in his life, perhaps bought and paid for with his "just in case" money. Just in case she didn't satisfy him. Just in case she wouldn't play his games. Just in case she and her sister-in-law weren't enough. Just in case...little Elizabeth.

Emily figured there wasn't much more about her husband that would surprise her, but that didn't last long. Behind the pistols and ammunition, she found a box full of cigarette papers and a bag of what she assumed was weed. She wasn't surprised, knew he had done drugs in college. But she saw another envelope leaning against the back wall of the safe. It was black like the safe and almost impossible to see. She dreaded what she would find there, but knew she had to look.

She wished she hadn't.

Emily didn't recognize the faces, but the empty eyes all looked the same—innocently sexy and terrified. Photo after photo of mere children—boys and girls in suggestive poses, almost or totally nude, alone until the final photo—an 8X10 glossy of Dan, sprawled back in a lounge totally naked, a young boy, ten years old perhaps, also naked and lying wrapped in Dan's left arm. A girl, maybe nine or ten, lying next to him on the right side wearing only a white cotton slip, her blonde curls spread out across his chest, his hand on her bottom, her face toward the camera, red painted lips not smiling. Emily retched into the trashcan over and over again until she was dry heaving and breathless. What kind of monster would do such a thing? What had he done to her boys?

Driving to the attorney's office in Wilmington, Emily wondered if Dan's secret life had anything to do with the phone calls. Would some sleazy slimebag he dealt with think he could have her, too? What had he said about her? To whom? She didn't know where to turn, whom to trust, what to do.

§ § §

"Hello, Mrs. Gillespie." The sign on his door had read Tony

Willoughby, Attorney at Law. He greeted her with a firm handshake.

"Please, call me Emily. Mrs. Gillespie is my mother-in-law."

He laughed. "I understand. Emily, it is. And please, call me Tony."

"I brought what paperwork I could find in the safe. I'm not sure if it's all there or not."

"Dan was very meticulous, Emily. But you probably already know that. Anyway, I have copies of most everything except the last few months of savings statements. For some reason, he neglected to bring those to me. I have the will, but that's pretty much a moot point in North Carolina. Since your name is already on the vehicles and the real property, they automatically become yours. And of course, the household items you've accumulated together are yours. Your name is on the bank accounts and you're named as beneficiary of the life insurance policies. This should be a simple process. Do you have the savings statements?"

"I do." She handed over the box of paperwork, and he rifled through it until he found the statements.

"Let me take a moment to look at these, then we'll talk numbers. Would you like something to drink?"

"No, thank you, I'm fine." Emily sat silently and watched the attorney. This was so different from the volatile scene with Norma over her parents' estate and the life insurance Norma was sure she would get but that went into a trust for the children. Emily could still not understand why her parents had left the farm to Norma, and in turn, why Norma was so outraged to receive it and determined to sell it. Norma wanted money, cold hard cash. Now the farm was on the market; the last thing they had of her parents would soon be gone.

"This is quite strange," Tony said. "The Dan Gillespie I knew wasn't much into spending money, and there are several rather large withdrawals made over the past few months. Did he buy anything that you know of?"

"Not that I can recall." Emily wondered how much child porn cost, especially personalized child porn. "How much money?"

"Ten thousand dollars a month for three months—nothing last

month. But an additional withdrawal of fifteen thousand back in June."

"I didn't even know we had that much money."

"Well, it's not a problem for you. He left you and the boys well taken care of. It just seems a bit out of character for Dan."

"Well, we never really know people, now do we?" Emily's mind was reeling. She thought about the new car Norma had just purchased, the fact that she had quit asking her for money every week. Maybe she was blackmailing him. But then why would she kill him?

"Emily."

"I'm sorry, what did you say?"

"I said Dan had two life insurance policies with face value of $500,000 each. They both have double indemnity accidental death clauses, making them each worth one million dollars since he died in a traffic accident. In addition, the house has insurance to pay it off, so you won't have any debt."

"May I ask you a question, Tony?"

"Of course."

"Did either of these life insurance policies ever have a different beneficiary than me and the boys, or did he have other policies?"

"As far as I know, he had no other life insurance policies, and I think I handled all of his financials. I am a practicing CPA as well as an attorney. I must say I'm a little shocked by your lack of reaction to the numbers. Insurance money is tax free. You are a very rich woman, Emily."

"Yes, I guess I am. Do we have any further business to take care of today?"

"Let me finish looking through this envelope, but I don't think so."

Emily watched and waited; saw the expression on his face change.

"Here's something I didn't know about." He opened the white envelope and pulled out what looked like another insurance policy. "You may be richer than I thought. Let me see."

Emily saw him open the policy. "Well, this is strange." She saw his facial muscles twitch. "This is just a copy. I'm not sure where the original is, but it's worth a million dollars as well." He read some more and Emily watched him. "It doesn't have double indemnity. In fact, it has a clause I've never seen before. If he died from anything other than natural causes, it wouldn't pay at all. Do you know a Norma Morino?"

"That's my sister-in-law."

"Well, your husband must have been a very thoughtful man who cared deeply for your family. This policy is made out to her, with the secondary beneficiary being Elizabeth Turner."

"My niece." It was all falling into place. The cash would run out. Norma wanted more, but Dan didn't trust her. "Is there anything else?"

"No, you're free to go. The insurance money will go into your accounts very shortly. You'll be needing investment advice. I hope you will call on me to handle your finances."

"I'll take that into consideration. Thank you."

Emily wasn't sure what to do next. She returned home from Wilmington the long way around, riding by her parents' farm. She drove down the dirt drive, past her grandparents' cabin, up to the house where her parents had been so happy. The fields were already overgrown, even though so little time had passed. The yard had not been mowed, and the grass, though dead this time of year, was far too tall. She didn't have to go inside to know the houseplants were all dead, and the furniture covered in dust. The property was Norma's, and Emily knew she didn't have a right to be there. But she walked up on the front porch and sat down in the swing, pushing off with one foot until she was swaying steadily. The one person she could always turn to for answers was her daddy, and he was gone. What would he tell her to do now? She sat for almost an hour, hoping she could feel his presence, hear his voice, but all she felt was a cold late October wind, and all she heard was the squeak of rusty swing chains.

She drove straight to school although she was almost an hour early. She wanted to make sure no one got near her boys. She needed to talk to them about their dad, needed to know if he had ever done anything to them, but she wasn't sure what or how to ask. Maybe she should talk to a counselor first, but then she'd have to divulge information she wasn't sure she wanted to share. Should she call the cops? Frank? What would she tell him? Maybe she'd just burn the pictures.

"Mommy!" Through her rolled down window, Emily heard Bobby's delighted squeal. "I made a hundred and two on my spelling test!"

"But I thought a hundred was perfect," she said, reaching over to open the front door for him. "Guess you're riding shotgun. How'd you make better than perfect?"

"Extra credit. I knew how to spell Halloween." He tossed his bookbag across the seat into the back. "Are we going to carve a pumpkin this year? Daddy's not here anymore. Do you know how to carve a pumpkin? We need a jack-o-lantern."

"Of course, we'll carve a jack-o-lantern. Mommies and sons can do lots of things together. Like...get ice cream. You want to?"

"Yeah, but we better wait for Danny."

"Where is your brother?"

"I don't know. I ain't seen him."

"Haven't seen him. He's late."

Moments passed like hours while they waited. Emily did not want to over-react, but she began to panic as the flood of children pouring out of the building slowed to a trickle, only one or two here or there. Most of the parents had driven away; the buses began to leave. Her heart pounded against her ribcage.

Then she saw him, dragging his bookbag down the steps, kicking the dirt dejectedly as he walked toward the car. She got out and walked to meet him, telling herself to watch what she said.

"What's wrong buddy, we were beginning to worry about you."

"It weren't my fault, but the teacher made me stay anyway."

"What wasn't your fault?"

"The fight."

"You were in a fight, Danny? With whom?" When they reached the car, they stopped. She wanted to finish this conversation before they went any further.

"Benny Bishop. He called me an orphan, Little Orphan Andrew. My name ain't Andrew. And I ain't no orphan. Am I?"

"No, of course not. You have me. And Bobby. We're a family and we'll always be a family. Orphans don't have families like us. But you shouldn't be fighting."

"It weren't much of a fight. I just pushed him and he cried."

"Did you apologize?"

"Yes, ma'am."

"To Benny and to Mrs. Fisher?"

"Yes, ma'am."

"Good. Bobby and I need some ice cream. You want some?" She opened the back door and helped him inside. "I love you guys more than anything in the whole world. You know that, right? I think we need some fancy ice cream, not just some old ice cream cone. You up for the Dairy Queen?"

"But that's all the way to Wilmington," Bobby said. "And it's a school night."

"Well, we can splurge every now and then, don't you think? We just need to stop by the house for a minute." Emily wanted to turn on lights so they wouldn't come home to a dark house, and she wanted to set up an appointment with Norma. She needed to talk to her sister.

"You boys run on in your room and put your bookbags away. Mommy needs to make a phone call, then we'll be ready to go, okay?"

She went into her bedroom and closed the door, then on second thought, stuck her head back out and yelled to the boys. "Stay in the house. You can turn on the television if you want, but don't go outside." She closed the door again when they responded and she knew they were safe. She picked up the phone and dialed.

"Hello?"

"Norma, this is Emily."

"Fancy that."

"I need to talk to you."

"You're talking."

"No, I mean I need to meet with you, talk to you in person. Can you see me tomorrow while the kids are in school?"

"I might have something better to do."

"This is important, Norma. Ten o'clock. I'll come to you."

"Important to who, little sister? The world doesn't revolve around you."

"Important to all of us, to Elizabeth."

"What's Elizabeth got to do with anything?"

Emily took a deep breath before continuing. "I know about Elizabeth, Norma."

"Know what?"

"What Dan did to her. And I know about what he did to you, with you. I know. I saw the tapes. Just say I can come over. We really need to talk. You and your kids are the only family we have left, Norma."

"Family's not all it's cracked up to be. Come now."

"I can't. I promised the boys I'd take them to Dairy Queen. I'll be at your house at 10 a.m. tomorrow. Be there." Emily hung up the phone not knowing if Norma would be at home when she got there or not. Then she turned on lights in several rooms, the back porch, front porch and garage, and loaded up the boys for a special treat.

While they were in Wilmington, she decided to see if the boys wanted to find store-bought Halloween costumes, if she could still find some, and eat supper before they had ice cream. The boys wanted pizza from Pizza Hut, and the best one in New Hanover County sat on the edge of the waterway at Wrightsville Beach.

The weather in North Carolina changed often, so much so that a favorite saying was, "If you don't like the weather, wait a few minutes." Despite the cold earlier in the day, the evening warmed up nicely, almost balmy for October, so they sat at the tables on the deck. The boys knew better than to feed the seagulls while they were eating themselves, but afterwards, they tossed bits of crust up into

159

the air, watching the gulls catch the offerings in mid-flight. They hovered just above head height even after the boys ran out of food.

Emily loved hearing her boys laugh, no sweeter sound to her ears. She wanted them to always be this way, carefree, innocent. She thought surely Dan couldn't have done anything to them and they still be so free-spirited. Anything like that would have damaged them, and as their mother, she would know. She could tell, couldn't she? She decided to wait and see, hope that nothing would change, that their father never made it to them. She ached for the children in the pictures, the boys he touched, but she was so very thankful that they were not her boys, not Danny and Bobby.

"Okay, guys, let's go get ice cream and head home before it gets too late. You'll be out past bedtime as it is. Dairy Queen or Shields?"

"Shields," Bobby responded immediately. "I want a clown!"

The ice cream shop made a special treat for kids. Rounded ice cream for the face, a cone for the clown's hat with a cherry at the top, jellybean eyes, a cherry nose, peppermint candy mouth, and a whipped cream neck ruffle covered in sprinkles. Emily didn't mind that choice at all. She savored the hot fudge turtle sundae—vanilla ice cream all gooey with hot fudge and hot caramel sauce, pecans, whipped cream.

"Shields okay with you Danny?"

"Sure, but I'm too big for the clown. Can I have a banana split?"

"I don't know. You think you're big enough to handle a whole banana split by yourself?"

Danny nodded.

"Shields it is."

Occasionally that evening, Emily thought about what two million dollars would do, and could not fathom the possibilities. All she knew was that as big a sleazebag as Dan turned out to be, he did one thing right. His boys would never want for anything.

"Let's go home," she said. "Both of you in the backseat this time, please."

"Ah, mom," Danny said, not happy to be missing his turn to ride shotgun.

"It's safer there."

Not many miles out of town on Hwy. 117, the road became desolate, not much traffic as it wound through a wooded area before running into the little crossroad town called Castle Hayne. Emily peered into her rearview mirror and saw the boys leaning inward toward each other, their heads already bobbing in sleep.

A car appeared quickly behind Emily, riding her bumper and glaring high beams into her rearview. She slowed a bit in hopes it would pass, but it didn't. The car got closer and closer until it bumped into her, then backed off. Emily wasn't sure whether she should speed up or slow down more. The car sped up and rear ended her again, harder this time. The boys woke up and began to cry, calling her. Emily sped up, but the car sped up faster, pulling alongside her and sliding into her, forcing her off the road. She went bumping off onto the shoulder and her car started skidding in the grass, down the embankment, toward the creek. Emily saw trees coming in fast and heard her boys' terrified screams. Then darkness. Silence.

Chapter 14

Emily heard sirens, but couldn't open her eyes, couldn't move. She heard her babies crying, but could not console them. Pain seared through every muscle, every nerve ending raw. She heard voices, but could not respond. In and out of consciousness, she heard tools crunching metal, someone say she was dying. *I can't die, I won't.* But she couldn't tell them.

Then bright lights through closed eyelids, frantic voices, "Code blue, code blue, we're losing her."

Then nothing.

The rusty chains on the porch swing squeaked as she methodically pushed with one foot on the wooden plank porch. Honeysuckle sweetened the air and a mockingbird fussed nearby. Gazing past the grape arbor, Emily could see her daddy bouncing in his tractor seat, plowing between the rows, corn tasseling, harvest still weeks away. But nothing would taste better than sweet, juicy corn on the cob with a pot of shrimp fresh from the ocean, boiled just until they turned pink and the water started to foam. She could hear her mother singing Amazing Grace, rolling biscuit dough in the kitchen. Molasses and butter mixed to sop it in. Butter beans boiling on the stove. Chicken frying in the cast iron skillet. Home. Nothing better.

Emily stood and stepped off the porch into the soft green grass. She needed to talk to her daddy, but she couldn't remember why. She walked and walked, but didn't get any closer—he kept bouncing along, Mama sang Amazing Grace, Emily walked. She could hear her boys laughing but couldn't see them. Then screeching tires, crumbling metal, screams. Daddy kept bouncing along and Mama kept singing. Emily kept walking, going nowhere.

Cool water on her face. A swimming hole? Rob was there, young, handsome, coaxing her under the water.

"Come on, Emily. You can do it. Open your eyes."

Darkness. Straining. Were they open or closed? She couldn't see. Couldn't talk.

"Come on Emily. Open your eyes."

She struggled to open them but the water held them closed. Was she swimming or drowning? Tired, so tired.

Nothing.

Emily rocked in the new white wicker rocker, the baby blanket she crocheted laying warmly across her legs, rows of pinks and blues, greens and yellows. She stopped when the fluttering started, the baby moving. A boy or a girl? She hummed a lullaby. Emily! Dan yelling. Where the hell are you? Mad. What's all this? Are you crazy? Towering over her. Glaring. The fist to her bulging belly.

"Mommy. Wake up. Mommy? Can you hear me?"

I hear you baby, mommy's here. But her mouth wouldn't move, the words wouldn't come. She couldn't lift her arms. Where was her baby? She needed to get to her baby. Struggling to speak, struggling to see, struggling to move. Tired, too tired.

Nothing.

"Her heart rate is normal, blood pressure normal, her body's working fine, but she's just not in there."

Yes, I am here.

"I don't know any more to tell you. She could come out of it tomorrow or stay like this for years. There is brain activity, but I can't guarantee anything. We won't know unless she wakes up."

I'm here. So tired. I'm here.

Nothing.

The light is so bright. The sun? She struggled to open her eyes. Concentrate.

"They moved. Nurse, nurse. Her eyes, they moved."

"Are you sure?"

"Yes, I'm sure. Emily, come on baby, do it again."

Struggling. Concentrate. Struggling. Motion.

"See. Did you see it?"

"I think so. I'll call the doctor."

"Emily? Emily, baby, do it again."

Rob? Struggling, concentrating, she could see a blur of lights, could hear

163

beeping. Struggling harder. The light hurts.

"Squeeze my hand, Emily. I know you can hear me. Squeeze my hand."

Concentrate. Fingers.

"You did it, that's great. Can you look at me, Emily? Open your eyes, please baby. That's my girl."

Emily blinked, but the light hurt so bad. She squeezed her lids tighter.

"Is it the light? Does it hurt? I'll turn it out. Try again."

Slowly she raised her lids, blinked. Closed her eyes, then opened them again. She could see him. Rob. It was Rob. Tears began to trickle down her cheeks, and he brushed them away.

"Welcome back. I was so scared."

She tried to speak, but her throat ached, something blocked her tongue.

"Don't try to talk. You've got a feeding tube in there. They'll take it out soon, I'm sure."

She squeezed his hand hard, stared at him frantically. She needed to know about her boys, but she couldn't ask. Her heart rate started to rise, the machine beeping faster and faster.

"Well, what do we have here," the doctor said.

"She looks so scared. She tried to talk. She wants to ask me something, I know it."

"I'm quite sure she'll have a lot of questions. But all in good time. You talk to her for a while. Tell her anything you think will calm her down. What would she be most worried about?"

"Her boys, of course, her boys. Emily, baby, the boys are fine. Your in-laws are staying at your house with them. They're going to school, doing just fine. They come to see you every day after school. What a surprise you'll be for them today. Bobby's arm is still in a cast, but he's so proud of it. All the kids at school signed it. And Danny's off his crutches, walking in a boot now. But you'll see, they're just fine."

Her heart rate settled into an even rhythm.

"You did good," the doctor said to Rob. "She needs to rest now."

164

"I can't leave her. I won't."

"I didn't say you had to leave her, just try to keep her calm and encourage her to get some sleep. Awakening can be very draining."

"Is she going to be alright?"

"All her vital signs are good. We'll try taking that feeding tube out in the morning and see how she does with some liquids. You might want to get her a pad and pencil in the meantime. Knowing Emily, she's going to have a lot of questions."

Emily looked around the room. There were flowers everywhere, but the paper pilgrims and turkeys caught her attention. They had not even carved their Jack-o-lantern yet. She looked from the turkey to Rob and back again, moving her head, pointing with her free hand.

"You've been asleep for more than two weeks. The boys have been working on their Thanksgiving decorations. But look over there and there. They left the Halloween decorations up, too. Everything but the jack-o-lantern. It was here, but the bottom started to rot, so we had to throw it out. Man, it's good to have you back." He bent over and kissed her on the forehead. "Now get some sleep so you'll be rested when the boys arrive. I'll be right here, I promise."

§ § §

Emily was awakened by small hands rubbing her arms—one son on each side. She opened her eyes to see worried faces staring back at her. She tried to smile, but couldn't. She lifted her arms slowly, so tired, so many tubes, but managed to pull her boys close to her chest and hold them.

"Mommy, are you okay?" Bobby was almost crying.

She nodded.

"Does it hurt?" Danny asked.

She nodded again, but with her fingers formed a small space to indicate a little bit. She didn't want to lie to them, but she didn't want them to worry any more.

She pointed to her decorations and crossed her arms over her chest, a universal sign for love. The boys understood and both grinned.

"We better go now boys and let your mother get some rest,"

Grandma G said. "We're so glad to have you back, Emily. The boys are doing fine. They've been so good. You've done an excellent job raising them, you and Dan. They are good boys."

The sound of Dan's name sent pain and anger through Emily's body, and she winced.

"Are you okay, Mommy?"

She nodded, and hugged her boys once again. She pointed to her chest, crossed her arms over her chest, and pointed to each one of her boys.

"I know what you said," Bobby squealed with delight. "I love you, too, Mommy!"

"See you tomorrow," Danny said, and kissed her on the cheek. "Love ya."

Emily didn't want them to leave, but she was so tired. As soon as they walked out the door, she closed her eyes and drifted off to sleep. But not dreamless. Memories tumbled in, old ones, new ones...

She stood on the edge of a mountain, her face tilted toward the sky. Snowflakes drifted down, landing lightly on her face. Her boys were building a snowman in the yard. But the snow turned to sand. The beach. Waves. Seagulls dipping down to catch Cheese Doodles. Fried chicken. Mama in the kitchen, singing. Daddy on the tractor, bouncing. Baby girl, my baby girl. Blonde curls, naked body. Dan.

Emily struggled to wake up, sit up.

"Emily, what's wrong? Be still, baby. You'll pull your wires loose."

Dan. Walking down the beach, shorts slung low, arms swinging by his side. Hurt. It hurts so bad. Ice cream clown. Laughter. Tires screeching. Metal crunching. Sirens. Boys crying. Can't talk. Can't see.

Emily thrashed in her bed.

Gotta get up. Boys need me. Don't die Mama. Daddy, I need my daddy.

"Calm down, Emily. It's alright. Everything's alright."

Rob.

Emily relaxed into sleep, restless, worrisome.

§ § §

Hospitals are never quiet, but the change of morning rounds created a clatter of noise all too familiar to Emily. Her eyes popped open easily, and she realized she was the one in bed, not her daddy. She lifted her hand to rub Rob's mussed hair, his head lying next to her on the bed. He lifted it and smiled at her, a crooked smile, sleep filled eyes.

"Good morning sleeping beauty. How you feeling?"

Emily nodded her head, pointed to her mouth. She looked around the room, then gestured that she wanted to write.

"The boys bought you a slate and some chalk down in the gift shop before they went home. Here, can you hold it alright?"

Emily's hands weren't strong enough to hold and write, so Rob moved the bed table over her bed. "Try this."

Emily fumbled, but managed to scrawl legibly—What happened?

"You were in a wreck. You remember taking the boys to town for pizza and ice cream?"

Emily nodded.

"You had a wreck on your way home."

What happened?

"You ran off the road, the car hit a tree."

WHAT happened? WHY?

"We can talk about all that later when you feel better. The most important thing is that the boys are fine, and you're getting better every day. You need to concentrate on getting well. Nothing else right now, ok?"

Emily nodded. She was too tired to argue, but she knew something wasn't right.

The doctor removed the feeding tube that day, but instructed Emily not to try to talk for at least twenty-four hours. The boys seemed to enjoy watching her write on her slate. They asked question after question until Emily wrote "my fingers hurt." Emily saw the way Mrs. Gillespie treated Rob—cold, detached. But the boys seemed to like him just fine. After they left, Emily wrote to Rob.

You. How long?

"Here you mean?" Emily nodded. "Since the morning after. My

mother called and told me about the wreck, and I drove down right then."

Where?

"Right here in your room. I wasn't going to leave you, not for a minute."

How explain?

"To who?"

Mother-in-law.

"Oh, her. I told her we were old friends from school, and that I wanted to help out. I told her I could stay at the hospital so she could take care of the boys. My mother came by, too, and talked about us being like family years ago, about how people from church wanted to do what they could. I think it softened it a little bit. But she doesn't like me."

I like you.

"That's all that matters. I'm going to stay as long as you let me, as long as you want me."

Tell me.

"Tell you what?"

Everything.

"When you're stronger we'll talk. Now close your eyes and get some sleep."

Emily was still too tired to argue. She slept more soundly that night, Rob's head and arms on her bed, her hand on his arm. For two more days, he refused to talk about any specifics, but Emily kept pressing. Her voice came back strong, and she kept asking. By the third day, she had had enough.

"You can't protect me forever. Something more than my wreck is really wrong, and I know it. Tell me now. Where's Norma? I know she isn't my best friend, but I thought she would come see me. I called her the night of my wreck, told her I needed to talk to her."

"Do you know something, Emily? Anything about Norma?"

"Yes." Emily wasn't sure how much she wanted to say, but if she were going to demand the truth, wouldn't she have to offer it back in return? Hadn't Rob proved his loyalty? If she couldn't trust him, who could she trust?

"Tell me what you know first," Rob said.

"Norma and Dan." Emily could hardly say it. The images of those films flashed through her mind, and she started to cry.

"We don't have to talk now," Rob said. "Let's wait until you're better."

"No," Emily said. "Now."

"There's so much to tell, Emily. You've been out of it for two weeks, and my PI friend's been working hard. He found out a lot of things. Things that aren't going to be easy for you. Are you sure you're ready?"

"I'm sure."

"It was Norma."

"What was Norma?"

"The phone calls. Dan's death. Maybe your parents, too. Your wreck. Norma did it all."

"No. I don't believe you. Not Mama and Daddy. Not me. I want to see her. I have to talk to her."

"You can't."

"Yes, I can. Give me that phone. I'll call her. She'll come. She has to come."

"She can't come, Emily. Norma died the night of your wreck."

"No."

"Yes, she ran you off the road. But there was a big truck coming from the other direction, a dump truck, and she couldn't get out of his way fast enough. Hit it head on. She died instantly. I'm sorry, Emily."

"No. She wouldn't do that. That's crazy."

"She was sick, Emily. On medication. And she had recently been diagnosed with something called manic depression. Have you ever heard of that?"

"No."

"Me neither, so I looked it up. It causes mood swings, something called manic and depressive episodes. You never know which person you'll get on a given day. It can cause increased involvement in sexual fantasies and behavior, even painful stuff. And—get this—excessive religious activity. Weird combination if you ask me. But it can also cause people to be violent, Emily, or suicidal."

"Where's Elizabeth. The boys?"

"They're in foster care right now, three different homes unfortunately. They did keep the boys in pairs. Not one of their daddies wanted the responsibility. I can't believe it. Not one of them. My buddy talked to the caseworker, told her about you, that you were their only family. When you're better, you can decide what happens to them."

"I can take care of them. I have money. Lots of money."

"We can take care of them. If that's what you want, but you don't have to decide that now."

"I don't know where I'll live. Not Dan's house ever again."

"What do you know about Dan?"

"What do you know?"

"I know a lot more than you might think. Where do you want me to start?"

"With Norma. Why did you say Norma killed everybody? How?"

"The money. Do you remember Norma dating an insurance guy?"

Emily nodded.

"Well, it seems he talked your daddy into a pretty hefty insurance policy with you and Norma as beneficiaries. They couldn't get him to do just Norma even though she tried to convince him that you were crazy and she needed to be guardian of your money. That's why the phone calls. We think she was trying to make you sick again, Emily." He paused.

"Go on."

"This guy she dated was pretty bent out of shape that she dumped him, so he didn't mind talking. Seems that sometime just before your parents' wreck, your daddy went in and changed the policy, said that wasn't the right way to do things. Your mother's policy kept your dad as primary beneficiary and you girls as secondary beneficiary, but he changed his policy to be for your mother if he died first and then a trust for the grandchildren."

"I know about the trust. I'm the trustee."

"Yes, but Norma didn't think you should be. She dated the attorney, remember, after the insurance guy? I guess when she thought she had the insurance like she wanted it, she dumped him and set her sights on the attorney so she could get the wills the way she wanted them, too."

"That attorney left his wife for Norma, then she dumped him."

"Well, lack of personal integrity aside, it looks like she couldn't get him to bend his work principles for her goals, but she damn well tried. She told him that you had been in a mental hospital and that you were showing signs of another breakdown, that you weren't fit to be executrix." Rob picked up Emily's hand, rubbed his thumb across her fingers. "You okay?"

"Uh-huh, go ahead. Tell me the rest."

"She told him that your daddy's insurance policy named you both as beneficiaries, but that she needed to be made trustee over your part of the money. She apparently didn't know he had changed it. We think she killed your daddy for the insurance money. The dark vehicle that ran him off the road could have been your parents' station wagon she had been driving. Your mother just happened to be in the wrong place at the wrong time."

"No, she wouldn't do that. She loved our parents. But she was using their car then. Her car had broken down again, and I wouldn't give her money to fix it. She blamed me."

"Blamed you for what?"

"Our parents' deaths. Said it was my fault they were in the little truck instead of the station wagon. That it wouldn't have been so bad if they'd been in the big car."

"That's ridiculous. Don't you believe for a minute that it was your fault."

"I know. I just miss them so much."

"After they died, Norma went back to the insurance guy, but he threw her out of his office. She went to the attorney to try to have you declared incompetent to handle the trust and the estate. She was not a good person, Emily."

"But they were the only parents she ever knew. She wouldn't kill them." Emily turned her face toward the window, pulled her hand away and rolled over slightly. "She wouldn't kill them."

"I'm sorry, Emily. Do you want me to stop?"

"No. Go on."

"Did she get along okay with your daddy?"

"He was a lot tougher on her than Mama." Emily rolled back flat and stared at the ceiling while she talked. "Norma didn't fool Daddy. He usually didn't give in to her demands, but he worried about her. Worried about Mama, too. She always caved in to whatever Norma wanted. She was even taking cash advances against a credit card to give money to Norma."

"I didn't know that."

Emily slowly turned and looked at Rob. "I don't think Daddy did either. I found the bills and Mama's ledger in her nightstand drawer."

"Did Norma ever say anything, do anything that was strange where your daddy was concerned?"

Emily closed her eyes, thought for a moment. "She did say something in the hospital. I didn't think much about it at the time." Emily squeezed her eyes tighter. Opened them wide, stared at Rob.

"What did she say, baby?"

Emily felt the tears rising, filling, overflowing. "She said Mama wasn't supposed to be with him. Oh god, Rob, did she really kill them?"

"Well, we don't actually have any proof. But we think so."

"I'm really tired. Can we stop now? Why don't you take a break, go for a walk."

"I don't want to leave you. I didn't protect you like I promised. I'm not going to leave you now."

"I want you to. If what you said is true, if Norma was making the phone calls and Norma's dead, I'm not in danger anymore. Please, just go. Go."

Emily felt bad for yelling at him, hated the hurt look on his face, but she needed some time by herself. She needed to think. She needed to cry. He turned back when he reached the door, a pleading expression on his face.

"Go." Emily was abrupt, firm. As soon as the door closed behind him, she began to sob, and cried until she was totally void of negative feeling—no fear, no sorrow, no anger, no hate. Then she slept.

§ § §

After the boys' afternoon visit, Emily told Rob she was ready to know more.

"Where do you want me to start?"

"With Dan. Norma and Dan. I know they were having an affair."

"You do? When did you know? How?"

"I found out the day before my wreck. That's why I called Norma and told her I needed to talk to her. I told her I knew."

"Did you know that Dan had a life insurance policy for a million dollars with Norma as the beneficiary?"

"Yes."

"Seems that she had been blackmailing him for several months, but we don't know why other than the affair. She had three $10,000 deposits that coincided with his savings withdrawals, but then they stopped about a couple weeks before he died."

"Your buddy's good."

"He is. Yes. But why would Dan pay that kind of money to keep the affair a secret? Why didn't he just leave you and go to Norma?"

Emily wasn't ready to tell him about Elizabeth. "Maybe he didn't want to lose his boys."

"How did you find out about the affair? If Dan was dead and you and Norma weren't talking."

Emily wasn't sure how to answer or how much to say. She wanted so much to trust Rob. "He made tapes. I found them."

"Oh, Emily. I'm so sorry, sorry you found out that way." He squeezed her hand.

"Keep talking. I need to know what you know."

"We think he called her bluff, said he wouldn't pay out anymore. The brake line had a clean cut, small to cause a slow leak. He must have spent Sunday afternoon with her before he left. Maybe she even drugged him so he'd fall asleep at the wheel. Or she might have run him off the road. She'd gotten away with that trick one time already. And that stretch of road is so desolate, no witnesses late at night."

"But why did she hate me so much? She claimed I was her sister."

"A rich sister. Jealousy. Entitlement. First you had the man she wanted. The house, the security. Then you had control over all the money from your parents—money she thought was rightfully hers, plus some. On top of that, you had all the money from Dan's insurance policies—boatloads of money. The policy he had for her wouldn't pay if he died in an accident, but she must not have known that. She killed him for nothing."

"You know about that money?"

"My man's good, remember?"

"But Norma wouldn't get my money if I died. My boys would."

"Not if she killed them, too. With them gone, Elizabeth would be your only heir. I guess Norma figured she'd have control of all your money, and her children would get your boys' share of the trust.

"Rob."

"I'm sorry, Emily, truly I am so sorry. Did she know the boys would be with you that night? Did she know where you were going?"

"Yes, she knew."

"If she had hit you a little harder; if the truck had not been coming; if she could have swerved back into her lane and kept going, she would have had everything—millions, your house, the farm, control of the trust. Money can make people do strange things, Emily. Terrible things."

"And she was sick."

"You're too forgiving."

Emily began to sob. "But how could she try to kill my boys?"

"You're right, Emily. She was sick. That was the reason. Now rest, okay? It's been a long day. You need to rest."

§ § §

The next day, Emily awoke from her afternoon nap to see not two, but seven young faces staring at her—Danny, Bobby, Elizabeth, Isaac, Peter, James and John.

"Wow, what a sight for sore eyes!" She smiled at them sleepily. Danny and Bobby were their normal jubilant selves, but Elizabeth looked haunted, and the other boys simply looked sad.

"My mommy's dead," Isaac said.

"I know baby. I'm so sorry."

"We don't got no home no more," Peter added.

"Aren't you staying with a nice family?"

"Not together," Elizabeth said.

James and John clung to their sister and didn't say a word.

"You know Aunt Emily loves you very much, right? And we're family. When I get out of here, we'll figure something out, okay? Just be good for your foster parents, and we'll work something out soon. I promise."

Rob was standing off to the side of the room, obviously not wanting to intrude. Emily motioned him to come closer.

"This is my friend, Rob. He's taking good care of me to make sure I get well fast. I want him to take you boys down for some ice cream so Elizabeth and I can have some girl talk, okay?"

When the boys were gone, Emily took Elizabeth's hands in hers. "I know this is hard to talk about, but I need to ask you something, okay?" Elizabeth nodded. "Did your mommy take you to talk to anybody about what happened with Uncle Dan?" Elizabeth jerked her hands away and looked angrily at Emily.

"It's okay, baby. It wasn't your fault. Uncle Dan did a very bad thing to you. But...I...I just want to make sure you're going to be alright. I didn't know about it, I swear, not until just before my wreck. I would have come to you sooner. I would have tried to help you. I'm so sorry Elizabeth. He was so, so wrong. He was a bad man. I didn't know. I didn't."

Emily started to cry. She just could not control her tears at all.

Her weakness made her mad at herself, but she just couldn't stop the tears.

Elizabeth reached out and touched her arm. "I'm okay," she said. "I'm okay."

"Did you talk to anybody about it?"

"I talked to Mom. She said to just forget it happened. That she would take care of it."

"Do you want to talk some more? Not to me, but to somebody else. A counselor, someone you don't know so you can say anything you want to say. Anything. Will you do that?"

Elizabeth nodded.

"Okay. I'll set it up with your social worker. I won't tell her why. Everything else that has happened is enough for you to need to talk to someone. I won't tell her about the other, okay?"

Elizabeth bent down and hugged Emily. Soon the boys came bounding back in. After a half hour of mayhem, Rob walked them down to adults in the waiting room.

"I want to adopt Norma's children," Emily said to Rob when he returned. "I have enough money, even without the double indemnity. The farm belongs to Elizabeth and the boys now. I can raise them there. I can add rooms and clear pasture, and we can have horses and cows and cats and dogs. It will be a nice life for kids. I want to raise them all. I'm sure neither of the boys' daddies will care. According to Norma, they only insisted on seeing them because they had to pay child support. They won't have to pay anymore. I won't need their money, and they don't know about the trust fund. I can get them all to sign over their rights. I know I can."

"Children need a daddy," Rob said.

"I can give them enough love," Emily insisted. "I can."

"But children need a daddy," Rob repeated. "And Mama might need a little love of her own. I'm pretty good with a hammer, you know. I can build rooms and fences and barns. I can play cowboys and Indians with little boys. You might have to do the girly things with Elizabeth, but I can teach her how to ride a horse."

His sincere expression changed to a sheepish grin.

"I know this isn't the most romantic place to do this, and it's probably way too soon. But I've loved you all my life, Emily. If you're going to insist on making plans for the future while you're lying in this hospital bed, then I'm dang well not going to wait and lose out on my chance. Will you marry me, Emily? Will you let me be your husband and your lover, and father to all those beautiful children? Can we add a few of our own?"

Emily stared into eyes full of promise and unmistakable devotion. She had married the wrong man the first time, and she wasn't going to make the same mistake twice. But what she really needed now was a friend.

Emily turned her head toward the window. The sun streaming through the glass felt so warm, but the limbs on the trees were bare. A contradiction. "Is it cold outside?"

"Very. Supposed to be in the thirties tonight." Emily could hear anxiety creeping into Rob's voice.

"Do Norma's children have their coats with them? We wear them so seldom around here someone might have forgotten to pack them."

His response was patient, gentle. "I'm sure they do, Emily. If not, their foster parents will make certain they have coats."

"Yeah, I guess you're right." She spoke softly.

"Emily," Rob whispered. "Please look at me."

"I can't."

"Yes, you can. Please."

Emily slowly turned her face toward Rob. "I can't." She saw the recognition of her response on his face, the disappointment in his eyes. Hers filled.

"Marry me, Emily. Please let me take care of you. I'll be a good husband, a good daddy. We've wasted so many years."

"I can't. Not now."

"Sometime? Is this a 'no' or a 'not yet'?"

Emily hesitated before answering. "It's an 'I don't know.'"

"I can live with that. As long as you don't push me out of your life."

She tried to explain. "I went from living with Mama and Daddy to living with Dan. I've always been dependent on somebody else. I know it's a stupid cliché, but I don't know who I am, who I could be, who I would have been, or should have been, or can be."

Emily sat up in the bed and her voice began to rise. "I can't do that anymore. It's too easy to get lost in what everybody else wants or thinks or needs. I want to know what I need."

"It's okay," Rob said soothingly, rubbing her back. "I understand."

Emily pushed his hand away and responded vehemently. "No, you don't. You can't. You're a man in a man's world. You've done what you wanted to do, lived your life your way. You didn't give up your dreams for somebody else. You haven't felt your only little girl die inside you. You didn't end up in a psychiatric ward. You haven't been scared to death every time the phone rang. You haven't felt like you can't breathe or couldn't stop crying. You haven't thought you were going crazy while everything around you was falling apart. You haven't lost your parents. You haven't been betrayed by your husband. Fucking your damn sister-in-law. Nobody killed your dog. You didn't have to worry every single day that somebody might kidnap or kill your children. You didn't find pictures of naked children in bed with the person you thought you loved. How sick is that? You don't have to live with the fact that you married a pervert. The father of your children. Your life was not one big lie. Your brother sure as hell hasn't tried to kill you. So, no, you don't understand."

"You're right," Rob said softly. "You're completely right." He reached out and stroked her cheek, brushing back strands of hair that clung to the tears.

Emily didn't resist. She let him help her lie back down, completely spent, her energy and emotions drained.

Rob continued. "You're right. I haven't experienced any of those things, and when you were going through most of them, I wasn't here, wasn't even part of your life. But I wanted to be. Remember how you told me you always knew when something was going wrong in my life because you could feel it, deep in here?"

Rob touched the blue silk of her gown where it dipped between her breasts. Emily nodded slightly, and he continued in his soft soothing tone.

"I felt it, too, Emily. I knew when you were hurting, I cried for you, ached for you. I know it's not the same and it didn't make up for what you were going through or even make you feel any better. But I knew it, I felt it, I wanted so much to be part of your life and make the hurt go away. But you didn't choose me, Emily, and I tried so hard to honor your choice. But I caved in last year to my need to hear your voice."

"I'm glad you called me that day."

"I am, too, but talking to you made staying away so much harder."

"Can I ask two favors?" Emily's ranting had been cathartic. She was calm now, content if not bordering happy. She tried to refocus on the present, the future, what she needed to do to move forward.

"Anything."

"I want you and your PI buddy to stop investigating. I want you to keep what you know a secret, not because of the double indemnity, but because of the kids. Norma's children need to remember their mother in a good way. They don't need publicity. They don't need their mother called a killer. It was just an accident that she hit me. I read in the paper a while back that two sisters hit each other head-on miles from their homes and it killed them both, so it can happen. I don't want anybody investigating Dan. I don't want them looking into my parents' wreck. The police think it was all just coincidence, bad luck, and I don't want them investigating anything. Please."

"Are you sure?"

Emily nodded. "It won't change anything that's happened. But it will affect the future, our future, the children's future."

"If that's the way you want it. We haven't gone to the cops. I'll tell him to back off, to just let it go."

"Thank you." She touched his face. An apology.

"And the other favor would be?"

"The other favor is a big one. You can say no, especially since I did."

"What is it, Emily? You know I'd do anything for you, anything at all."

"I'm being released in a few days. I can't live in Dan's house anymore. It's full of lies, full of betrayal."

"I know," he said. "I can take you to the lake house, or the mountains. We can have an awesome Thanksgiving and a white Christmas on the mountaintop—you, me, the boys, Elizabeth."

"What I really want to do is go home to the farm. Will you find out if that's okay? It did belong to Norma, but doesn't that mean it belongs to her children now? Maybe I can buy it back. Put the money in a trust. Can you go clean it up for me? Move some of the boys' things over? Maybe we will visit you in the mountains as soon as the kids get out of school for the holidays. It will do us all good to get away. But for the next few days, I'd like to be back close to Mama and Daddy. I need to sort through some thoughts, put the past behind me so we can move forward, me and the kids. Does that make sense?"

"Absolutely."

He pushed a stray lock of hair from her forehead with his fingertip. The innocent gesture sent ripples of pleasure through Emily's body. A contradiction to the pounding that had begun in her head.

"Don't worry about a thing, I'll take care of it," he whispered. "I'll start tomorrow. It's been a tough day. Right now you need to rest, and I want to be right here when you wake up from your nap."

In spite of the headache, Emily was beginning to feel empowered, ready to test her independence. She insisted he leave. "The worst is over, the mystery solved. I'll be fine. There's hours of good daylight left. Please go and start getting things ready for us. Please."

"I don't want to leave you."

"Go. Come back after dark. You can even sneak in a pizza for supper. And you can sleep in that dumb recliner again tonight."

As soon as Rob closed the door, Emily rang for the nurse and asked for pain medication. When the pounding in her head began to ease, Emily felt relaxed, totally safe for the first time in over a year. She closed her eyes and daydreamed, making plans for a future filled with a dozen kids, herds of animals, beach camping, mountain hiking, horseback riding, summer gardens, ballgames, dance recitals. She couldn't help that the images included Rob.

Chapter 15

The door to Emily's room flew open, and the boys came bounding in, full of energy and excitement, followed by their grandmother Gillespie. Emily saw her scan the room and heard the question she spoke only with her eyes.

"He's cleaning up the farmhouse for me," Emily said. "The boys and I will be moving out there when I'm released in a couple of days. He'll be coming by the house to pick up a few things."

"We only have the rest of this week and two more days before Thanksgiving break," Danny said. "We're having a party."

"Me too," Bobby piped in. "Grandma G said she would help me make cupcakes for my party. Can you come, Mommy, can you?"

"I would love to come to your party. But we'll have to see what the doctor says, ok?"

"Grandma G said we're going to her house for Thanksgiving," Bobby said. "We're going to help Grandpa G put up a big Christmas tree and the lights down the sidewalk and the snowmen and everything. Grandma G said she could tell Santa to deliver my toys to her house this year."

Emily shot her mother-in-law a "how dare you look" but spoke directly to her boys. "Come here, I need a hug." She snuggled Bobby up on the bed with her and held Danny's hand. "That sounds like a lot of fun. If Grandma G wants to take you home with her for a couple of days after Thanksgiving, that will be fine, but we're having Thanksgiving and Christmas here as a family—you and you and me and Elizabeth and Isaac and Peter and James and John. We're going to move into Granny and Poppy's farmhouse just as soon as I get out of here. Doesn't that sound like fun?"

"Don't be ridiculous," Mother Gillespie said. "You can't take care of yourself, much less a bunch of children and everything they need for the holidays."

Emily continued to speak directly to her children. "You remember my friend, Rob?" The boys nodded. "He's cleaning up the house right now. He's going to move our stuff over there. Just as soon as I get out of the hospital in a couple of days, we can start planning our Thanksgiving dinner and get ready to decorate for Christmas. How does that sound?"

"But what about our house?" Bobby asked.

"What about our friends?" Danny added.

"Everything will be fine, I promise. Just think of it as an adventure, like a camping trip but in a house—a very special house. Can you do that for me?"

Encouraged by their nods, Emily continued. "Elizabeth and the boys can't live with us right now, but I'll make sure they can spend Thanksgiving and Christmas with us."

"But how will Santa know where to bring all our toys now?" Bobby looked worried.

"He'll know," Emily said. "But just to be on the safe side, you can write him a letter. You want me to help you?"

"Nah, Danny can help me." Bobby looked at his brother. "You'll help me, Danny, right?"

"Yeah, I'll help you. Just like I help you tie your shoes, and brush your teeth, and pick up your toys, and make up your bed."

Emily ached for what she was missing with her boys.

"We need to go now, boys, and let your mother rest." Mrs. Gillespie looked at Emily and mouthed the words, "I'll talk to you later."

Emily spoke firmly. "Please call me after the boys go to bed. We need to talk about what I've decided will happen in the next few days."

An hour or so later, Rob arrived carrying a large pizza box. "Pepperoni, mushrooms, ham and extra cheese, right?"

"Bring it on," Emily said. "I'm glad you're back. I missed you."

"You just want pizza."

"Well, I did sleep through lunch."

Rob sat the pizza box on the over-the-bed table and pulled his chair closer to the bed. He kissed Emily lightly on top of her head before sitting down.

"You okay?" he asked.

"Yeah, just a bit perturbed at my mother-in-law. I know she means well, and I owe her so much, but she can be so frustrating."

"Tell me about it."

"Can we eat first?"

"No reason we can't do both at the same time."

Emily told him about asking for pain medication, then falling into a deep sleep. She explained how the boys came right after she woke up. She vented about Mrs. Gillespie's gall in telling the boys they'd spend Thanksgiving and Christmas in Raleigh. She told him she stood her ground.

He told her he saw a black bear in her daddy's garden cleaning up what was left of the corn. He told her impatiens were still blooming in her mama's garden at the end of the house and explained how he tossed some cheesecloth over them hoping to protect them from that night's cold so they'd be there when she left the hospital. He told her he made a lot of progress and the house would be ready.

She told him that she wanted to cook turkey and dressing in her Mama's kitchen for Thanksgiving and have all the kids around her parents' huge dining room table. Then she wanted them all to hang garland on the porch rails and put candles in the windows. She wanted a big tree in the living room and lighted snowmen and deer in the yard.

She told him he could retrieve their things from the house when Grandma G brought the boys to see her the next afternoon, said she would stall them so he didn't have to deal with her. Grandpa G would be fine, she said. She told him just where to look in the attic for the Christmas decorations and asked him if he was okay with going there, being in the house she shared with Dan.

He told her he'd do anything for her. She said she knew that. He told her he talked to the real estate agent and the lawyer about the farm and that they'd work on what she wanted. She said she needed to be there. He told her he took the "For Sale" down. She said thank you.

And they finished their pizza.

§ § §

Three days later, Emily prepared to leave the hospital. Grandma G had come by to see her while the boys were in school and argued that they should go to Raleigh for Thanksgiving like they had always done. Emily said no. She said if they wanted to spend the holidays with the boys, they were welcome to stay, then take the boys with them the day after Thanksgiving.

As she packed the few things in her bag and waited for discharge papers and a wheelchair, Rob went down to bring the car around. Emily sat down on the side of the bed, already exhausted from the effort. She wondered how she could possibly get ready for Thanksgiving.

She hoped Elizabeth's and the boys' foster parents wouldn't argue about the kids spending Thanksgiving Day with her. She wasn't ready or strong enough to take them full time just yet, but they needed to be a family now, and hoped it would be official before Christmas.

"Can we go now?" Emily buzzed for the nurse, then sat down in the wheelchair. "I'm so ready to be out of here."

"When are the boys coming?" Rob asked as he rolled her to the elevator. The nurse aide followed pushing the flower cart.

"Grandma G is bringing them to the house late this afternoon. I wanted to get home and get settled, maybe take a nap before they arrive."

"Need company?"

"Was counting on it."

Emily was quiet, and Rob didn't intrude into her thoughts, as they left the hospital and drove through the crazy holiday traffic in Wilmington—last minute shoppers getting ready for a big

Thanksgiving feast. As independent as she wanted to be, she knew she'd have to ask for help. The busy streets became country roads and Emily soaked up the feeling of freedom—from the hospital, but more importantly freedom from fear.

"I hope you like what I did at the farm," Rob said. "I wasn't sure what to bring, but I tried to make it comfortable enough until you could put your own magic touch to it."

"I'm sure it will be fine. Dan rarely visited there, so that alone will make it comfortable. I just have so much to do. I should have made more phone calls while I was still in the hospital. I'm not even sure Elizabeth and the boys will be able to come for Thanksgiving."

"Are you sure you're up to a house full of kids?"

"I have to be. We're the only family they have."

Emily felt slight apprehension as they neared the drive to her parents' farm. So much had happened since she'd last been there. Rob slowed and made the turn down the long two-rut drive. He reached out to hold Emily's hand, rubbing her fingers with his thumb.

"You okay?" he asked.

"I think so."

Her grandparents' house appeared on the left decorated with garland and wreaths. A pine tree stood on the front porch adorned with pinecones and gum balls, popcorn and holly garland, and a grapevine star on top. Cardinals flitted in and out underneath the porch roof, landing on the railings and the bare crepe myrtle bushes flanking the house.

"Peanut butter in the pine cones," Rob said. "A trick my granddaddy taught me. I know it's a little early for Christmas decorations, but the birds like it."

"It's beautiful," Emily said, knowing the words were trite and inadequate, but failing to find better ones.

Her parents' home looked even better. Emily saw every little thing she had mentioned to Rob and more—garland on the porch railings, wreaths on every window, lighted snowmen and deer in the yard, plus spirally trees. She could hardly wait for night to come so she could see them glow. "Wow," she breathed softly.

"I hoped you wouldn't mind me taking care of some of the details."

"No, it's beautiful. I wanted to let the kids help decorate for Christmas, but it's probably better this way. I need to save all my energy for just taking care of them."

"Give me a minute inside, then I'll come back and help you in. I know you're exhausted."

Emily waited patiently until Rob returned. He helped her out of the car, up the steps, and to the front door. "Close your eyes," he said.

"What?"

"Close your eyes. Trust me."

"You know I do." Emily did as he asked and let Rob lead her into the house. She could hear and feel and smell what she could not yet see—a freshly cut tree, oak logs crackling in the fireplace, fresh sweet potato pies, chocolate chip cookies, the special little things that made a house a home.

"Okay," Rob said after leading Emily several steps into the house and positioning her where he apparently wanted her to be. "Open your eyes."

Emily gasped and turned in a slow circle. The house was a mixture of her things and her parents'. Her favorite pictures of the boys on the wall. The floor pillows the boys laid on while watching TV leaned against her parents' sofa. The green and purple quilt her mother had made for her hung across its back. Her parents' recliners were still there, but held her pillows. Huge golden mums encompassed each end of the stone hearth, and the boys' stockings hung on a rough-hewn mahogany mantel decorated with magnolia leaves, candles and berry-laden holly.

In front of the picture window, a huge spruce stood fully lit, void of all decoration but one. Boxes Emily recognized as hers in addition to ones she did not remember flanked the tree. On top stood the angel her Mama and Daddy placed on their tree every year as long as Emily could remember. She was speechless.

"I thought you'd want to decorate the tree with the children. You know these boxes came from your house, but these are Norma's. I thought it might be good for her children to have some of their own things."

"You're right, of course. But where did you get them?"

"When Norma's rent ran out on her apartment, the landlord was going to toss all her stuff. My buddy and I told the landlord we'd take it. That would give us a chance to go through it for clues, and the landlord didn't care as long as it was gone. We moved all of it out here to your daddy's shed."

"Oh." Emily was dumbstruck by how thoroughly Rob had taken control of her life and the things she should have been doing. She stared at him.

"You were in a coma, Emily. I was just trying to help. Everything's here. When you're up to it, you can go through it and decide what to do. Your parents' things that I moved out of the house are in the shed as well. I wrapped it all up really good to protect it."

Emily ran the gamut of emotions in lightning speed—anger, hurt, sorrow, helplessness, gratitude, love. She smiled at Rob and touched his cheek with her fingertips. "Thank you."

"Whew, you scared me there for a minute. Thought I had really messed up."

"No, it's perfect. Everything you've done is perfect. You're perfect."

"Look up."

Above her head, mistletoe hung from the light her daddy had created using deer antlers shed in the woods around the house. Emily had always thought it gaudy. Now it was a reminder of his gentleness, his love and awe of nature, his creativity and resourcefulness. Now it was also an invitation, a promise, maybe even a challenge from Rob. She wasn't ready.

"I'm really tired. I think I'll just nap here on the couch."

Rob took the afghan from the back of the couch and covered her with it. Emily fell into her first dreamless sleep in months.

§ § §

"The boys! What time is it?"

"About two-thirty. You've been asleep for a couple of hours. Missed lunch. I think they're supposed to be here about five or six. I was hoping you'd wake up in time for me to show you a few more things before I had to leave. Are you hungry? Up for a little walk around?"

"Ravished."

"Good. I'll go heat up the soup and make you a sandwich while you freshen up. Need any help?"

"I think I can handle it. Thanks."

Rob had not changed much in the kitchen, and Emily was glad. That was the perfect place to be close to her mama. She finished off the homemade vegetable soup, a lightly grilled pimento cheese sandwich, and a piece of homemade sweet potato pie with a dollop of whipped cream.

"Thank you. You're a very good cook."

"Comes in handy. Now, are you up for a tour?"

"Where do we start?"

"Right this way." Rob led Emily to her parents' bedroom. Everything was the same except for her clothes in the closet.

"I thought you'd be comforted by their things for a while," he said.

Then they went to the only other bedroom in the small house.

"This was a challenge," he said. "I figured Elizabeth would just have to sleep with you for a while. But fitting six boys in one room, now that was a puzzle."

"Looks like you solved it just fine," Emily said, seeing two sets of bunks, each with a double bed on the bottom and a single bed on top. Not much room in between.

Rob opened the closet door to show sets of built-in shelving and double clothes rods. "I built drawers under the big beds, too. That should be enough room to store seasonal clothes anyway. We can pack the others in the shed and trade them out until I have time to add some rooms."

"Sounds like you have it all planned out."

"I'm not taking anything for granted, Emily. I know you refused my proposal and that's fine. I really do think I understand why you have to do this on your own. But you'll need a carpenter, so why not me? And I hope you need a friend, so why not me?"

"Why not, indeed."

"Come on, there's more."

"Can't be much more, this is a very small house."

"Outside. A few more surprises." Rob took her by the hand, led her through the kitchen and onto the back porch. "I parked it out back so you wouldn't see it when you got home. Do you like it?"

"A van?" It was large, white, and with big windows. "It looks like a church bus!"

"A mother of seven needs enough room to transport her kids. I would have waited for you to help pick it out, but you're going to have to go get them all very soon, so you just wouldn't have time. And besides, your car was totaled in the wreck so you didn't have anything to drive."

"But I don't know if they're even coming."

"They're coming. I worked it all out—with the help of your attorney, the social worker, and the foster parents. You're going to have a full house for Thanksgiving and Christmas, Emily, just like you hoped."

"I'm speechless."

"There's more. Come on. Watch your step." Rob grabbed her hand and walked toward the packing shed. "I know it's a month before Christmas, but I also know you were already worrying about presents, so I helped just a little. It'll give you more time with the children without having to worry about going shopping. The foster parents had purchased some things, so I reimbursed them and moved the presents over. Apparently, they had been talking to each other and all the boys wanted bikes. They were on layaway at Western Auto, so I finished paying them off and picked them up. I thought since they would all have new bikes, Danny and Bobby might like new ones, too. And Elizabeth, of course, although her foster mom said she wouldn't ask for anything at all.

Rob unlocked the door and switched on the light. Emily stared at seven new bikes lined up in the shed—each one slightly different than the next.

"It's too much. And I wanted to shop."

"Oh, you still have plenty to shop for. These are just a few of the big things, things that would be harder for you to handle by yourself."

Emily nodded.

"The kids' stockings were in the things I brought from Norma's house. I just didn't want to hang them yet and spoil the surprise."

"Well, you're certainly full of surprises."

"You don't seem very happy about it."

"Oh, Rob. I'm just a little overwhelmed. So much has happened in the last year that I can't even begin to process it all, and then you ask me to marry you and I turn you down, even yell at you, and you just keep doing all these wonderful things for me. Too many things."

"Look, your boys will be here soon, and I need to disappear. There's a casserole in the fridge that you can put in the oven for dinner. I've left a list of all the phone numbers you might need on the table beside your bed, in the living room next to your chair, and on the wall in the kitchen next to that phone. I'll be at the lake, except when I'm at my mother's for Thanksgiving dinner. She still wants us all in the house like when we were children. I'm not going to intrude on your time with the kids, but if you need me, need anything at all, call me, okay?"

"I will."

"Promise?"

"I promise."

And then he was gone.

Chapter 16

Emily walked through the house and surveyed her new home. She knew they would need more room, but for right now, this was perfect. Pleased with what she saw, she retrieved the quilt from the back of the couch and a pillow from the recliner, walked out onto the front porch and bundled up in the swing to wait for her boys.

She must have dozed, and was awakened by a car door closing. Expecting to see her in-laws' silver Cadillac and hear her boys' excited voices, Emily was surprised to see the rear half of a dark blue sedan, the rest half hidden by the house. She could not see who was there. Determined not to let her old fears consume her, Emily walked down the porch steps and followed the brick path to the car. She saw no one. She continued around the side of the house, peering past the corner into the back yard. She continued around the house, slipped quietly up the back steps, into the house and locked the door. Before she could reach the front door, someone rapped loudly. She heard the screen door squeak open. Another knock.

"Emily, are you there?"

Relief washed over her as she recognized Frank's voice—the officer who had helped her take Winston's body to the vet. She opened the door and invited him in.

"I heard you had been released from the hospital and wanted to check in on you."

"How did you know I was here at the farm?"

"Your in-laws. In fact, I was expecting to find them here, too. I have a report for Mrs. Gillespie, and she said she would just meet me here."

"A report?"

"About Dan's accident. The Gillespies wanted it investigated, and since Dan and I had been friends in school, they ask me to do it. I was the only person they knew in the department. They wanted someone they could trust."

"Oh." Emily was flustered. "Excuse my manners, please, sit down. They should be here any minute. Can I get you something to drink?"

"Iced tea?"

"I haven't been home long, but I think there's some in the fridge."

"You here all alone? Drive yourself home?"

"No, a friend helped me, but I was expecting the children soon so...."

"Rob left you alone."

"Yes, Rob. He's been very helpful."

"And very attentive. You haven't been alone much at all since the wreck, have you?"

"No, I haven't. I've been very sick, but you probably know that. Not many secrets in a small town, and you being law enforcement and all. Rob and his mother and all the ladies from the church have been very helpful."

"Yes, indeed."

"And Mrs. Gillespie. She's been staying with the boys. But you probably know that, too. What's this about a report? I thought Dan's death was an accident."

"Why don't we wait until the Gillespies get here to talk about Dan. When do you expect them?"

Emily looked at the clock. "Anytime now. They said around five, and I thought they'd probably get here before dark."

"Are they staying here with you?"

"I don't think so. Not much room. They'll probably stay in Dan's house."

"Dan's house?"

"Yes, in town. Dan's...our house in Burgaw."

Emily heard several car doors slam. "That must be them now," she said, rising quickly.

Frank caught her as she began to sway. "Whoa, there."

"Guess I stood up too fast. Thanks."

"Anytime." He hesitated before letting her go.

With equilibrium intact, Emily broke his embrace and hurried to the door just in time to see her boys running up the steps. After quick hugs and kisses, she reluctantly sent them to their new room to unpack and watch TV, with a promise of popcorn and tree decorating just as soon as everyone else left.

"I don't know why in the world you'd drag the boys all the way out here." Mrs. Gillespie started in on Emily as soon as she closed the boys' bedroom door. "You have such a nice home in town, and you would be even better off in Raleigh with us. You have no family here to hold you. In fact, you should just move in with us. You and the boys move in for good."

"Catherine, please." Mr. Gillespie was a man of few words, but when he spoke it was with authority. "No more. Not now."

"As a matter of fact," Emily said. "I do have family here and the boys do, too. Norma's children are coming for Thanksgiving and Christmas, and as soon as I'm stronger, I will be adopting them."

"Ridiculous," Mrs. Gillespie said.

"Catherine!" Mr. Gillespie addressed his next words to Frank. "Please, tell us what your investigation uncovered."

"Without an autopsy, we have no way of knowing whether or not Dan was drinking or on drugs."

"Of course he wasn't," Mrs. Gillespie interrupted.

"Let the officer continue." Mr. Gillespie spoke firmly, authoritatively.

"We have no reason to believe that Dan's death was anything but an accident. He could have dozed off while driving or, perhaps a deer ran out in front of him and he swerved to miss it. That's the most likely explanation. Deer are prevalent in that area. They can jump out at any time and it's easy to over-react."

"But Dan was a good driver, he drove all the time. He would not have over-reacted." Mrs. Gillespie was obviously not satisfied.

"The officer has done what you asked him to do." Mr.

Gillespie's voice was tender, but firm. "He's gone, Catherine. We have to accept that. Having someone to blame won't bring him back."

"Mommy, can we come out now?" Bobby was peeking out the bedroom door. "Me and Danny are hungry."

"Absolutely," Emily said, standing slowly. "The nice officer was just leaving. You and Danny come give Grandma and Grandpa G a goodbye hug.

"You're throwing us out?"

"Of course not, Grandma G," Emily said with the nicest tone she could muster. "But I haven't been alone with my boys for weeks. I would like to spend a little bit of time with them. You're certainly welcome to come back tomorrow, and I hope that you plan to spend Thanksgiving Day with us. We will have a full house, but as Mama always used to say, the more the merrier."

"Will he be here?"

"Family will be here—me, my boys, Norma's children. You are family, and you are welcome."

"That sounds wonderful, Emily," Grandpa G said. "Doesn't it Catherine?"

"But what about tonight's dinner? The boys haven't had their dinner."

"I have a hamburger casserole ready to go in the oven for our supper," Emily explained. "But I could certainly use some help with Thanksgiving dinner. You always do such a great job with traditional holiday fare, and I've never had to do that by myself before. We've always eaten with you on Thanksgiving. I don't want the children to miss out on that tradition. Do you think you could cook here? Maybe I could help out and learn some of your secrets."

"Well, at least let me put the casserole in the oven for you," Grandma G said, already heading into the kitchen. "Come boys, help me set the table."

"It's going to be hard for her to let go," Grandpa G said to Emily. "Taking care of the boys has been her salvation."

"I'm sure it has, and I appreciate everything both of you have done. But it's time for me to be their mother again."

"I know it is. I'm so glad you're okay, Emily. Just don't shut us out of their lives, please."

"I would never, ever do that. But I'm sure she won't agree with every decision I make. Maybe not any decision I make."

Emily looked into the kitchen and watched for a few moments. Grandma G had somehow found cloth napkins and was showing Bobby how to fold them properly, then place a full formal setting of silverware.

"I know how much she loves them, but we will be living a different life than you do, than Dan did growing up. A much more casual life, a country life. I will not allow anyone to undermine my decisions."

"Point well taken."

Grandpa G gave Emily a rare hug, then spoke to his wife. "Come on Catherine, I'd like to find some dinner myself before it gets too late."

§ § §

Emily secured the house after everyone left and sat down to have supper with her boys. They caught up on everything short visits to the hospital had not allowed. The boys seemed excited that the refrigerator was covered with their schoolwork and art, and that their clothes and favorite toys were in their new room. They asked questions that were easy and questions that were more difficult. Emily answered each one as honestly as she could—so many unanswered questions still raced through her own mind.

"Why do we have so many beds in our room?" Danny asked.

"Well," Emily chose her words carefully, taking one step at a time. "Elizabeth and the boys will be spending Thanksgiving and Christmas with us."

"Will Santa know where to find them, too?" Bobby asked.

"Santa knows everything," Danny said to Bobby, then turned to his mother and gave her an over-exaggerated wink.

Emily's heart ached at the knowledge that Danny had been forced to grow up too fast. She vowed to let him be a kid again as long as possible. She would not let anyone tell him he had to be the man in the family.

"When are they coming?" Danny asked. "How will they get here?"

"Come here and let me show you something," Emily said. She motioned them to the back door, switched on the outside light, and pulled the curtain aside.

"A bus!" Bobby squealed.

"It's actually a van, and it's ours," Emily explained. "Enough room for everybody. The foster parents whom Elizabeth and the boys are living with right now are bringing them to meet us in Burgaw for supper on Wednesday night. Then we'll all be here for Thanksgiving."

Emily added a couple of logs to the fire, made some hot chocolate, and cuddled up on the couch with her boys to watch A Charlie Brown Thanksgiving. All of them were dozing before the show ended. She woke the boys and tucked them into bed, then spent a few moments alone in the living room, lit only by the undecorated tree and the embers dying in the fireplace.

Emily was content, happier than she had been in longer than she could remember. But her body ached all over and her head was beginning to pound, so she acquiesced to the doctor's orders to take the pain medication on a regular basis for the next few days. At midnight, she stirred the smoldering embers, unplugged the Christmas tree, and went to bed.

Emily was sure she heard the phone ring, but when she reached for it in the dark and lifted the receiver to her ear, all she heard was a dial tone. She looked at the clock. Two a.m. She fell back to sleep quickly. It rang again. Dial tone. Four a.m. She fell asleep again. Ringing. Dial tone. Six a.m. Emily lay back in bed trying to clear the cobwebs from her head.

It had to be the medication.

§ § §

The Monday after Thanksgiving, when Emily entered the house after taking the boys to school, the phone was ringing. She started not to answer it.

With a shaky voice, she said, "Hello?"

"Hi there." Rob said. "I've been working on Granddaddy's cabin down at the lake the last few days. You remember it?"

"Yes," she replied, recalling its secluded location as a favorite hangout for couples in high school. "But you never took me there."

"Well, I mean to remedy that error today. Are you free?"

"I don't know if I should."

"I'll grill you a burger. No strings attached."

"You don't understand."

"Please, Emily."

"You don't understand, Rob. Everything's different now. I'm different."

"You will always be my friend, Emily. Maybe we went a long time without seeing each other and things have changed, but we are the same people. Just a little older, wiser maybe. At least I hope I am. Do you know the way?" he asked.

"I think I remember. I came to the graduation party our junior year."

"Oh yeah, that night. Not a good image to leave with you all these years."

"Forgettable," she said.

"So, will you come?"

"I want to, I do. I just don't know."

"I won't tell."

Emily smiled as she clung to the phone. How many times had Rob said that to her when they were growing up, sharing secrets. *I won't tell.* And he never did. Never betrayed her confidences. Never betrayed her trust. Never hurt her. She wanted to see him. Rob had always made her feel smarter, stronger, trusted, loved. She craved that feeling.

Emily showered and shampooed, but stood staring at her clothes for an indeterminable amount of time. The day was unusually warm for November, even in North Carolina. She finally settled on madras bermudas, a white blouse with Peter Pan collar, and a long-sleeve navy cardigan. She pulled her long, straight, dark hair back loosely with a scarf, donned a little blue eye shadow to highlight the color of her eyes, mascara, lipstick and perfume, then slipped on her weejans and stared at herself in the full-length mirror. Okay, she thought, then walked out into the bright autumn sun.

The drive took about half an hour. Morning fog hung heavy, droplets of dew streaking the side windows of her car, running and drying as she drove. When Emily maneuvered her van off the blacktop onto the narrow two-rut dirt road that led through the woods to the lake, she slowed and rolled down the windows. She breathed deeply. The sun sent slithers of light cascading through the leaves of the trees, shattering the shadows of the driveway. Cobwebs glistened in side shrubs, not yet dried by the sun. The drive twisted and turned, but ended abruptly, emptying into a sun-bathed clearing where the small pine-slat cabin overlooked an expanse of water sparkling almost white in the morning light.

As Emily parked her van next to Rob's dark green Jeep and stepped out, he walked around the side of the cabin. The tension that had been building during her drive dissipated like the fog, and she laughed out loud when he appeared wearing madras shorts, a white button-up and a navy pullover.

"You are a sight for sore eyes," he said grinning. "We still have it, don't we?"

"Looks that way," she said.

He greeted her with a tight embrace, full-bodied and intense, but released her quickly before she had time to push him away.

"Come on," he said. "Let me show you what I'm up to." He took her hand lightly and guided her around the cabin to the back.

"Wow!" she said in response to the newly built deck that spread out in three levels toward the water. "You did that?"

"Yep, been working on it for a week now, sunrise to sunset."

"I'm impressed."

"Part of the plan," he said. "And I cook, too."

The inside of the cabin was much the way she remembered it, absent the partying kids, beer bottles and chips. The pine-plank floor had been swept and oiled, an oval braided rug added between the worn and faded brown corduroy couches. A large stone fireplace claimed the majority of one wall and knotted pine cabinets hung between the windows across the front. A bouquet of fresh-cut multi-colored fall flowers sat in the middle of a round, claw-foot oak table. Window after window framed the back wall overlooking the lake, the expanse of glass broken only by the door through which they had entered.

Emily walked left toward the only bedroom, sunken one step down. An antique four-poster bed held center stage, covered with an intricately stitched double-wedding ring quilt. She saw her stare reflected back in the oval mirror that hung above the dark walnut dresser. Then she saw Rob walk up behind her and felt his hands on her shoulders. She flinched at his touch, but tried to calm herself. This was not Dan. Rob leaned in close, his chin resting on the top of her head.

"What do you think?"

"I like it a lot."

"Good." He stepped down into the room and turned her around, keeping her close, too close. "What time do you have to be home?"

"The boys have scouts after school. Three, maybe?" she said. The guilt, the fear, were squeezing her heart, but Emily fought the feelings. She knew she shouldn't be there at all, and certainly not so close to Rob that she could feel him breathe. But she wanted to stay as long as she possibly could.

He smiled, then turned her around and nudged her up the step and toward the back door.

"Wanna go out in the boat?" He grabbed her hand and strode to the edge of the lake, helped her into the canoe, then shoved it off the shore and climbed in. Rob rowed them out onto the lake, away from the cabin, and up into a cove. There, he slid down into the bottom of the canoe and leaned back on the seat facing her. He grinned, crossed his arms over his chest and said, "Let's catch up."

They talked about all the good times they had shared as kids, and focused on the good times since. Their easy banter felt as though neither time nor events had ever separated them. Emily even laughed.

She told him how wonderful Thanksgiving had been having all the children together. She shared her shock at how Grandma G made herself at home in the small country kitchen and how together they prepared a traditional Thanksgiving feast. She told him how they went around the table before eating, each one naming one thing they were thankful for this year, and how some memories brought tears.

When the conversation slowed, he said, "Are you hungry?"

"Yes, very." Emily couldn't remember the last time life felt so simple.

Rob rowed expertly toward the cabin, the canoe splitting the glassy surface of the dark water. A vast number of stubborn leaves still clung to trees along the shore, their brilliant colors standing out against the foliage of the evergreens. Emily watched him watching her, wondered how he could steer so unswervingly toward their destination without even a glance backward. He even knew when to stop rowing and let their craft slide gently into the grassy bank.

They strolled up the hill, climbed the steps of the deck, and entered through the back door. Before she could even ask, he said, "Bathroom's in the bedroom. Door's on the right of the dresser."

"I remember," she said, but as she walked through the bedroom and past the bed, she paused. Her heart began to race. Get a grip, she thought. He's your friend, nothing more, not before, not now, not yet. But he's not Dan. No reason to be afraid. She hurried into the bathroom. When she came back out, she took time to absorb the atmosphere of the room—the perfectly detailed quilt, the high mattress, the crocheted doilies on the nightstands, rows of family pictures on the chest of drawers—great grandparents, grandparents, aunts, uncles, brothers, sisters, Rob as a baby and as a little boy holding up his catch of the day. In the far corner, a white cloth covered what looked like an easel. Emily walked over to it, lifted the cloth, and peeked underneath. She gasped.

"Snooping?" Rob asked from the doorway. Emily jumped.

"It's okay," Rob said. "I hoped you would. Do you like it?"

"I love it," Emily said, never taking her eyes off the oil painting that portrayed the cabin and lake in perfect detail. "You did this?"

"Yeah, I took some art classes in school. Kind of liked it."

"I'm impressed," she said.

"Part of the plan," Rob answered. "The burgers are almost ready."

They ate lunch on a picnic table by the lake. The remaining fall leaves painted a perfect backdrop for the sparkling water.

"This place is so beautiful," she said.

"So are you," Rob responded. "I've really missed you."

"I missed you, too. I could have used a friend all these years. How could we ever get so out of touch?"

"You know the answer to that," Rob said softly. "But I don't think we ever were completely out of touch, not really. Do you know what I mean? Want some mustard?"

"Yes," Emily said. "I do. Know what you mean, I mean. No mustard." She took a big bite of her burger. "This is good."

"Glad you like it." Rob dipped a French fry in ketchup and plopped it in his mouth.

They finished eating in a comfortable silence clipped occasionally by fish breaking the surface of the lake and a couple of wood ducks taking flight.

"Your art," Emily said as they carried the remnants of lunch into the cabin. "Do you have more? May I see it?"

"Hoped you would ask." Rob walked toward the bedroom. "Come on," he said.

Emily hesitated.

"It's ok, Emily. No expectations. Just sit." He pointed her toward the bed. She climbed up on the high mattress, kicked off her shoes, and drew her feet up under her. Rob handed her a sketch pad. It was large and hard to handle the way she sat, so she turned over onto her stomach, placed the pad on the bed and started turning pages. Rob lay down beside her, close but not touching, and placed several more sketch pads on the bed.

"These are so good," Emily said, turning page after page of still life, landscape, and abstract sketches. Pad by pad, his work amazed her. Opening the last sketchpad, she felt her eyes fill and tears threaten. Her face stared back at her, first years younger, then aging slightly with each turn of the page, hairstyles changing, facial expressions different, but all her, all the years she had not seen Rob. On the very last page, there she was, sitting on the deck of the cabin, looking exactly like she did at that very moment. "How?" she asked, staring straight into Rob's deep-set eyes.

"I dreamed you," he whispered, then leaned in and kissed her lightly on the forehead. "Now, come on, it's late and you've got to go get those boys."

Emily looked at her watch. It was time. Rob walked her to her van, gave her a tight but quick hug, and said, "Go."

§ § §

The next few weeks passed in a blur of busyness preparing for Christmas. Emily could feel herself getting stronger every day. On Thanksgiving afternoon, all the children had helped decorate the tree with ornaments from both families. The Gillespies had brought each of the children—including Norma's—a new ornament with their names and the year—1968.

Since Christmas was on Wednesday the following week, Friday would be their last day of school before a two-week Christmas break. Rob had called a few times just to check on everyone. He never pushed, never asked for more than Emily had to offer. The marriage proposal, offered far too soon and rejected, never entered their conversations. But Rob had asked if they could spend one more day together while the children were still in school.

On Thursday morning before their last day, she dropped the boys off at school then hurried home, threw some clothes in the washer, made the beds, slid breakfast dishes in the sink, showered, dressed and was out the door in less than an hour. Driving the last stretch up to the cabin, she saw Rob sitting on the steps.

"Hoped you'd be early," he said, walking toward the van. He gave her a quick hug and said, "Come on."

"Where are we going?"

"Treasure hunt."

"Are you crazy?"

"Maybe. Come on."

Emily hurried to catch up with Rob walking briskly into the woods and down a narrow path that wound around the edge of the lake. The leaves were brown now, but many clung stubbornly to their branches. Others crunched under her feet.

"Look closely," he said.

"What am I looking for?" she asked.

"Treasure."

They walked on.

"Oops, you passed one. Go back."

Emily turned around and started back in the opposite direction. She looked under leaves and behind trees. Then she spotted a rectangular gold package tied with purple ribbon stuffed inside an old stump.

"Bingo," Rob said as she picked it up. "One down, three to go."

"What is it?" Emily asked.

"I'll never tell. Gotta find them all first."

She walked down the path, rustling leaves, circling trees, peering in stump holes.

"Look up," Rob said.

Emily saw a silver package, larger than the first one, tied with green ribbon and hanging from a branch over her head. She laid the first on the ground and reached as high as she could, but she wasn't quite tall enough. As she stretched, Rob came up behind her and placed his hands on her waist.

"Let me help." He lifted her up, then slid her slowly back down, her back to his chest. He kept his hands on her waist a little longer than necessary, but just when Emily started to say something, he did. "Two more."

She found the next package, blue with white ribbon, under a pile of leaves. She was having fun—excited, but nervous. Like a teenager's jitters, she chided herself.

"I'll take those. One more. Keep walking," Rob encouraged.

In a clearing on a ridge overlooking the lake, a bright red package sat in the middle of a quilt spread on the grass, with a picnic basket and cooler beside it. Breathless, Emily knelt down on the quilt and looked up at Rob who handed her the other presents.

"Brunch," he said and began spreading out an array of fresh fruit, croissants, cheeses, juice, and chocolates. "Now, open them."

Emily started tearing into the presents with the enthusiasm of a child. After she had opened them all, she spread the pictures out on the quilt and looked up at Rob who had been silent. He wiped the tears from her face with a white cloth napkin and plopped a grape in her mouth, letting his finger slide down her trembling lip.

"Like them, do you?" He grinned.

Emily looked back at the four pen and ink drawings of her favorite beach creatures—the sand dollar, the ghost crab, the sea gull, and the pelican. She ran her fingers across the glass, taking in details of every single little stipple.

"When? How?" she asked. "These would take so long."

"I haven't been able to sleep much the last few weeks. They filled the time." Rob stretched out on his side, elbow bent with his head resting in his palm. "Eat."

They spent the morning on the quilt beside the lake, eating, laughing, reminiscing about the friendship they had shared since childhood. They stretched out on their backs and looked up at the sky, naming the shapes they saw in the clouds just like they had done as kids.

They talked about mundane things. They talked about important things. They talked about his art. She told him about spending every spare minute at the beach during the summer. How she could walk for hours, inhaling the salt air. How the sand felt sensuous beneath her feet. How she envied the seagulls. So free. He told her what it was like to live in the mountains. How he could sit on his porch and see four states. How the blazing reds and fiery yellows of autumn always amazed him. How he loved to stand with his face tilted upward as the first flakes of winter snow settled on his cheeks, his eyelids, his tongue. How he wished she could see it.

"What time do you have to leave?" Rob asked.

"Mmmm," Emily said lazily. "What time is it?"

"Quarter of one," Rob replied.

"Oh, no!" She almost yelled. "The boys get out early this week. I forgot." She grabbed her pictures and rushed down the path toward her van. She left in a cloud of dust.

§ § §

The boys went home with their grandparents the Saturday after Christmas. Emily was still recuperating, but feeling stronger. And now she felt lonely. She watched the phone all morning. It didn't ring. Good, she thought. She walked to her room and retrieved a present from the top shelf. She touched the gold paper and twirled the red ribbon round and round. Then she put it under the tree, grabbed her coat, put on her tennis shoes and went out the door. She walked for an hour and a half, returning only after a cold drizzle had drenched her hair and settled in her bones. She slept most of the weekend.

On Monday morning, the phone rang early.

"I'm sorry I didn't call sooner," Rob said. "Everybody's been home. Somebody's been at the cabin every day. I couldn't even get away long enough to call. Can you come?"

Emily thought about all the ways she had decided to say no. Pick one, she thought.

"What time?" she asked.

"Sooner the better," he replied.

"Give me thirty minutes."

She quickly chose her favorite slacks and purple sweater, slipped on her weegans. She took the clasp from her hair, brushed it out and let it fall across her shoulders. Grabbing the gift from the closet, she was ready and out the door in fifteen minutes, glad that the weather was still mild this late in the year.

Rounding the last curve going up to the cabin, she could see smoke swirling up from the chimney. When she opened the door, she smelled the rich aroma of burning oak. Rob met her in the doorway, placed his arms around her and held her gently. Emily could hardly keep from dropping the package in her hand.

"Your present," she said, pulling away. "Here." She handed him the gift.

"Thank you." They walked into the house and Rob laid the gift underneath the tree. "Now, come here and let me look at you," he said. He led her to the fireplace. They stood facing each other. For a few minutes neither said a word. Rob touched Emily's cheek. She shivered.

"Are you cold?" he asked.

"No."

He let both hands wander around the back of her neck and began running his fingers through her hair, lifting it and letting it fall. Emily closed her eyes and concentrated on breathing. Rob leaned a pillow up against the couch, gently guided her around, sat down and pulled her in, back to him, close between his legs with his arms around her waist. She let her head fall back against his shoulder, and he lowered his face until their cheeks met.

Rob was the first one to break the silence. "What's in that present you brought?" he asked.

"Mmmm," Emily sighed. "Want to see?"

"Think I better," Rob replied. He slipped from behind her and went to the tree. Emily followed. It was a small pine, cut from the woods and decorated without lights. Sycamore balls covered with tin foil or dipped in glitter, small pinecones tied with red ribbon, popcorn and holly berry garland, and obviously old paper stars with glued on macaroni decorated its limbs.

"Stuff we made when we were kids," Rob said as Emily touched the ornaments. "Except the garland. We redo that every year."

"I love it," Emily said. "Want your present now?"

"The one in the box?"

"Yes." Emily reached for the perfectly wrapped present with a slightly smashed bow and smiled.

"Thank you," he said. "After I open my present, I'll fix you lunch. Steak this time."

Emily gave Rob pastels, oils, watercolors, pens and charcoal.

"Ulterior motives," she said.

Rob cooked steak and baked potatoes while Emily fixed the salads. He covered the table with a white cloth, lit candles and poured champagne. "Merry Christmas, Happy New Year, happy to spend time with you," he said as he handed her a glass.

"Me, too."

They ate in relative silence. Every time Emily looked up, Rob was staring at her.

"My brother's coming over later," Rob said as they cleared the table. "I'm not sure when."

"I'll go," Emily said. "I need to anyway." She walked to the fireplace and backed up to it, relishing the heat. "Just getting warm before I go. Nice out, but still a little cool," she explained.

"Wish you didn't have to. I couldn't tell him not to come."

"It's okay," Emily said and started toward the door.

"Wait a minute," Rob said. "Stay right there." He went into the bedroom and came out with a large frame. "This," he said, "is your present." He turned it around.

Emily was speechless. Watercolors bled across the painting into dunes and sea oats, sandpipers and ghost crabs, ocean and sky, pelicans and sea gulls. In the lower right hand corner just above his name it said, "Flying free."

The next day was New Year's Eve. Emily was up before dawn. She hung her new painting in the den, opposite the wall with the smaller pen and ink drawings. She needed to start packing for her trip to Raleigh to attend the New Year's celebration with her boys and their grandparents. Watching the acorn drop in the "City of Oaks" had been a Gillespie family tradition forever, it seemed. She could hardly wait to see her boys and bring them home. Then, she would be ready to start the process of adopting Norma's children.

Emily turned on Mama's radio that sat on the kitchen counter. As The Rascals sang *A Beautiful Morning*, she said a little prayer that 1969 would be a better year.

Chapter 17

Emily found herself actually dancing and singing to the music as she washed clothes and started packing while the Billboard Top 100 played. She had promised the boys she would leave the tree up until they came back home, so she didn't have much cleaning to do just yet.

She danced her way from the kitchen to the bedroom as Sly and the Family Stone sang *Dance to the Music*, then dropped a pile of clean laundry on the bed. By the time Otis Redding started belting out *Sitting' on the Dock of the Bay*, she was packed and ready to go.

Emily started making herself a ham and cheese sandwich for lunch just as the Beatles began singing *Hey Jude*, and she had almost finished eating it by the time the song ended. She never really liked that song. It kept repeating the same words over and over and just felt like it would never end. But it was the number one song that year. Go figure.

Emily preferred listening to beach music, but Mama's radio didn't pick up that station. She had always wanted to learn how to shag. The one time she dared mention it to Dan, he had laughed at her. Emily decided that she would either find a better radio or buy a lot of records so she could listen to more beach music. She wondered if Rob knew how to shag.

After checking every room to make sure the windows were locked, unplugging everything but the refrigerator, and turning off all the lights, Emily carried her suitcase out the kitchen door to the back porch. She laid her coat on the suitcase, hung her purse over her shoulder, and was locking the door when she heard a vehicle approaching. Emily walked down the steps and around the side of the house, only to see a dark green truck with tinted windows coming down the drive. She froze.

The truck pulled up to the front of the house and stopped. Emily told herself everything was fine, the horror was over, she didn't need to be scared anymore. She forced her feet to move, walking around the house toward the truck. When the door opened, Phillip Morino stepped out.

"Hello, Emily," he said. "How are you doing?"

"I'm fine," she said. "I'm surprised to see you. I thought you were in California."

"I've been around for a while. Doing a little work with the sheriff's department."

"So you know about Norma, right?" Emily asked.

"I didn't come to see Norma," he said. "I came to see you."

Emily's southern upbringing overtook her in spite of her angst.

"The house is all locked up. I was just leaving, but I can spare a few minutes. Would you like to sit on the porch?"

Without answering her, Phillip slammed his truck door and took long strides toward the porch. He was tall and thick, Emily noticed, bigger than she remembered the few times she had seen him when he was married to Norma. She followed him up on the porch.

"Would you like to sit?" She motioned to the rocker, then sat on the swing. "What can I do for you?"

"Oh, not much," he said. "Two million should be enough."

"I don't understand."

"The way I see it, you owe me," Phillip said. "Norma and I had it all planned out, but either she was stupider than I thought or you were smarter. Not crazy, after all. Or maybe crazy like a fox."

"Norma said you had a plan, but I don't know how that involves me."

"Oh, it involved you alright. You would have been safely out of the picture if she hadn't botched things up so bad. You were supposed to be tucked away back in that asylum, and she would be in charge of the insurance money. Norma screwed all that up and then screwed your husband. I'd been waiting two damn years, and she just kept messing it all up. I gave her one last chance—you and your boys. But she couldn't even do that right. Got herself killed in the process and left me high and dry."

Phillip stood up, took one step toward Emily. She bent her head and covered her face with her arms.

"Don't cower from me," he said. "I'm not like Dan. I would never hit a woman. Now stand up."

Emily did.

"We're just going to take a little ride to Burgaw. That's where you bank, right? Good to see you have your pocketbook. You'll need it. You didn't know you'd be buying some beachfront property today, did you? Such a good investment."

"I don't understand."

"You keep saying that, so let me explain. You have the money that was supposed to be mine. I have a deed for some very valuable property in California. It doesn't really belong to me, but that's just a technicality. Let me show you my card."

Phillip handed a business card to Emily. It read, "Phillip Morino, Esquire" and the name of a real estate investment company with an address in California.

"You're a lawyer?"

"Of course not, but that's only a technicality, too. Come on."

He reached for her arm, but she pulled away from him.

"I can't go anywhere with you. I have to go get my boys."

"Yes, you will go. They are safe right now with their grandparents," he said. "Raleigh, right?"

Emily cringed.

"They will continue to be safe as long as you do what I say, but if not," Phillip paused and reached out his hand toward Emily. "Accidents happen in Raleigh, too, you know. Much worse traffic there. And this being New Year's Eve. Terrible tragedies happen on nights like this. A lot of drunk people, you know. Now, come with me. We have a transaction to make."

Emily walked with Phillip to his truck.

The drive to Burgaw took less than twenty minutes, but seemed like a lifetime to Emily. Phillip pulled into a parking place on

Fremont Street next to the First Citizens Bank.

"Now, you're going into the bank and do exactly as I say, understand?"

Emily nodded.

"That's a good girl. I'm selling you property for 1.75 million dollars, so the check will need to be for that amount plus attorney's fees, closing costs, prorated taxes, all the normal stuff. I'm thinking a nice number would be $2,015,201.83. He handed her a closing statement sheet. A cashier's check for that amount to Phillip Morino, Esquire. Understand?"

Emily nodded.

"I'll wait for you right here. Don't be stupid."

Emily walked into the bank and followed Phillip's instructions. She never cared about the money anyway. She would live the rest of her life dirt poor to save her boys, would rather have nothing if she could only see her Mama and Daddy again.

When she walked out of the bank, Phillip was standing next to the truck. He opened the door for her, and she climbed in. When he got behind the wheel, she handed him the check.

"Will you take me home now?" she asked. "I need to go get my boys."

"Not yet."

"But they're expecting me. If I don't show up, they'll be worried."

"We have a few hours before they miss you. I'll take you to a phone booth so you can call them and tell them you're running a little bit late. That will give us a few extra hours. I have to deposit my check, after all, and this hick town doesn't have the bank I need. A little ride to Wilmington should be enjoyable, don't you think?"

Emily rode in silence, scared to do or say anything that would infuriate Phillip. So far, he had not hurt her, and she prayed he would let her go.

Phillip made her go into the bank with him when they reached Wilmington. After he finished his transaction, he pulled into the Chic-Chic drive-in on the way out of town.

"What do you like on your burger?" he asked.

"I'm not hungry," Emily answered.

"Well, I am, and you might as well eat. It's going to be a long night."

"I will eat when I get to my boys."

"But you're going to get hungry long before then. You might need your strength. What do you want on your cheeseburger?"

"Chili and mayonnaise," she said.

A few minutes later, when Phillip handed her a burger, fries, and a drink, she thanked him.

Emily tried to choke down the food. She kept glancing at Phillip who seemed calm. She couldn't detect any anger, but she knew from experience that a man's anger could flare up unexpectedly.

"Will you take me home now?" she asked as he crumpled up his cheeseburger paper.

"Just a little detour," he said. "But don't worry. I'm not a violent man. I don't intend to hurt you as long as you do what I say."

Phillip drove back to Burgaw and turned down Walker Street. Dark came early this time of year, and even blocks away, Emily could see the Christmas lights surrounding the Pender County Courthouse in the center of Burgaw, occupying its own city block. The three-story brick building was surrounded by towering aged oak trees and huge azaleas.

She let her mind drift back to happier times as Phillip kept driving. Right after Thanksgiving each year, the four gigantic magnolia trees were decorated with large multi-colored lights, and the baby oaks that bordered the sidewalks on all four sides of the square were decorated with white lights. Then, on Christmas Eve, the Boy Scouts lined the sidewalks with small white bags weighted with sand and each holding a candle—around the square and diagonally from each corner to the courthouse in the center. The luminaries were lit at dusk and burned long into the night.

A week ago, it was a magical scene that Emily now relived in her mind, recalling the oohhs and aahhs from all seven children and even her ever-so-formal in-laws.

Phillip drove several more blocks and entered the gates of the Burgaw Cemetery.

"Don't look so scared," Phillip said to Emily. "I told you I don't hit women."

"Please take me home. I need to get to my boys. They'll be so worried."

"You'll see them soon enough. But I have a ways to go before that happens."

Phillip left her in the car and walked around to the back, opened the trunk. She sat frozen in place, staring out the back window. He came walking around to her side of the car, opened the door. The last thing she saw was a hand coming toward her face.

§ § §

Emily awoke slowly to total darkness. Heard nothing. She shook her head trying to clear away the grogginess. Her whole body shivered—from cold and from fear. Where was her coat? Then she remembered—laying her coat across her suitcase sitting on the back porch, locking the door, Phillip coming, her boys. They would be so worried. She had no idea how much time had passed.

"Phillip?" she called out, hoping he would not answer, afraid that he would.

Nothing.

She felt around on the floor. Cement. Neither her hands nor feet were bound, so she slowly pushed herself up, with her back against the wall. She turned carefully, keeping her hands on the wall, feeling her way along, trying to find anything that would tell her where she was. Anything to help her escape. Her hand felt a switch, and she flipped it up. Light filled the room from a single bulb overhead.

She found herself in a large room with no windows. Several sets of bunks were lined up against one wall. A small couch sat in the middle. She saw shelves filled with canned goods and large jugs of water, a small kitchenette in one corner, and a door. She walked slowly toward the door, opened it slightly, and peeked in. A toilet and a wall-hung sink.

Emily looked at herself in the mirror. Then surveyed her body.

Her hair was a mess, but she saw no signs that Phillip had hit her or physically hurt her. She was fully dressed. And no new pains.

She walked back into the larger room. On a table in the corner, she noticed a piece of paper.

Emily,

I told you I was not like Dan. I do not hit women. Since you did as I asked, your boys are safe. As far as I'm concerned, this whole nasty mess is over, and you will not hear from me again. Make sure I don't hear from you—or anyone else.

Now, for your little dilemma. I know you want to get home so you can go to Raleigh. Not in 1968, you won't.

You should have slept for at least 12 hours, I'm thinking. Maybe longer. By the time you wake up and read this, it will be 1969, and I will have touched down near a beach somewhere neither you nor the law can touch me. So don't even try.

There's plenty of food. Help yourself. You'll need your strength after all for the task of freeing yourself. There's a key hidden somewhere in the room. It will get you where you need to go.

Happy hunting, and have a Happy New Year.

Phillip

Emily wasted no time opening doors and pulling out drawers, moving cans and boxes, looking under blankets and tearing off sheets. She searched until she was exhausted and had to sit down. She thought she had left no place unsearched, but like the princess and the pea, felt something in the cushion underneath her. She ran to the cabinets, opened a drawer, and took out a knife. Shredding the cushion, she found a single door key.

When she unlocked the door, light spilled into a corridor rising toward darkness. But it didn't shine far. The echo of her footsteps told Emily the corridor was long. She walked as fast as she could, not wanting to run headfirst into a door she couldn't see. The elevation of the climb winded her. With the precious key in her left hand, she felt along the corridor with her right.

Emily felt the floor beneath her level out. A few yards later, she bumped so firmly into a barrier that the key fell from her hand. She felt back and forth across the surface. It was a door, the knob would turn, but it would not open. She felt above the knob and found the deadbolt, one that only opened with a key. Emily knelt down and started searching, rubbing her hands back and forth across the floor. Panic threatened.

She scrambled around on the floor, sliding both hands back and forth across the cement until she finally felt the key she had dropped. Standing, she tried to insert it in the deadbolt. It fit, but it would not turn. She needed a different key. She felt her way back to the room and started searching all over again.

She ripped through the cushions on each of the other three table chairs. Nothing. She took the knife to the small couch and started shredding the cushions, the seat back, the arms. Nothing. She went to the lower beds and one by one, cut pillows and mattresses until she was sweating and hyperventilating. She climbed the ladders to the upper bunks and started tossing pillows and mattresses to the floor. On the last one, in the corner, hooked to the springs underneath the mattress, she found not one key, but a keychain full of them—at least a dozen that all looked the same.

Emily cut loose the wire tie that held the key ring to the springs and climbed down the ladder. She felt her way back down the corridor to the door. She tried one key, then another and another and another, shuffling through them with both hands until one finally fit into the lock and turned. Emily pulled the door open and felt a blast of cold fresh air. She walked into the early evening twilight, found herself standing in a small covered enclosure leading to a short set of cement steps. Emily climbed step by step and instantly recognized where she was—she had been held prisoner in the bomb shelter under the Pender County Courthouse right there in the middle of Burgaw.

Enormous snowflakes floated gently to a snow-covered ground glistening in the soft glow of the lampposts lining the sidewalks. Snow—a Southern miracle. Emily wandered into the square where children were building snowmen and having snowball fights. She dropped to her knees, spread her arms, tilted her head back, closed her eyes, and opened her mouth. Snow settled softly on her eyelids, her cheeks, her tongue.

It tasted like freedom.

Epilogue

July 1969

Emily rolled down her window and let the wind blow her hair as she drove her VW Beetle down Hwy. 117 toward the road that led to the lake house. The thought of Grandpa and Grandma G driving off in her van full of children at daybreak made her smile—inside and out. So much had changed in the past few months. She thought about the new life they were building and precious memories they were making.

The adoptions for Norma's children were in process. The laughter and bickering of seven happy, rambunctious kids filled her little house. She had been so surprised and so happy when, after Thanksgiving and Christmas, Grandma and Grandpa G made regular visits to the house and included all seven children in everything they did.

Emily was glad that Grandma G had loosened up a bit, seeming to enjoy helping Emily and Elizabeth plant flowers and decorate the multiple new bedroom and bathroom additions to the house. She even seemed a little less hostile toward Rob as he helped with the construction.

Her heart warmed when she thought of Grandpa G learning to drive the tractor and seeming to relish the fact that everything he planted was not just growing, but thriving.

The Gillespies still stayed at the house in Burgaw when they came to visit, but Emily hoped that one day they would consider staying in her grandparents' cottage when Rob finished repairing and remodeling it as a guest house.

But today they were taking the children on a week-long trip to the Outer Banks to ride the ferry, climb up the lighthouse, and see the wild horses. Grandpa G said that if this trip went well, they were thinking about buying a motor home and making special grandchildren trips every summer. Emily wasn't so sure about that— she might insist on going along.

She would join them later in the week, but for now, she was happy to be alone, driving in the early morning sunlight toward Rob. He had been so patient with her. They spent a lot of time together. The kids loved him, and he was like part of the family. Just not the part he wanted. She knew what he wanted, but wasn't ready yet. Did not know when she would be.

Emily parked next to Rob's green Jeep. His johnboat and trailer were hitched to the back, filled with gear and a cooler.

"Where are we going?" Emily asked Rob when he came bounding out of the house, his smile slightly crooked but captivating. He had told her to pack her bathing suit and towel, but he had been mysterious about his plans for the day.

"To your island."

"You know how to navigate the creeks?"

"I grew up here, remember? Besides, the tide's high."

Emily grabbed her small cloth tote scattered with colorful seashell images and threw it into the backseat of the CJ-5, then opened the door and hopped in.

They chatted easily during the thirty-minute trip to the boat landing on the Intracoastal Waterway. Rob backed the trailer expertly into the water, and Emily maneuvered the unloaded boat to the wooden dock, holding it steady with the red and white braided rope while Rob parked the Jeep. He returned and climbed in, taking the back seat so he could steer the motor. When Rob yanked the cord and the outboard roared to life, Emily flipped the rope into the boat, stepped onto the bow and pushed away from the dock.

Sitting in front, Emily savored the tingle of salt air on her face as they sped down the waterway and quivered involuntarily from the chill of water sprays each time they passed a larger boat, its wakes causing turbulence. High on the bluffs of the Intracoastal Waterway, large rambling homes overlooked the water—occupants of the ones with the best views could see not only the waterway, but the sound and marshes, and in the distance, the Atlantic Ocean breaking on the shores of two small spits of North Carolina land, long and narrow, lying between the elite community of Figure Eight Island to the south and the Mayberry-esque town of Topsail Beach to the north. Emily sometimes imagined herself in one of those homes of glass walls, surrounded by ancient oaks, boughs arching up and out, then dropping down to rest upon the ground and growing upward again—large limbs, powerful, protective.

Rob expertly maneuvered the boat out of the waterway into a creek, then through a maze of narrow ditches bordered with grasses, tiny crabs crawling in the mucky edges. When the water receded with the falling tide, the ditches would become mere mudflats. Emily silently acknowledged Rob's skillful style, how he kept the small boat skimming level atop the water even through sharp turns to reach the center of the southernmost barrier island. She knew that if he slowed, even slightly, the stern of the boat would settle lower in the shallow water and they would be stuck. After he steered the vessel into a cove on the backside of Hutaff Island, Rob grabbed the cooler in one hand and beach chairs in the other.

"Can you carry my bag and yours?" he asked.

"Yep, I'm an old hand at this."

Emily had passed countless days on that very island, but no matter how many times she trekked from the boat, through rich marshes to arid white sand that shifted under her feet as she climbed the rise of the dune, she became breathless— not from exertion, but wonder. At the top she paused, always amazed at the view. Grey-blue ocean stretched into eternity, greeted at the horizon by a sky as soft and dusty as blueberries before they're touched. Waves rolled timelessly onto the shore, lapping, foaming, retreating, repeating. In either direction, left or right, the beach stretched for miles, no other person in sight.

She still cherished the time her little family had spent there on the uninhabited island, often camping for days at the time, usually seeing no one else during their stay. The islands, accessed by inlets on each end, were long and narrow. Storms and shifting sand changed the inlets every year. Sometimes navigation was treacherous, always it was an adventure. Neither sun-worshippers nor fisherman usually wandered far from either end of the island. Being caught when the tide went out was a deterrent for most.

Only one house occupied the island. A few other shanty shacks had long since washed away. Emily often contemplated how many boat trips it would have taken to transport the materials across the sound to build the house. She wondered who owned it. In all the time they spent there, she had never seen anyone in it. It was a small A-frame on stilts with large expanses of glass facing the ocean. She smiled at the thought of someone carrying all that glass through the creeks that led to the back of the island. More amazing were the stones used to construct the chimney. How could someone have done that? Sometimes Emily wondered if the whole house were just a mirage.

"Enough daydreaming. I bet you've seen that view a zillion times." Rob spoke cheerfully, walked past her across the dunes, then turned left.

"Let's go this way," Emily said, a few steps behind. "I don't usually set up right in front of the house. I've never seen anybody there, but you never know."

"I really want to see it. Come on."

Emily followed him. When they reached the front of the house, she stopped. Rob kept walking. He leaned the chairs against the stair railings and started up.

"What are you doing?" Emily asked. "We can't go up there. It belongs to somebody."

Rob reached the top of the stairs, set the cooler down and leaned over the railing. He dangled keys at Emily. "This week," he said, "it belongs to you."

"Where did you get those keys?"

"Research. Found out who owned it at the tax office. Then I called them up and rented it. Took some fancy wordsmithing and a pretty pocket of cash. But here we are."

Emily hesitated, glanced toward both ends of the island, surveyed the sand along the dune line. Seeing no one, she climbed the steps and followed Rob through the door. The rugged stone fireplace was even more beautiful than she had imagined. Candles nestled in conch shells and glass holders of varying shapes and sizes lined the hearth and the rough-hewn mahogany mantle. Flowers filled a tall smoked-glass vase on the table. Emily walked toward the tiny kitchen and saw fresh fruit piled high in a crystal bowl. She opened the small refrigerator to find it well stocked.

"How?" she asked.

"Generator."

Emily wandered through her mirage, into the small bedroom, past the double bed and entered the bath where new toothbrushes, soap, shampoo and lotions lined the shelves. She ran her fingers across the fluffy white towels hanging on wrought iron rods. Leaving the bath, she rounded the end of the bed to the opposite side of the room, walked through the sliding glass doors onto a deck that overlooked the ocean. She watched a formation of pelicans glide in low across the water, searching for fish.

"Put on that bathing suit, grab your oil, and let's go," Rob said from behind her. Emily jumped, not realizing he had followed her.

She reached down and pulled up the cotton knit dress she wore, revealing a bold black and white geometric two-piece, the waist riding low on her hips. "It's on."

"I'll say. You ready?"

Emily nodded.

At the bottom of the stairs, Rob grabbed the chairs and carried them close to the edge of the receding water.

Emily stretched a quilt out on the sand, took off her cover up and tossed it on one of the chairs. She twisted her long brown hair up on top of her head and fastened it with a clasp pulled from her beach bag. Retrieving an oversized bottle of Johnson's baby oil laced with iodine, she started slathering her arms, across her chest, her bare midsection, and down her legs. She sat, then lay back on the quilt, legs outstretched, sandy feet staying just on the outer edge of the quilt. She slipped on her large dark-framed sunglasses and closed her eyes.

After a few seconds, Emily lifted her sunshades slightly and saw Rob still standing in the same spot staring down at her. She smiled, slid the glasses back over her eyes, reached out her left arm and patted the quilt. "There's room," she said.

They lay side by side, not touching, not talking. The crashing cadence of the waves, lilting laugh of the gulls, and soft sweep of southern sea breeze swept away all apprehension, and Emily dozed.

The child ran, lifting arms into the air, twirling and laughing, her long brown hair sun-kissed with streaks of gold, her delicate skin beautifully bronzed. She skipped along the water's edge, skimming the shore, searching for sea treasures. Mommy, mommy, look what I found. She ran. She stumbled. The sand dollar crumbled in her tightly clinched hand. I broke it. I let the doves out. She cried. Her mother reached for her, pulled her close. It's good luck, she said. They bring peace, good will. But the doves took flight. One. Two. Three. Four. Five. Soaring, circling, swooping down to peck at the child. Her mother tried to protect her, wrapped her body around her, cried out. The birds relentlessly attacked. Blood flowed. The mother cowered. Cried.

Emily flinched at Rob's touch. She abruptly opened her eyes to see him sitting up staring down at her.

"You're shaking," he said.

"I couldn't save her," Emily whispered.

"You want to talk about it?"

"Talk about what?"

"Her. Your dream."

"I miss my little girl," she said, "even though I never knew her, you know? I loved her, and I miss her."

Emily picked up the bottle of oil, handed it to Rob, and rolled over.

"You want me to oil you?" Rob asked.

"Yes."

He started with her legs, rubbing slowly up and down her calves, working his way up her thighs, his fingers grazing slightly inside the legs of her suit. He poured oil into the small of her back; it was warm and tickled slightly as it ran.

Rob rubbed rhythmic circles on her back, small at first, then gradually larger and firmer up onto her neck, across her shoulders, then back down farther than where suit met skin. He poured oil on one arm then another and rubbed from shoulder to wrist across each hand, clasping his fingers between hers. He kissed her softly on the cheek.

"Your skin is so beautiful," he whispered.

Emily sighed. She took a deep breath, the scents of salt air and seawater soothing. But she didn't want to risk falling asleep again. She sat up and donned her white floppy-brimmed hat and sunglasses.

"Let's walk."

They strolled the beach for a couple of hours, sometimes talking, often silently basking in the aura of the island, the presence of each other. Rob didn't ask for explanations, and Emily was grateful for that. He had such a gentle, unassuming nature. She had always loved that about him. Emily began to relax. She deserved some fun.

After lunching on Vienna sausages, Cheese Doodles and M&Ms, they started the cycle again. They lay in the sun, walked on the beach, ran and laughed, swam in the waves, threw scraps to the seagulls, searched for shells.

The tide returned, reaching its highest point and washing away the names they had scrawled in the sand. As it began to recede Emily said, "I guess we better go while it's still light enough and the water's high, or we'll be stuck."

"Part of the plan," Rob said with a burned face grin.

"Seriously," Emily responded.

"I am serious, Emily. Stay with me." He took her by both hands, staring straight into her eyes. "Stay with me, Emily."

"I don't know. I really need to go home. I need... I have to..."

Rob silenced her with a kiss. "There's no one there, Emily, no one waiting, no one coming."

"But what... what if..."

"What if you stayed, Emily? What if you forget about everything else? What if I told you…"

He paused, looked out over the ocean, then back at Emily.

"You know how you feel about this place, Emily? How it makes you feel to be here. How your skin tingles with the thought of it. How your breath catches at the sight of it. How you feel most complete when you're here."

She nodded slightly.

"You are my island, Emily."

With little hesitation, she slipped one arm around his waist, turned and guided him down the beach, away from the house, away from the boat, away from her desire to leave. They walked the three miles to the inlet, sat on the sand and watched the orange flame of sun extinguish itself in the sound.

"Come on," Rob said. "Let's go eat." They walked back more briskly than they had come, the evening air surprisingly chilling for July. Emily laughed as ghost crabs scampered from their path, disappearing into sand caves.

"You've got goose bumps," Rob said.

"You're sunburned," Emily responded. "I'll lotion your back later."

"I'll warm you up later."

"Deal," Emily whispered.

When they reached the house, Emily started lighting the candles inside, leaving Rob on the deck to douse the charcoal with fluid and strike a match. Emily saw reflections in the glass as fire leapt from the grill. She walked to the open sliding glass door, leaned against the jamb, and silently watched.

"There you are," Rob said. "Go look in the bathroom and bring the blue bag in the corner."

Emily went inside and returned with the bag. "Sit here," Rob said, pointing to the plastic lounge chair. From the bag, Rob pulled out a burgundy chenille throw and wrapped it around her. He delved into the bag again and brought out a brush. Emily reached for it.

"Let me." Rob unloosed her hair and let it fall over the back of the chair. Then gently, he worked out tangles of salt water, sand and brisk breezes. Emily closed her eyes as the bristles began to sweep away her reservations. Rob slipped the brush up under her hair and brought it down in long slow strokes, bristles tickling the nape of her neck. Too soon, he stopped.

"Everything you need is on the shelf," he said. "Towels on the rods, clothes in the closet."

Emily reluctantly left him, went into the bathroom, showered and shampooed, then looked in the closet. She took out the long-sleeve white peasant blouse and flowing cotton eyelet skirt and slipped them on over her otherwise naked body.

The night had turned unusually cool, and by the time she was dressed, Rob had a fire blazing in the fireplace.

"If we leave the windows and doors open, I don't think it will get too hot," he said.

He carried their burgers to the picnic table on the deck where all the condiments and side dishes were ready. They ate in companionable silence, listening to the crashing waves and haunting calls of the birds. A slither of moon rose over the dark water and stars punctuated the ebony sky.

"Breathtaking," Emily said as rose and stood by the railing, looking out at the ocean.

"Yes, you are," Rob replied.

"I'll clean up while you shower," Emily offered, and watched him go into the house. She tried not to think of joining him, of running soapy hands up and down his body, of kissing him as hot water ran down their faces.

"Damn," she heard him say and hurried into the house. He walked out of the bathroom with a towel slung low on his hips. "Sorry," he said, "ran out of hot water."

"Come in here by the fire," Emily said. "I'll doctor that sunburn."

She took a quilt from the back of the couch and spread it on the floor. "Be right back." She retrieved a dark blue jar of Noxzema from her beach bag and set it on the hearth to warm.

"Sit," she told him. "This may tingle, but it's good for you."

Emily sat down behind him with her legs folded under her. She dipped three fingers into the jar and began spreading the white cream in soft slow circles on his back.

"I kept you out too long," she breathed closely into his ear.

"Worth it," he said.

Emily stroked the cream across his shoulders, down his arms, then slowly down his back, running her fingers barely under the edge of the towel to reach the red where his wet suit had sagged. Then she crawled around in front of him and started with his face, gently smoothing the tingly cream into the tiny creases around his eyes.

"Does it burn?"

"Like fire."

She deftly massaged the cream down his chest to where the towel was stuffed inside itself. He shifted slightly and it pulled loose, fell to the floor. He stood and brought her up with him, slipped his hands inside the elastic waist of her skirt, and slowly slid it down her legs. Emily did not resist, could hardly breathe.

He slid his hands under her blouse, rubbed them up and down her back, moved them to her sides, his thumbs working their way forward. She lifted her arms and he swiftly carried the blouse he had chosen for her up and over her head. He stepped back and stared. Emily was motionless, watching his every move. She felt his eyes caress her bronzed body, saw his body respond, felt the path of his gaze. He took her in his arms and guided her gently to the floor.

They lay closely curled together, barely moving, barely breathing. Then hands began to roam, lips began to search and find. But as Rob raised himself above her, reaching the fringes of the only intimacy they had never shared, Emily bolted.

"I can't." She sat up, stood up.

"What do you mean, you can't?"

"Not that. I thought I could. I wanted to. I can't."

"Why not? What about everything else? Doesn't that matter?"

"It does, I know. But this is different. It's more, more than I can give you. I'm sorry."

"Damn this madness, Emily. I've done everything I know how

to prove to you that I am not Dan."

"I know. I'm sorry," she cried as she gathered up her clothes and ran out the door, down the steps, and across the beach. Only after she had run as far as she physically could, did she stop and put on her clothes. She sat on the sand and drew her knees up under the skirt, pulling them close to her body. She watched the gentle waves of low tide lap the shoreline and sobbed. She thought about her children. She thought about her husband. She thought about Rob.

He was nothing like Dan.

She curled up in a ball on the sand and cried herself into a dreamless sleep.

The rising sun glinting on her face, swelling tide tickling her feet and the call of a gull splitting the silence woke her at dawn. She felt the pillow under her head, the blanket warming her body. She opened her eyes and saw Rob sitting there in the sand beside her.

"I didn't want to wake you," he said. "So I just watched over you. I won't pretend to understand anymore. I've done everything I know how to do to prove to you that I am not like Dan. I will never hurt you. I will never hold you back or keep you from being anything you want to be. Do you still want to be a doctor? Fine. Go to school. I'll help with the kids. We'll go anywhere you need to go for medical school. Don't want that? Fine. We'll live at the farm, raise the children we have and add a few more."

"That sounds nice," Emily said.

"You are a beautiful, strong woman, Emily. I just want to be part of your life. A real part—your husband, their father. Being together doesn't mean one of us has to be less. Being married means both of us are more."

Emily looked into eyes that said far more than words could ever say. She smiled, but she didn't speak.

"Tide's up," he said. "Let's get you home."

ABOUT THE AUTHOR

Cindy Horrell Ramsey lives with her husband in Southeastern North Carolina where they grew up, married, and raised a family. After all their children were grown, Cindy attended the University of North Carolina Wilmington where she earned a BA in English and a Master of Fine Arts in Creative Writing. She now spends her time writing, enjoying retirement, and being Mimi to five beautiful granddaughters.

CINDY HORRELL RAMSEY

BEYOND THE EDGE

Chapter 1

July 1969

"Tides up," Rob said. "Let's get you home."

Emily's eyes felt gritty from sleeping on the beach. She squinted at Rob sitting on the sand beside her, the ocean waves nearly reaching their feet. Morning rays created a multilayered orange glow behind him, brighter streaks of sunlight dancing through his unruly hair. Exhaustion and pain stared back at her.

"Thanks for the pillow and blanket," she whispered. "How long have you been here?"

"Most of the night," Rob said. "I gave you time to come back to the cottage, but when you didn't return after a couple of hours, I was worried. With the tide rising, anybody in a small boat could have slipped up behind the island. I'm sorry if that smothers you, but I couldn't just leave you out here alone."

"No," she said. "You have nothing to be sorry about." After a slight hesitation, she added. "But I do."

"I won't pretend to understand what happened last night or why you keep pushing me away," Rob said. "I know you've been through a lot in the past year – the past dozen years if we're honest."

Understatement of the decade, Emily thought, staring out at the Atlantic Ocean glistening in the early morning light. The sun

233

had crested the horizon and cast shimmering silver streaks on the turquoise water rolling timelessly toward her. A seagull squawked overhead, his white body in stark contrast to the clear cobalt sky. She wondered what it would be like to be that free, that untethered to humans.

"I've already packed your stuff in the boat," Rob said, standing up. He offered the towel off his shoulder and the bag sitting in the sand beside him.

"Here's a change of clothes. I'll go back to the boat and wait so you can rinse off in the ocean and change, or we can return to the cottage if you want a shower. But we need to get going before the tide falls too low for us to navigate the creeks. Tide's already turned, and there's that one shallow spot that gets tricky about half-tide."

"Go ahead," Emily said, standing up. "The ocean will be fine."

She watched Rob become smaller and smaller in the distance as he walked away from her down the beach toward the cottage and climbed the dune. She thought he might have stopped and turned back toward her before he walked into the sea oats and out of sight, but he was too distant for her to be sure.

She didn't realize she had run that far.

The cottage appeared so small in the distance but still stark against the bright morning sky — the only cottage on the barrier island separated from reality by inlets and mud creeks and ocean. Rob had worked so hard to surprise her with a whole week there — a getaway, a celebration, a new beginning. She didn't even make it through one night.

Emily brushed at the white eyelet skirt hanging limply around her legs. It was heavy with wet sand. Slipping her hands inside the elastic waistband, she slid it down her legs and let it pool at her feet. She pulled the matching top up over her head and let it drop from her hands.

Standing naked, Emily ached with the rising turmoil, memories from the night before flooding her mind with confusion and regret. Drowning her. She sucked in her breath and rode the waves of emotion through defiance and fear and sadness until they laid her soul bare on the beach.

It would be so easy, she thought, staring out at the endless edge of the world. She started walking, the waves pushing against her legs, sand pulling at her feet. When she could no longer stand, Emily gave into the call of the water and dove under the crest of foamy waves.

***

Rob sat in the boat and waited. He watched the fiddler crabs crawling in the mud, fending off unseen predators with the big claw while raking minuscule marine life into their mouths with the tiny one. Maybe there was a metaphor for life there somewhere, but he couldn't come up with one.

The sun baking down on his bare back made him drowsy, and his mind wandered – back to the previous day that seemed so idyllic, so romantic, so safe. He thought that's what Emily needed. What she wanted. He thought he could bring her here and she could finally let go of the horrors and memories of the past few years. All seven children were safe and on a grand adventure with their grandparents. Her stalker was long gone. Her abusive husband dead.

Rob wanted this week away to give her the gift of sand, salt air, sunshine, and solace — nature's remedy for the soul. But most of all, he wanted her to feel safe again. And truly loved.

Finding the owners of the cottage wasn't so hard but convincing them to let him rent it took a little bit of finessing plus the promise of an original painting of said cottage on the beach. Planning for the week and hauling everything over when he could only get there by johnboat on high tide took a little more work — and many trips. He wanted everything to be perfect, and Emily's first reactions when she found out they were staying at the beach and not just making a day trip told him he had succeeded.

Sitting in the boat as patiently as he could, Rob relived every moment of the last twenty-four hours starting with the sight of Emily driving up to his house in her cute little VW Beetle all sunshine and smiles, her long blonde hair blowing in the wind. Buying that car was probably the only frivolous thing she had ever done in her life — the only time she had purchased something just for herself, just because she wanted it.

She had hopped out, excited and carefree — or at least pretending to be. Now he wasn't so sure. It had only been seven months since her nightmare ended, after all. She was pretty amazing, the way she moved forward — making a life for her two children and Norma's five. Their adoptions were moving forward without any hiccups — at least so far. The boys' absentee daddies could still cause problems if they wanted to, but with Emily having no more money to entice them, the prospect of child support payments ending was probably enough to keep them at bay.

Rob could tell she was daydreaming as they rode down the waterway, saltwater spraying up every time they crested the wakes of other boats. She hummed a little, turned to look at the huge houses on the banks of the waterway, pointed up at pelican patrols flying past. Smiled as she turned to look back at him from the front bench seat.

When they left the boat and trekked through the marsh toward the ocean, Emily stood at the top of the dune taking in the expanse of sand and sea as if she'd never seen it before — even though she'd been there countless times. Her ability to remain innocent and inspired after what she had been through filled him with overwhelming respect and love and admiration.

They had stretched out on a blanket in the sun, rubbing oil on each other's bodies, stirring desire. They talked about old times when life was simple and they were best friends who could read each other's minds, feel each other's emotions. He yearned to feel that connection again. Thought surely she did, too.

They dozed in the warm sunshine, and he comforted her when painful dreams interrupted her sleep — visions of the precious little girl she had never birthed. The little girl she sees daily — long blonde curls blowing in the breeze, bright blue eyes sparkling with mischief and joy, the precious child her husband's abuse had murdered in her womb.

Walking along the shore for miles, they held hands, kicked water into the air, watched the seagulls dive for food, and the ghost crabs scurry sideways into their holes. They marveled in awe as the sun sank into the water and its afterglow turned the sky and sound into a canvas of pink, orange, and yellow slashes of brilliance in the fading light.

They held hands and stopped for brief embraces as they strolled back several miles to the cottage, then teased and flirted as they showered and dressed and ate dinner on the deck with a slither of moon and millions of stars punctuating the night sky. Crashing waves matched the beating of his heart, anticipating what would come next.

But he must have misread her cues. Expected too much. Maybe that unidentifiable connection they shared all their lives wasn't so magical after all. Or maybe Dan destroyed it – Dan and Norma and Phillip.

A mullet jumped out of the water, and the return splash broke Rob's train of thought. Mud banks had become exposed as the tide fell fast. *Where was she? What was taking so long?* Rob clung to all the restraint he could muster to keep himself from jumping out of the boat, running back across the dune, and making sure nothing bad had happened to her. Again.

Rob thought back to a day almost two decades ago when Emily was injured trying to protect him. He should have been protecting her. They had talked about it so often that Rob could see it through Emily's eyes as easily as through his own. He could not help but smile slightly when he remembered Emily's multiple retelling of the events—moment by moment from the time she walked out on the porch to wait for him.

***

July 1950

Ten-year-old Emily sat in the porch swing of their large home in Burgaw. Her legs were barely long enough for her feet to touch the wooden flooring, but she pushed with her tiptoes to make the swing move. Shade from the huge ancient oaks and a light summer breeze helped make the sweltering heat almost bearable, but the mosquitoes were biting, and she kept slapping her legs and arms and neck. She would look like a polka dotted monster when those bites started swelling and turning red. And they would. They always did.

"Where are you?" she yelled into the street, hopping out of the swing and plopping herself down on the bottom step. Emily fumed internally. *I am old enough to ride my bike to the drug store by myself.* But then in her head she heard daddy's defiant declaration that she was not to ride away from this house by herself and knew she wouldn't. It wasn't the first time she wished she was a boy. They could do anything they wanted anytime they wanted, and nobody ever said they weren't old enough. True, her brother Charles was three years older, but still. She knew she wouldn't be able to go anywhere on her own when she was his age either.

Emily stood up, stomped back up the steps, and started marching around the porch that spanned the entire circumference of their home. She had ridden her tricycle round and round the house when she was little. Now she used it as a timing tool. She decided she would walk all the way around one more time, and if Rob did not show up, she was going to get on her bike and ride to get ice cream all by herself. Her long blonde ponytail swished back and forth as she strutted around the wicker table and chairs, the porch swing, and half a dozen wooden rockers. When she rounded the last corner of the house, she saw Rob rolling up into the yard.

"What took you so long?" Emily yelled so loudly her voice

squeaked.

"Sorry," Rob said. "Mama made me clean my room."

"Well, you shouldn't be so messy," Emily said, "and if you woulda just yelled, I coulda come helped you."

Grabbing her bike and hopping on, she said, "Come on."

"You don't understand," Rob said as they rode down their street. It had not yet been paved, but the clay was packed tight like hard brown sugar, so their bikes rolled easily. But their knees would get bloody strawberries if they fell.

"What do I not understand?" Emily asked.

"That you can't create art without being messy," Rob explained. "And if I have to clean up my canvases and paper and paints every stupid day, then I don't get anything done."

"You're an art snob," Emily said, laughing. She stood up on her bike and pedaled away as fast as she could, her bike swaying back and forth from the effort.

"Wait up!" Rob yelled.

Emily stopped at the end of their street where it ran into the wider, busier Wilmington Street and grinned as Rob pulled up beside her, braking so hard that his back tire slid around and threw up dirt.

"Hey!" Emily said. "You got dirt in my eyes."

"Oops," Rob said. "Serves you right for leaving me."

Wilmington Street was the main road through town and paved, so the ride was easy. They turned left down Wright Street and headed toward Dees' Drug Store where they leaned their bikes up against the building and walked in.

"Uh-oh," Emily said when she caught a glimpse of who was sitting on the stools at the counter —the three bully boys. "Let's ride a while and come back," she said.

"Yeah, maybe," Rob said, turning back toward the door. But it was too late.

"Yo, Pillsbury!" Greg shouted. He hopped off the stool and strutted toward them, his five-foot-eight-inch ten-year-old body long and lean but firm as a lightweight boxer. "You running?"

"No," Emily said. "We're riding our bikes, and we have no time for you."

"She your bodyguard or something?" Sam asked, walking up beside Greg. He was not nearly as tall as his friend, but strong and muscular from working on his grandpa's farm after school and all summer.

"No," Rob said.

"She your girlfriend?" Willie said, with a drawl. He nudged his buddies. "No girl gonna like that flab."

They all started howling with laughter. Emily watched Rob clench his fists so tightly his face turned red.

"Let's go," Emily whispered.

"No," Rob whispered back. "We came for ice cream, and I'm getting some. Follow me."

He started walking toward the counter, but the other boys spread out shoulder to shoulder, entirely blocking the aisle.

"You kids take it outside," Ms. Ruby said from behind the soda fountain counter. "Or I'm going to call your parents. All of them!"

"Yeah, outside," Greg said.

With no way to go forward, Rob and Emily turned around and started toward the door. The others followed.

"Ignore them," Emily said as they reached their bikes.

"Yeah," Rob said. He grabbed his handlebars and pushed up the kick stand.

"Hey, dough face," Greg said, walking right up to Rob's back. He towered at least a foot over the top of him. "Turn around."

"Leave him alone," Emily shouted. She left her bike, walked up to Greg with her hands on her hips, and stomped her foot. She was lean and wiry, but Greg looked like a giant in front of her. "You're nothing but a stink-faced bully. Just because you're bigger than everybody else doesn't make you better."

She turned on her heels and headed back to her bike.

"Let's go," she said.

They mounted their bikes to ride away, but as they started to pedal, Greg shoved Rob causing him and his bike to topple onto Emily. She broke his fall but slammed into the brick wall of the building. The bullies cackled loudly and ran.

Untangling himself from the bicycle debacle, Rob helped Emily up.

"Are you alright?" he asked.

"Yeah," Emily said. But then she stood up.

"You're bleeding!" Rob said.

Blood dripped onto her white eyelet blouse from a cut on her forehead. Her elbow was scraped raw and oozed blood. She fought back tears.

"Come on," Rob said. "We'll get some ice and napkins from Ms. Ruby."

Rob righted their bikes and led Emily into the drug store, straight to the counter where he helped Emily up onto a stool.

The longtime waitress turned from the milkshake machine and saw the kids sitting there.

"Lordy be child, what happened to you?" Ruby said, bustling her two-hundred-fifty-pound body around the end of the counter, her brightly colored flamingo print moo-moo swishing around her knees.

Rob gave Emily the 'don't tell' glare so she said simply, "I fell off my bike."

"Well, that was a hard tumble," Ruby said. She grabbed some napkins from the dispenser on the counter and pressed them against Emily's forehead.

"Hold this," she said, "and let me get some water to clean you up. She hurried around the counter, reached under, and placed a box of first aid supplies on top where she could reach them from the other side. Then she hustled back around to Emily.

"This won't sting at all," she said, placing a wad of gauze under the cut on Emily's head and pouring hydrogen peroxide on it. "I just gotta wash it out."

Emily winced as Ruby put a clean piece of gauze on her cut and said, "Hold this. It don't look like it needs any stitches, so we'll just fix it right up."

She began plundering through her supplies and not finding what she wanted, gave Rob instructions.

"Go over there on aisle three and pick me up a little bottle of that Merthiolate. It's on the second shelf from the bottom. And bring me a box of those Band-aids, too. The one with all the sizes in it. Mine are all gone."

Rob hopped off the stool and hurried to gather the

supplies. When he returned, he handed them to Ruby then looked the other way. He knew what came next would not be good.

"Ok," Ruby said, "now this will sting a bit."

"Do you have to?" Emily said, tears already streaming down her cheeks.

"I'm sorry," Ruby said. But she kept right on working, applying the Merthiolate across the cut and placing several small Band-aids on Emily's forehead crossways to close the cut.

Emily's shoulders began to shake as she sobbed.

"Let me see that elbow," Ruby said. "You know we got to do it, too."

Blood oozed from the abrasion on her elbow and forearm creating little red bubbles on a sea of scraped skin. Ruby soaked gauze in peroxide and started dabbing at the scrape.

"Now that one don't look too bad," she said to Emily. "Maybe I'll just smear a little Vaseline on it and put a big Band-aid over it. How does that sound?"

"Yes, please," Emily said, sniffling. "Not Merthiolate."

After she finished doctoring Emily, Ruby secured her supplies below the counter and said, "I think you kids deserve a bit of ice cream or a shake after that ordeal. What'll you have? My treat today."

***

Rob's patience was beginning to wane. The tide had fallen so much that the boat sat solid on a mud flat. Going anywhere had become an impossibility. They'd have to wait at least four or five hours for the tide to come back in enough to maneuver through the creeks back to the waterway. *Where was she?* Rob

244

stepped out of the boat and sunk up to his knees in pluff mud. So many people thought it stunk to high heavens, but for Rob, the rich, earthy, salty smell simply flooded his mind with memories.

***

July 1953

The Turner and Waters families loaded their station wagons and pickup trucks with chairs, coolers, fishing gear, and suitcases for their annual week at the beach. They'd buy groceries when they got to the island, but inside the Turner coolers were various pop-in-the-oven dinners like lasagna, spaghetti bake, and chicken pot pies. Mary Waters would have a plethora of desserts in one of her coolers. They'd cook fresh-caught fish almost daily and start each morning with a huge breakfast. This was their favorite week every single year.

When they neared the swing bridge, they would always roll down the windows and breathe in the fresh, salty air—unless the tide was low. That's when the earthy odor of pluff mud would fill the car with a rich pungent scent created by decaying Spartina grasses and marine life. While his brother would complain and pretend to gag, Rob thought it smelled like adventure.

Emily and Rob had both become teenagers earlier in the year, so they hoped they would have more freedom that summer – be able to leave the rental house and venture out by themselves, maybe go to the pier to get a hotdog, hang out with other teenagers, and watch the surfers – like Emily's brother, Charles, and his friends.

The first day when they arrived at the beach house was

always a crazy rush to get everything unpacked. They could never check in before four in the afternoon, so much of the day was already a bust. Being the only girl, Emily had a room to herself, but her older brother, Charles, had to share with Rob and his younger brother, William. All four were required to make sure everything was in its designated place before they could leave the house—a rule laid down by both moms.

He definitely enjoyed their "let's get this vacation started" tradition, though, when all the chores were done, and the kids went running down the steps that crossed the dunes and raced toward the ocean seeing who could reach the waves first, dive headlong into the salty water, and pop up past the breakers. At least that's what Charles and William did. Emily and Rob usually stopped when the waves reached their knees. They preferred easing into the ocean. That year, Rob and Emily had made a pact that they would not stop, and they didn't.

***

Emily's lungs ached as she floated beneath the water. She could see the sun's rays streaming in, glistening off tiny silver mullet and menhaden swimming past. Subconsciously, she knew feeding fish would follow—maybe even sharks. She surfaced and breathed deeply, gagged, coughed, and turned in circles, finally finding the shoreline and judging her distance. She knew she had to choose—keep swimming out until she was beyond return or swim toward shore and face her future. She was just so tired.